Mari Jungstedt is one of the most successful crime fiction authors in Sweden, and has sold over three million copies of her books worldwide. Barry Forshaw writes that her Inspector Knutas novels are 'among the most rarefied and satisfying pleasures afforded by the field'. This is her seventh novel set on the island of Gotland and featuring Knutas.

Mari lives in Stockholm with her husband and two children.

For more information on Mari Jungstedt and her books, see her websites at www.jungstedtsgotland.se and www.marijungstedt.se.

Also by Mari Jungstedt

Unseen
Unspoken
Unknown
The Killer's Art
The Dead of Summer
Dark Angel

and published by Corgi Books

THE DOUBLE SILENCE

MARI JUNGSTEDT

Translated from the Swedish by Tiina Nunnally

CORGI BOOKS

TRANSWORLD PUBLISHERS
61–63 Uxbridge Road, London W5 5SA
A Random House Group Company
www.transworldbooks.co.uk

THE DOUBLE SILENCE
A CORGI BOOK: 9780552168755

First published in Great Britain
in 2013 by Doubleday
an imprint of Transworld Publishers
Corgi edition published 2014

Addresses for Random House Group Ltd companies outside the UK
can be found at: www.randomhouse.co.uk
The Random House Group Ltd Reg. No. 954009

The Random House Group Limited supports the Forest Stewardship
Council® (FSC®), the leading international forest-certification
organisation. Our books carrying the FSC label are printed on
FSC®-certified paper. FSC is the only forest-certification scheme
supported by the leading environmental organisations, including
Greenpeace. Our paper procurement policy can be found
at www.randomhouse.co.uk/environment

Typeset in 11/14½pt Giovanni Book by
Kestrel Data, Exeter, Devon.
Printed and bound by
CPI Group (UK) Ltd, Croydon, CR0 4YY.

2 4 6 8 10 9 7 5 3 1

For Anna Samuelsson, beloved little sister

Can you be one and the same person, at
exactly the same time? I mean, be two people?

from Ingmar Bergman's *Persona*

The car turned off the main road and continued along the tractor path, which led straight into the woods. Dark had fallen, and only the cold beam from the headlamps showed the way. Here the pines were taller than usual on Gotland. They stood close together, with thick brush in between, their branches reaching out for each other to form a shield from the wind when storms swept across the island. Although right now there was no wind. The solitary car jolted along, only to stop in the glade near the small marsh, which was actually little more than a boggy patch of land. The moon shone round and white above the mirror-smooth water. Mist slowly rose up from the surface towards the sky, where it dispersed and vanished into an empty nothingness.

The couple tumbled out of the car, already immersed in their game. She clung to him, lips against lips, body against body, feverish hands reaching under their clothes. She laughed, and the sound travelled across the water, ricocheting between the gnarled tree trunks and the boulders, aimlessly scattering here and there, as if coming out of nowhere. An old willow stretched out its branches over the black and cold water, grazing the motionless surface.

She leaned against the trunk, spread out her arms and closed her eyes. The smell of damp earth in her nostrils, the cool, dewy air against her bare skin excited her even more. When he bit her hard on the shoulder, she cried out, pulled out of his grasp and ran off towards the woods. Up on the hill across from the marsh, he caught up with her and pressed her against a pine tree. The bark scraped at her back. His eyes glittered in the dim light. Slowly he began unbuttoning her clothes. He ran his fingers along her shoulder until the cloth gave way and fell in a heap at her feet. She hadn't bothered to wear a bra. She had been longing for him for days.

She shivered. His face was so close. In the moonlight it looked like the face of a stranger. They didn't speak during their game. He sighed as he slid his hand over her body, touched her breast, stopped, circled. He carefully caressed her with his fingertips, following the line where her ribs joined, moving down to her navel, then wandering upward again. Slowly, back and forth, until she began to moan with desire. Without her noticing, he reached into the bag sitting in the grass at his feet. With his hand behind his back, he cautiously rummaged among the contents until he found what he was looking for. The minuscule, nearly transparent, thong she was wearing barely covered her sex. You naughty girl, he thought excitedly. You knew what was coming. He circled her navel with his tongue, then cautiously bit the lower part of her stomach, which was smooth and firm, like a boy's. Then he moved up, caressing her, holding the blindfold behind his back. He kissed her breasts, reached her slender throat. Such a vulnerable spot, he thought as he tenderly nibbled and licked the delicate skin. He could feel her veins under the tip of his tongue, her blood vessels just below the surface. Then he raised his arms and in a flash tied the blindfold around her eyes. The black mask covered them securely. He knew that everything had now gone dark for her.

'What are you doing?' She giggled uncertainly. 'What are you up to?'

Her hands automatically flew up to her head. Her palms glowed white. He thought they looked like two lost birds, fluttering through the air without knowing where to go.

'Now, now,' he admonished her. 'Take it easy. Never a danger if you're careful with a stranger,' he hummed, taking the phrase from an old nursery rhyme. At the same time, he pulled out the rope, which had been hidden inside the bag. The clumsy fumbling of her hands stopped abruptly when he took a firm grip on them, tying the rope tightly around her wrists and hoisting her arms above her head.

A moment later she was tied securely, bound to the tree, and unable to escape. She was helpless, in his power, which was something he enjoyed. It was just the two of them here, the trees their only audience. Far away from everyone and everything. A separate universe. He did as he liked. She was tied to the tree, unseeing, like a newborn baby.

And he exploited her vulnerability to the fullest.

The moment that Andrea Dahlberg turned on to their usually peaceful residential street, she was struck by a feeling of unease. The affluent community of Terra Nova, just outside of Visby, was an area where nothing much ever happened. Life proceeded at a predictable tempo among the gardens surrounding the detached homes and the sites of the terraced houses. But suddenly there was something different in the air. She stopped, wiped the sweat from her brow, removed the water bottle from her belt and drank a few gulps. She glanced around, studying the façades of the houses and the few cars parked along the road. Not a soul in sight. On the surface everything seemed calm.

She was on her way home from her usual exercise routine: power-walking at a furious pace. For once she hadn't managed to persuade any of her neighbours to come along. On this particular morning all the women who usually accompanied her were busy. Why? Was it because of the rain? she thought with annoyance. She had never let the weather deter her. And besides, it was only a light drizzle.

Since she was without a companion, she had been

forced to confine her ten kilometres to the small paths around the neighbourhood. How dreary. She preferred the woods but didn't dare go there alone because she couldn't relax. She always imagined that a rapist was about to appear as soon as she heard the slightest rustling in a nearby thicket.

Her stomach was growling. She always walked before breakfast. That way she burned off more fat, which was something that Andrea Dahlberg was extremely interested in doing, even though there was no sign of any extra kilos on her toned body. She had almost reached home now and was thinking about how much she longed for some freshly squeezed orange juice and vanilla yoghurt with her own homemade muesli. Along with slices of kiwi and fresh raspberries from the bushes in her greenhouse in the back garden. Espresso and the morning paper. Always the same routine. Today she could also enjoy greater calm than usual because she was home alone and didn't have to go in to work. Her holiday had already started. Sam was up in Fårösund working on a film and was expected home the following day. The children were going to spend the next two weeks in the Stockholm archipelago with their maternal grandmother and the man she had been married to for so long that the kids forgot he wasn't Andrea's father. They had left yesterday. She should have plenty of peace and quiet.

But then that feeling had come over her. So subtle that it was barely noticeable. Like a whispering at the back of her neck. Andrea again glanced around, looking in all directions. Nobody was behind her. She was the only one on the road. The only person she had met since nearing home was a man wearing a straw hat and sunglasses who had been walking towards her on the opposite pavement. He had raised his hand in greeting, but she hadn't recognized him. Maybe he was visiting someone. She straightened the visor of her baseball cap and stretched her back, trying to shake off the sense of unease.

She was relieved to see in the distance one of her neighbours coming towards her. Pushing a pram, as usual. Even though Sandra was not one of Andrea's best friends, she was always pleasant, and she and her husband were part of her general circle of acquaintances.

She greeted Sandra cheerfully. They exchanged a few words about the weather and the upcoming summer holidays. Nothing special. Sandra seemed stressed and kept evading her eyes, her smile a bit strained. A few minutes later she excused herself, saying that she was in a hurry and had an appointment at the social services office.

Andrea was almost home. She passed the Halldéns' house, which was made of sand-lime brick painted pink. It was much bigger and showier than the neighbouring houses, with its luxurious, pillar-lined driveway, curving staircase and a fountain on the lawn. She remembered how she and Sam had laughed at such an ostentatious display. Who did the Halldéns think they were? The Ewings in *Dallas*?

The rain had stopped, but the air was still heavy with moisture. The street was deserted. The grass was fragrant from the rain. The vegetation in the resplendent gardens was a sumptuous green right now, at the beginning of summer. Things had looked quite different when she and Sam and the kids had moved into the new development fifteen years ago. Back then the land around the houses consisted mostly of heaps of dirt and scraggly, sparsely planted shrubs meant to provide a semblance of hedges along carefully plotted property lines. By now the area was lush and flourishing and spacious houses with neatly mown lawns lined both sides of the street. In a second she would be home. Their house was at the far end, with a wooded area behind. It was a white-painted wooden house, built in an early-twentieth-century style, in spite of the fact that it was only fifteen years old. It had a pitched roof, gingerbread trim, mullioned windows and a glass veranda.

As Andrea got closer, she gave a start. The front door was open. Just slightly ajar, but enough so that she noticed it as she passed their bright-red postbox, which Sam had bought in New York in the spring.

She stopped short. Listened intently. Not a sound except for the quiet dripping from the drainpipe on the garage wall. She fixed her eyes on the door. Had she forgotten to close it when she left for her walk? That was impossible. She was always so careful. An inveterate worrier who regularly checked that the balcony door was locked, that all the windows were closed and the lights off before she left the house. She always set the security alarm that had been installed next to the front door, under the key cupboard. She would not have neglected to lock the door or set the alarm.

Soundlessly she crept closer. No signs of a break-in. Her brain was registering data and the exact time in case she would have to notify the police and the insurance company. Wednesday, 25 June, 9.35 a.m. As quietly as possible she went up the steps to the porch, cringing at every creak. She paused to listen for any sound from inside. Still nothing. She held her breath. Then she stretched out trembling fingers towards the crack in the doorway. Slowly she pulled the door open.

And stepped inside.

The shadows moved like elongated, intangible figures across the kitchen floor. Stina Ek sat on the floor with her bare feet on the cool tiles and leaned against the kitchen cupboard in the corner between the sink and the pantry. Her knees were drawn up, her arms folded. Her eyes followed the erratically rippling patterns, dissolving and merging, all depending on the capricious play of the tree branches outside the window. The light was lovely, and the house was completely silent. The sun had suddenly peeked out from the heavy cloud cover. The babysitter had picked up the children right after breakfast. She ought to pack but couldn't get herself to move. She just remained sitting here, incapable of doing anything at all. As if the air had gone out of her when the house had emptied and she was left alone with her thoughts.

Her controlled façade crumbled, the muscles in her face relaxed, her shoulders drooped, and she found it easier to breathe. She no longer had to make an effort, and that made her feel tired.

On the following day she and Håkan were going away with their best friends: Sam, Andrea, John and

Beata. They were neighbours in Terra Nova. All of them had moved in at the same time, when the houses had just been built and the area had the air of a new development. Back then their children were young, and they had met at the day nursery or the playground. The years had passed with a countless number of parents' meetings, children's parties, dinners and celebrations that had brought them close, so that over time they had become practically indispensable to each other. They helped each other out by taking the kids to and from school and football practice; they exchanged recipes and borrowed high-pressure washers and circular saws. In the autumn they set aside special days to rake leaves together, then burned the leaves and grilled sausages. They helped each other put up wallpaper and finish DIY projects. And it wasn't just daily chores. They had dinners and parties together, including the annual crayfish feast, *glögg* parties at Christmas, and celebrations on Walpurgis Eve and at Midsummer. They steadfastly clung to traditions, and everything always had to be done in the same way. A few times they had diverged from the customary festivities, with unfortunate consequences. None of them wanted to risk losing the deep-seated sense of community that they'd established, so now they all kept to the unspoken rules. At least outwardly.

A few years back they had created a new tradition. Three couples in the neighbourhood who were particularly close friends decided to take a brief trip together each summer. A grown-up trip without the children. Sam Dahlberg was the one who had come up with the idea. He was the driving force in the group, inventive and creative. He thought that since the children were older now, they could treat themselves to a holiday without them for a few days once a year. But it wasn't supposed to be just an ordinary trip. It had to include some sort of activity, something original. And they couldn't be away very long, since they had to find someone to take care of the children. Just a few days.

They had gone horse riding in Iceland and river rafting near Jukkasjärvi in northern Sweden. They had bicycled through the vineyard areas of Provence and gone mountain climbing on the North Cape. This year they had decided on a simpler holiday.

First they would attend the annual Bergman festival week on the island of Fårö, then continue on to Stora Karlsö to see the thousands of young guillemots that, at this time of year, glided down from the steep limestone cliffs to set off for their winter habitat in the southern Baltic Sea. The phenomenon was a famous event.

Stina got up with a sigh. Outside the window she caught sight of Andrea walking past, dressed in shorts and a top that fitted her tall, toned body snugly.

She was walking at a frenetically brisk pace, looking unabashedly alert and energetic. Sometimes Andrea's efficiency wore Stina out, and she didn't feel like going along. She had declined Andrea's invitation when she had phoned earlier. Stina had clearly heard the disappointment in her friend's voice, but she couldn't help the fact that she didn't want to go. Things weren't the same as before.

Nowadays she mostly went running by herself. When she was alone in the woods her thoughts had free rein, often wandering to the other side of the world. Stina had been adopted from Vietnam, and for as long as she could remember, she had yearned to rediscover her roots. Fragmentary images danced in her mind. The smells of Hanoi's slums still clung to her nostrils. She had memories of her grandmother's sinewy hands washing dishes in the sink, of her own feet touching the stone floor, of the privy out in the yard. Just after Stina turned five she had been left on the steps of the orphanage with a note hanging from a string around her neck and a toy rabbit in her arms. When she was six, an unimaginably big couple had come and taken her away from there. She had no memory of her biological mother, or her father. But her grandmother's face still appeared to her in the night. A wrinkled, toothless old lady with tiny black streaks for eyes, and rough but warm hands. She missed those comforting hands. She had longed for them all her life. For her, they were home, although they undoubtedly no longer existed. Stina was now thirty-seven, and back when she was five, her grandmother had already been old. Not that she had any plans to try to find her. As a teenager Stina had attempted to get in touch with the orphanage, but it had been shut down years before. She had tried to get help from the embassy, but that proved difficult. There was no information about her. All she had was the address where the orphanage had once been located. And her adoptive parents had convinced her that it wouldn't be a good idea to go there. She wouldn't find what she was looking for. Sorrow and a nostalgia for her origins and her grandmother's hands had settled like a dark weight inside of her, casting a shadow over her life.

She tried to gloss over it, to think about how fortunate she had been. She could have easily died of starvation on the streets or been sold to one of Hanoi's many brothels. Instead, she had enjoyed a secure and sheltered life and never lacked for anything.

Her adoptive parents were calm and nice, although slightly reserved in a way she had never been able to understand. They always kept a certain distance; it felt as if deep in their hearts they regarded her as a stranger, no matter how much they tried to show that they loved her, that she was their very own daughter. Really and truly. They treated her well and with respect, but their good-night hugs had seemed more obligatory than heartfelt. Her adoptive mother frequently said that she loved Stina, but there was no warmth in her voice. Her maternal solicitude was marked by an uncertainty that Stina was aware of throughout her childhood. Sometimes she would catch her mother surreptitiously studying her. On those occasions, the look in her eyes was surprised, almost frightened, with even a trace of aversion. That look told Stina more than all the years filled with assurances of love, the splendid birthday presents, and generous pocket money. At times Stina wondered why her parents had adopted her. She sensed that, in any case, she had never met their expectations.

As soon as she had turned eighteen, she had moved away from home and applied for a job with various airlines; the biggest of them hired her. It wasn't long before she met Håkan on a flight across the Atlantic. He looked to be at least ten years older than her and projected a self-confidence that she had never before encountered in a man. They chatted more than she usually did with passengers, and before he got off the plane, he had given her his business card.

A few days later Stina was seized by an impulse and phoned him. He sounded happy to hear from her and invited her to lunch in Stockholm. A year later she moved in with him on Gotland, in the house where he and his ex-wife had lived. At first that bothered her. Håkan already had two children and a dog, and living all around them were neighbours and former friends that he and his wife had known. And then she arrived. A mere slip of a woman, sixteen years younger than Håkan, and to top it all off, Asian in appearance – as if directly imported. Of course people had made an effort to be nice, but she was aware of what they said when her back was turned. It was a relief to move away from there to the newly developed Terra Nova, where everyone was starting from scratch. Nobody knew anyone else. She had been pregnant and immediately found new friends. All it took was one visit to the antenatal clinic. There she met Andrea, who had just moved in and was also expecting a baby. They became best friends, and gradually their group of acquaintances expanded.

As her family and social circle grew, Stina began to feel more secure. And they had a good life, she and Håkan. Two wonderful daughters, a big house with a garden and a swimming pool that they'd had installed last year when the company gave Håkan an extra big bonus. She still enjoyed her job as a flight attendant. Maybe it was because the atmosphere on board suited her. It was a temporary situation; everyone was always on their way somewhere else, and she had only superficial contact with the passengers. She forged no permanent bonds with anyone. Her colleagues came and went, and she was always working with new people.

She had filled the emptiness in her own way. No one had any idea what went on underneath, but soon everything was going to change. Her life was about to take a dramatic turn. Although she was terrified by the thought of the consequences, she realized that this change was inevitable. She had reached a crossroads. With one blow her secure existence would be turned upside down, and she was the one who had made that choice.

There was no going back.

At the foot of the stairs, she stops abruptly. She is staring upwards, nervously biting her lower lip. Her expression is rigid, focused. Her body is on high alert, like a hunted animal, listening, watching. Not a sound. She is pale but beautiful; her lips are painted red. Her dark tresses reach all the way past her waist. Her body is slender; she has long bare arms; she is wearing a skimpy top and shorts. She has kicked off her shoes. She puts one foot on the stairs made of Gotland limestone. Her red-painted toenails look like ripe wild strawberries – a lovely contrast with the grey. The light falls in from the side, creating a suggestive shadow play.

Just as she's about to go upstairs, she hears a sweeping sound behind her and she freezes. In a second the man is upon her, grabbing hold of her long hair and yanking her backwards. She falls on to the hall floor.

'Cut!'

Sam Dahlberg lifted his eyes from the monitor, relaxed, and brushed the hair back from his forehead. The actors cast him enquiring looks. Was he finally satisfied? This was the twelfth take of the same scene. The lead actress, Julia Berger, was starting to get a headache.

'We'll take it one more time.'

Stifled sighs, resigned expressions. One person dared to shake his head, cursing the director who was never satisfied. And the cinematographer felt the same way. It was stuffy and hot in the house near Bungeviken where they were shooting the very last scenes, and the crew was running out of patience. It was past seven in the evening, and they'd been at it since dawn.

Everyone was exhausted and hungry. Julia Berger shrugged and turned her hands palm up as she spoke to the director.

'First, I'm going to need a cigarette and a glass of water. Just so you know.'

She and her fellow actor disappeared out to the veranda facing the sea. A crew member rushed to take them some water. It was important to keep the star in a good mood. She was a temperamental diva, and on more than one occasion she had simply walked out, leaving the whole film crew in the lurch, because she'd lost patience and didn't get her own way.

Sam Dahlberg refused to be deterred. He could feel in his gut that this movie was going to be good. Really good. That was why he didn't want to take any risks. Retakes were necessary. He and the cinematographer had agreed to make sure that they had enough footage when they went to the editing room.

Sam quickly finished off a bottle of mineral water. In spite of the heavy downpour, it was damned hot. The crew relaxed, chatting to each other. One person ran to the toilet; another went out for a smoke. Everybody knew that the break would last a few minutes.

When Sam once again took his seat in the director's chair, the effect was immediate.

'OK, let's do it again,' shouted the director's assistant.

The hum of voices stopped at once. Everyone turned to look at Sam, then at each other. Their posture changed from relaxed to alert, their expressions attentive. An air of concentration filled the set. Sam looked at the people around him. It was like a dream play every time. The actors, the script, the cinematographer, and the rest of the film crew: everyone with an important part to play in completing the scene. He loved it, the way everybody joined forces in one intense moment. There was something magical about it. And an unpredictability. It was impossible to tell what might happen. Often something unexpected would occur, no matter how well he planned the production, going through the script in great detail with everyone involved, spending weeks in advance with the cinematographer and checking out all the film locations. He had to know how the light fell at various times of the day, what sounds they could count on hearing, how the site would function in practice for everyone involved. He liked to be well prepared. Only then was there room for spontaneity. Sam Dahlberg had spent years learning these techniques. He loved his job. For him, it was the very heart of his life, giving him the space to breathe. He surveyed the set one last time. Everything was ready. A giddy feeling filled his stomach; everyone was awaiting his signal. All of these people. They were waiting for him and no one else. He cast a quick glance at his assistant director.

'Quiet. Rolling. Camera.'

The same scene was repeated. In Julia Berger's defence, it had to be said that even though she might be feeling annoyed, she gave her all every time the cameras rolled – no matter now many takes it took. He admired her professionalism. When they finished the scene, everyone waited in tense silence. Now Sam had everyone's attention. He hid his face behind a handkerchief and wiped away both the sweat and a few tears that had trickled from his eyes. Then he looked at his colleagues and his face broke into a happy grin.

'Bloody good job. I think, by God, that we've just done the last take on the film. Just a second.'

He motioned for the cinematographer, and together they watched the scene on the monitor, accompanied by some indistinct murmuring. Then they nodded and slapped each other on the back. Everyone waited tensely. Sam raised his eyes.

'I think we've made a movie here.'

A grateful cheer rose from the set. The lead actors, who had just been involved in a fight, embraced each other a bit longer than might be considered purely professional, if anyone from the film crew had bothered to notice. But everybody was busy congratulating each other, hugging and patting one another on the back.

'Unbelievable,' exclaimed Sam happily. 'That's a wrap. Two months of filming are over. You've all been amazing. Now it's time to celebrate.'

Håkan Ek left the office early on that Friday afternoon. He had five weeks of holiday ahead of him. He couldn't remember when he'd been away from his job for so many weeks in a row. If ever. He enjoyed his work as the sales manager for a large electronics company in Visby, but now he felt he needed a holiday.

His mobile beeped before he'd even left the car park. A message from Klara. *Phone me.* He frowned. What now? His daughter from his first marriage was his only real worry. She was a restless young woman who lived in central Stockholm and suffered from an eating disorder. She'd also had problems finding a job and coping with various boyfriends. But Håkan was used to it. By now Klara's troubles were an inevitable aspect of his life, like a body part that was always tender and needed care.

But his daughter was not his only child from a failed relationship. From his second marriage he had a son who was now in his late teens, but he had little contact with the boy. The divorce had been a painful and long-drawn-out affair. He hardly ever spoke to his second wife, Helena. After they divorced, she and their son had moved in with her parents in Haparanda in the far north. But he was in regular touch with his first wife, Ingrid. Their marriage had fizzled out so many years ago that it felt like another lifetime. After they went their separate ways, it had taken years before she decided to remarry. She said she was very picky. She used to quip that she was used to the best. Håkan appreciated the fact that they were able to joke about their past, sometimes talking on the phone for hours. Nobody could make him laugh the way she did. The thought regularly occurred to him that he'd actually been happier with Ingrid than he was with Stina. They both belonged to the fifties generation and had a lot in common. They had watched the same TV programmes, gone to the same dance clubs. They knew the same dances, songs and bands. They liked the same musicians, and they had the same sense of humour.

As Håkan drove home, he grew pensive. He ought to be looking forward to the summer holidays, but something was preventing that. Almost like dirt on the windscreen that was impossible to remove. His thoughts turned to his third wife.

Everything was different with Stina, and in many respects more complicated than with either of his ex-wives. It was because of her childhood and upbringing, her rootlessness and insecurity. He was aware that she needed to view him as a father figure. He had been fascinated by Stina from the first moment he saw her on board the plane, with her shiny, raven-black hair reaching to her shoulders in a blunt cut, her slim figure in the attractive uniform. Her soft, dark eyes had fixed on his, and after that he didn't want to let her go. Not for anything in the world. Divorcing his second wife seemed like such an obvious decision that he wanted to get it out of the way as quickly as possible. Helena became a mere shadow for him. In hindsight, he could see how selfishly he had behaved.

But that was all in the past.

Right now he and Stina were anticipating a long holiday. And it would start off with the annual trip with their closest friends. In reality he would have preferred to do something all on their own, just the two of them. They needed time together; for quite a while now they had spent far too little time with each other. That must be what was worrying him, causing a deep disquiet. He could hardly remember when they'd last had sex. Sometimes that was what happened with Stina. She would distance herself from him, almost as if she was avoiding him. He had tried to talk to her about it, asking her what was wrong, but she assured him that it was nothing special. She was just feeling tired.

Stina had to work a couple more weeks before she could take an extended holiday from her job. But they could at least spend a few days together. Later their summer holiday awaited them, and they were planning to go island hopping in Greece with the children. He was looking forward to that. Since Stina had a hard time relaxing at home, they needed to go on a trip together, preferably abroad so that she could leave all her obligations behind.

He tapped in the number for home and felt both relieved and a little uneasy when he heard her voice. She didn't sound happy, but not really sad either.

No, he didn't need to stop for groceries. If they weren't going away he would have bought her flowers.

But it wouldn't be worth it just now.

He saw her from far away as she came walking towards him with her rather sauntering gait on the other side of Norra Hansegatan. Detective Superintendent Anders Knutas stopped to wait for her, observing her slender form as she approached. His colleague Karin Jacobsson always walked to work because she lived in the middle of town. She was wearing her iPod earbuds, as usual, and jeans that sat low on her hips. She had on a white T-shirt with a drum set printed on the front and trainers. The wind had tousled her cropped brown hair. Her eyes were fixed on the pavement, and she hadn't yet noticed Knutas. He wondered what she was thinking about, wondered what he was going to do with her.

Karin was the colleague he was closest to at work, and she acted as his deputy when necessary. But it was no exaggeration to say that she had really made a mess of things. A little less than a year ago she had confided a secret that Knutas couldn't possibly ignore. He knew that eventually he would have to do something about it – and sooner rather than later because her confession had placed him in an untenable position ever since.

Of course he was grateful that Karin had finally unburdened her heart, but he wished the circumstances had been different.

He, on the other hand, had trusted her right from the start, and she knew almost everything about him. All about his personal life as well as his professional career. Karin was always willing to listen, and Knutas considered her one of his best friends. But she had always found it difficult to talk about her own private life. She was forty-one years old, lived alone with her cockatoo in a lovely attic flat on Mellangatan, played football, and devoted herself to her job. He had never heard her mention a man or a boyfriend in her life. Or a woman, for that matter.

Then one evening last summer, when they happened to be in Stockholm in connection with a difficult murder case, they had been sitting in a restaurant drinking wine and she had suddenly fallen apart. She told him that as a teenager she had been raped and became pregnant. By the time her pregnancy was discovered, it was too late for an abortion, so she had carried the child to term. It was a girl, and her parents had forced Karin to give the baby up for adoption. Against her will, the child was taken from her immediately after the birth, and she had never seen her again. All her life Karin had kept this sorrow to herself. But now she had decided to search for her grown-up daughter.

It was as if a dam had burst, and Karin had wept and talked non-stop all night. She had also revealed something so serious that she risked being sacked if it ever came out. To Knutas's horror, Karin told him that the previous year she had allowed a double murderer named Vera Petrov to escape. Part of her explanation had to do with her own trauma. The police had been hot on the heels of Petrov, but during the chase Jacobsson had discovered the woman in the throes of labour in a cabin aboard the Gotland ferry. Instead of alerting her colleagues, she had helped bring the baby into the world. Since a tragic story had prompted Petrov to commit the two murders, Jacobsson had let her go. She had kept her actions secret until confiding in Knutas on that night in Stockholm.

Knutas was shocked when the truth came out. Certainly it was a distressing case, and of course he understood feeling empathy for the killer, but what Karin had done was the most grievous dereliction of duty, and his first thought had been to suspend her immediately. But then he had relented. He couldn't bring himself to do it. Vera Petrov was still being sought by international authorities; so far no trace of her had been found. Time had passed, and now Knutas was also implicated. He still didn't know how to solve the problem, but he realized it was inevitable that sooner or later he would be forced to do something about the matter. It was no exaggeration to say that Karin had placed him in the greatest dilemma of his life.

Yet he still felt a tenderness for her as she approached. She raised her head and looked straight at him with those eyes, nut-brown and doe-like. Her face broke into a smile, revealing the gap between her front teeth. He found it worrisome that her charm had such a powerful effect on him and that he had become dependent on her. They shared a deep bond. It had grown stronger over all the years they had worked together. Sometimes he almost mistook it for love. Even though he loved his wife, Lina, part of his heart belonged to Karin.

And no doubt it always would.

The shower water poured over her sweaty body. Goosebumps appeared on her skin as Andrea Dahlberg reached for the soap container. With brisk, light movements she massaged in the expensive shower gel that Sam had brought back for her from his latest trip. He was always so thoughtful, even after twenty years of marriage. He'd been to a film festival in Berlin. Just as a spectator. None of his own films had won any prizes. Not yet.

She stepped out of the mosaic-lined shower stall and wrapped herself in a thick terrycloth towel. Then she paused in front of the mirror and noticed to her satisfaction that she was already nicely suntanned. A few aches and pains after yesterday's evening workout at the gym, but she was in perfect bikini shape for the summer. She let go of the bath towel and it dropped to the floor. Then she turned around so she could see herself in profile in the mirror; it was the angle she liked best. She still looked just fine after passing forty and having three children. Her breasts were large and well shaped, but that was because she'd had work done on them after Mathilda was born. She couldn't stand the thought of spending the rest of her life with those flabby, drooping sacks that her breasts had become after all the breastfeeding she'd done. Now the part of her body that made her most proud was her bosom. She smiled at herself and went through the bedroom to the walk-in closet that Sam had built just for her. There was plenty of room for all her shoes and clothes, lined up in perfect order. An enormous mirror covered one wall so she could stand there in peace as she chose what to wear. Later today they would be going out to Fårö for the Bergman festival, and then continue on to Stora Karlsö.

Andrea's eyes paused on a photograph of Sam and herself on the yacht in Stockholm's archipelago last summer. How handsome he was, looking so tanned in his white tennis sweater and sunglasses. He had his arm around her and was smiling at the camera. He was still the most attractive man she could imagine. She was proud to walk at his side whenever they were out socializing. Sometimes she would sit for a long time and just stare at him across the breakfast table. There they sat, on an ordinary morning, and suddenly it would seem to her so unreal that she was allowed to be there with him. Day in and day out. Of course they'd had some bad patches, just like everybody, but for the most part things had been good. They led an orderly life with few surprises – exactly the way she wanted it to be. She was looking forward to growing old with Sam.

Their home was just as flawless as her appearance.

She loved decorating and furnishing the rooms, and she insisted that everything should be perfectly arranged. Sam laughed at her for pressing their bed sheets and ironing his underwear. Every six months she would remove all the books from the shelves so she could dust behind them. Once a month she would take the rugs and cushions out to beat the dust out of them with an impressive frenzy. She changed the bed linens every week, and during the summer months even more often, since she thought that everyone sweated more during the night at that time of year. She arranged the tinned goods and pasta packages according to a specific pattern in the pantry, which was always well stocked.

Every Sunday morning she would sit down at the kitchen table and fill out the family calendar with the activities and meetings scheduled for the coming week. She wrote down a menu for each day, checked to see what they had in the cupboards, and then went out to shop for the rest of the groceries they would need. Preferably with one of the neighbouring wives. She loved her predictable life. It made her feel secure; she always knew what to expect.

Right now she needed to finish packing for the trip they were taking with friends. She hummed to herself as she placed Sam's shirts in a neat pile inside his bag. She cast a glance out of the window. Sandra was walking past with the pram, as usual. That poor woman. Andrea didn't envy her. At the age of forty-two, dealing with young children was now part of the distant past, and she wouldn't for the life of her want to start again. Her neighbour already had two teenagers when she got pregnant again. Even though she and her husband claimed it was wonderful to add a latecomer to their family, Andrea didn't really believe them. She couldn't imagine anything worse than being tied down again. That was probably why Sandra seemed so stressed lately.

The sight of her made Andrea think about the strange experience she'd just had. That inexplicable feeling of being watched, and the fact that she'd not only forgotten to lock the front door but left it slightly ajar. It was so unlike her. Maybe she was starting the menopause, which could make a woman a bit absent-minded. Hormones and so on. But wasn't she too young for that? Didn't the change happen to women in their fifties? The 'change' – what an unpleasant word. She had no desire to change and enter another stage in life. She would be happy if time stood still for twenty years. She had never felt so good.

She went into the kitchen and put on the coffee. It would be several hours before Sam came home so they could leave on the trip.

This holiday was coming just at the right time. Sam had been busy with a lengthy film shoot that was finally done, and now he could take some time off before starting on the editing. He'd been away from home a lot lately, but that was always the case when he was shooting. During those periods he was 'married to the film', as he put it. That didn't really bother her because she was busy too. She ran a trendy clothing shop on Adelsgatan, and there was always plenty to do. It was with relief that she had turned over responsibility to her colleague, the other part-owner, several days earlier than she had planned. She'd wanted to take it easy and get in the mood for the trip. And take care of Sam after he'd worked so hard. They would enjoy relaxing together, watch movies that they'd seen before but that were worth another viewing. And enjoy the company of good friends and other people interested in film on Fårö.

She was also looking forward to spending more time with Stina. Maybe they could take morning walks together on Fårö. Have a proper talk. It had been a while, for they were both so busy with their own lives. She realized how much she had missed her friend. They knew everything about each other, had shared so much over the years, and there was a strong bond between them. In fact, Stina was the one she felt closest to, aside from Sam and the children. Now they would finally have the opportunity to be together for a few days. After that the nature trip to Stora Karlsö awaited them. She smiled to herself. They were so good about tending to their marriage, she and Sam. They had always been that way. When the kids were little, they had regularly hired a babysitter so that several times a year they could take a long weekend together, just the two of them. It was undoubtedly the sort of thing that had helped to keep their love alive. Over the years they had evolved into a single unit that was rock-solid. As she filled her coffee cup, she thought: We belong together. That's how it had been ever since they first met, and that's how it would always be.

Johan Berg reached for the package of nappies on the shelf in the bathroom. Anton lay on the changing table, gurgling happily. His round, sunny face was turned towards Johan, and his brown eyes sparkled with contentment. He chattered nonstop, constantly producing new sounds. Right now he lay there, waving his chubby little arms about. All of a sudden a stream shot up into the air. Johan felt it drenching his shoulder.

'Bloody hell!'

Quickly he wiped up the piss that had landed on the changing table and was trickling over the edge on to the bathroom floor. To think such quantities of fluid could come out of a baby only six months old. He dried off both himself and his son and then returned to Emma in the bedroom.

'Good morning,' she said sleepily, automatically pulling out one of her breasts as Johan carefully placed Anton in her arms. 'Ouch,' she complained as her son eagerly grabbed for her nipple. He was such a greedy little thing.

'He peed straight up in the air,' said Johan with a

44

yawn as he sank back against the sleep-warm pillows and covers.

'He did? What a rascal,' said Emma tenderly, caressing the baby's soft cheek. 'Aren't you going to work?'

'Sure. Just give me five minutes,' murmured Johan, turning his back and pulling up the covers.

For the past month he'd actually been on paternity leave from his job as a reporter for Swedish TV's regional news programme, but his editor, Max Grenfors, had phoned from Stockholm and asked him to come in over the weekend. They hadn't yet found a replacement for him at the local editorial office on Gotland, and so far they'd solved the problem with temporary substitutes who flew over from the mainland. Johan had nothing against going into the office. Spending his days with a baby was wonderful in many ways, but it could also get a bit tiresome.

But he had to be happy for every small step forward. For instance, now he shared the bed with only two others. A few months ago Elin had been relegated to her own room, and lately that had worked fine, without any fuss. When they brought Anton home from the maternity clinic, their three-year-old daughter had been extremely jealous and refused to sleep anywhere but with her parents. For two months they had all crowded into the same bed. Gradually Elin had calmed down and realized that things were going to continue as usual, even though the family had increased in number. Besides, she had her older half-siblings, Sara and Filip, to play with. It was so touching to see how they took care of Elin whenever Emma had to feed Anton or change his nappy.

Emma stretched out in bed and smiled at her son. She was relieved that everything was going so well, even though she'd been shocked to discover that she was pregnant again, and even though both she and the baby had been through a life-threatening experience before he was born, when Emma had accidentally ended up in the middle of a police manhunt.

During the spring she'd been on maternity leave from her job as a teacher at the small Kyrk School in Roma. Now the school was closed for the summer holidays, and Johan was also on leave. Elin had eventually agreed to go back to the day nursery, where she actually loved being with all of her friends, and Emma treasured her time alone with the baby. She could cuddle and feed her son as much as she wanted, without the risk of any jealous outbursts from his big sister. At the same time, she was longing for her adult life. She wanted to go back to teaching, spend time with her colleagues, and work out again. Even the teacher conferences now seemed attractive. But first she and Johan were going to enjoy a whole summer together. When Elin was born, everything had been in such turmoil. Back then she had lived alone in the house and taken sole responsibility for the newborn while Johan worked in Stockholm. It was true that she had chosen the arrangement herself, and Johan would have liked nothing better than to move in with her and share in caring for their daughter. But at the time Emma had felt so insecure, after the divorce and everything else. Now the situation was totally different. Her ex-husband, Olle, had met a new woman, the children had settled down, and her relationship with Olle functioned well. And besides, her kids loved Johan, who treated them as his own.

She sighed and looked down at her baby. Anton abruptly let go of her breast and his head fell back. The hair on his forehead was sweaty from the effort, his cheeks flushed. He was sound asleep.

His father was too.

Andrea Dahlberg opened the front door and lugged her suitcase out to the car. Would she never learn? Afraid of being without something, she always packed too much. Sam laughed at her as he passed, carrying a simple sports bag, which he elegantly tossed into the SUV. He had quickly removed half of the things she had packed for him.

'Is it heavy, sweetheart?'

He turned around and stretched out his hand to take her suitcase. When she handed it over, he grimaced and dropped it on the ground with a thud, as if it were impossible to hold. She smiled. She was happy to see Sam in such good spirits. He'd been unusually tired lately. The new film had taken most of his waking hours. Leaving on a trip right after the film wrapped was clearly exactly what he needed. The fact that he was the one who'd come up with the idea for their destination contributed to his good mood. They had never gone as a group to the Bergman festival, which was held on Fårö every year in late June. Sam had gone ever since the first one five years earlier, since he was a devoted admirer of

Ingmar Bergman. This year the festival was dedicated to Bergman's memory, since the world-famous director had peacefully passed away at his remote residence on Fårö in July of the previous year.

Andrea went back inside the house to get a few last items and make sure all the doors were closed and the lights turned off. Across the street she saw Håkan and Stina going through the same procedure. She waved happily to Stina, who was running from the house to the car, hunching her shoulders against the rain. Andrea paused to watch her friend. How lovely she was. Her hair was pulled back in a ponytail and she was dressed almost like a child, in a pink raincoat, short skirt, and flower-patterned wellington boots. Even though she was thirty-seven and the mother of two, she looked like a young girl.

Stina knew things about Andrea that no one except Sam knew. Her innermost and deepest thoughts.

She would never forget the time when Stina's own candour and sensitivity had made her reveal everything about herself. They were alone in Stina's house. Both Håkan and Sam were out of town, and Stina had invited Andrea and her kids to dinner. The children had played noisily until they all fell into bed. Then Andrea and Stina had sat in front of the fireplace with a bottle of wine. They'd talked about life's problems. About guilt and shame. And then, for the first time, Andrea had told someone other than Sam about her darkest secret. Stina's face looked so soft in the glow from the fire; she had listened attentively and they had talked all night. Andrea had never felt so close to anyone before. Stina became the sister she might have had. She would always cherish their friendship. There were no barriers between them.

Andrea shook off these thoughts. She was glad that in spite of everything she now had such a good life and such good friends. Their extended social circle included a dozen couples with children of more or less the same age. Within that circle was the core group, whose friendship was even stronger. It consisted of her and Sam, Håkan and Stina, John and Beata. Six adults who jointly had eight children, and it often felt as if the group was big enough. That was why they frequently held their own dinner parties and celebrations – something that the others in their social circle did not really like, just as they did not like being excluded from the trips that the three couples took together.

She looked in the children's rooms, and noted with pleasure that they had tidied things up before they left. Amazing that they'd become so neat and orderly. She affectionately pictured her children's faces. In a not-so-distant future they would be moving away from home. Several of her acquaintances were already worrying about that prospect, when they would be alone in the house, at the dinner table, and in front of the TV in the evening. That wasn't something that bothered her.

She and Sam often talked about everything they were going to do, all the trips and excursions they would take when they finally had plenty of time for each other. She longed to have her husband all to herself. Sometimes she even felt jealous when he laughed and talked too much with the kids. It felt as if he had forgotten about her. Occasionally it worried her that she was so envious, but she couldn't help it.

Their bedroom looked fine. She touched the handle to the balcony door; it was locked. Through the window she could see across the street, and she watched as Sam stowed their wellingtons and raincoats in the car. Later in the summer they were going to celebrate their twentieth wedding anniversary. She had secretly booked them flights to Florence. That was where they had got engaged, and this time they would be staying at the same hotel and having dinner at the same romantic restaurant where they had celebrated their engagement. She had even phoned the owner to make sure the restaurant would be open, and he had promised to seat them at the exact same table. Sam had no clue. She was taking along a special card that she would give to him when they were on Stora Karlsö. She had spent time drawing, cutting and pasting to make the card that would tell him all the details. He was going to be so surprised. She could hardly wait to see his expression when he opened the envelope. Several times she'd been on the verge of giving him a hint about what she was planning, but she had managed to stop herself at the last minute. Now she quickly went through the rest of the rooms to make sure all was in order. Everything had to be perfect when they left the house.

Only then could she relax.

It had rained steadily all day long. On his way home from work, Knutas turned his old Mercedes towards the Solberg swimming pool. He usually swam once a week during the winter months. Not as often during the summer, although there were few things he enjoyed as much as swimming. To cover lap after lap in the pool, metre after metre, was an undemanding type of therapy. The water infused him with calm, and he moved easily, at a leisurely pace, even though he was aware that he'd put on a few kilos. Whenever he encountered any problems, he gained weight. Eating was a consolation and a compensation; it gave him strength. Right now his mind was buzzing with contradictory thoughts and worries about both his job and his private life. First and foremost was his concern about Karin. Her personal trauma, the rape and the child that she'd had: her well-kept secret. And also the professional secret that she'd kept to herself for almost a year: the fact that she had allowed a murderer to walk free without saying a word to him about it. Month after month they had worked side by side, talking and joking as usual, solving problems, discussing cases, and not once had she mentioned it to him. They'd had coffee and lunch together – he didn't know how many times – as if nothing was wrong. And he'd had absolutely no idea.

On numerous occasions they had talked about the murder case and the hunt for the killer. He had told her about his conversations with Interpol and Europol. How the search was ongoing in several countries. He had talked about the tips that had come in, some more interesting than others. He had shared all the information with her. And the whole time she had been hiding the truth from him. He felt like an idiot. He still didn't know how to deal with the dilemma. He wished there was someone he could consult. A few times he'd thought of talking to the National Criminal Police inspector, Martin Kihlgård, who had come to Gotland on several occasions to help the Visby police with homicide cases. Martin also knew Karin well. He really should talk to him.

At the same time Knutas was forced to admit that he was worried not just for Karin's sake but about himself. He was concerned about the consequences for his own position. He would be accused of letting too much time pass before reporting the matter. And the police investigation would certainly question why he hadn't discovered earlier that Karin had helped the killer on board the ferry from Gotland. That made him look even more pathetic. Scorn for himself churned in his stomach.

He began swimming harder to escape from his

discomfort. With long strokes he swam towards the end of the pool, keeping his eyes fixed on the tiles. Not looking to either side, where only a few other people occupied the lanes, ploughing through the water just as he was doing, lap after lap. There were seldom many swimmers in the pool at this time of year.

After finishing a few laps at a furious pace, he slowed down. Depression weighed on him.

What had so far functioned best in his life wasn't going very well either. His marriage. Lina had always stood for security in his world, and she was the love of his life. An attractive Dane with red hair that reached to her waist, she loved her job as a midwife and had always been devoted to her family. She was always there when he needed her. Never before had he felt any doubt about their relationship. But lately a change had crept in, and it scared him. They rarely did things together any more. Lina was so busy, and he was too. Days could go by and they wouldn't even see each other. Knutas had begun to speculate about things that he had previously never questioned, including what Lina said and did. He had started listening in a new way. What they said to each other in the morning, what words were spoken at the dinner table, in front of the TV, in the bedroom. He had become more aware and alert, almost as if he were still on duty. And that bothered him. He'd begun to see Lina in a different light, and all of a sudden he'd discovered new aspects and sides of her personality that he'd never noticed before. He realized that when it came right down to it, his life was no longer the same. He couldn't take anything for granted. It was possible that things might not be as they seemed, that at any second the ground might begin to shift under his feet. All it took was to alter his perceptions a bit. Make a slight adjustment to the way he viewed the world.

He recalled a conversation he'd had a few days earlier with an old friend he hadn't seen for a long time. When the man's children had left home, he and his wife had sold the house where they'd lived all those years. They had watched their children grow up there, celebrated birthdays, weddings and graduations. Over the years, they had experienced so much in that house, both sorrows and joys. Knutas's friend told him that when they moved out, it felt as if their whole world was turned upside down. He saw his wife in a new light, as well as his job and his friends – in fact, his entire life. He could no longer assume anything. It was like starting over from scratch. He ended up getting a divorce, quitting his job, and moving into his own flat. He started a whole new life. How much of his wife lingered in the walls of that house? How much of their shared life existed only in their home, in the possessions they'd acquired and the routines they had become accustomed to? The thought terrified Knutas. He tried to reassure himself that things were different with him and Lina. Very different. On the other hand, who was to say that his friend had been happier back then than he was now? Maybe life demanded change once in a while. Required a person to shake things up, let in fresh air. Open the door to something else, something more enriching.

Knutas glanced at the clock on the wall. Five thirty. He'd been swimming for half an hour, but he wasn't tired at all. He decided to keep going for another fifteen minutes. Rain was pouring down outside the big windows of the swimming hall. That never-ending rain.

Sometimes he wondered whether he was going through a mid-life crisis. Nothing seemed to give him real joy any more. Now summer had arrived, and later he would go on holiday. He was supposed to have the entire month of August off, and he was planning a two-week trip to Italy with his family. Knutas had never been to Italy. But he was having trouble mustering his usual enthusiasm. He seemed overcome with apathy. That was also the accusation that Lina had flung at him when they argued the night before.

'You don't react to anything any more,' she'd told him. 'You have no opinions, there's nothing you want, you just don't care. As far as you're concerned, the world can go ahead and fall apart and all you'll do is shrug. Your indifference is driving me crazy!' And, as usual, she'd shouted and waved her arms about. Lina was so temperamental. She'd always been like that, with that flaming red hair of hers, and her pale complexion that flushed crimson whenever she got angry. In the past he had always admired her fiery temper.

Nowadays it merely made him tired.

At first glance the inn looked like an ordinary house. A small sign with the name 'Slow Train' painted on a piece of driftwood appeared right next to the turn-off. They just managed to see it in time, or they would have driven past. The name made Andrea think of an old tune by Bob Dylan, 'Slow Train', and the minute she got out of the car, she sensed a nostalgic air about the place.

The rain in Visby hadn't yet reached here. The clouds looked threatening, but so far no rain. Several horses were grazing in a pasture, a man in a straw hat was pottering about in the garden filled with flowers, and a slender woman wearing a long white skirt was taking in the laundry hanging on a line between the apple trees. From an open window in the large stone house came the scent of freshly baked bread. The woman stopped what she was doing and came to greet them.

'Hi. Welcome.'

Her gentle voice clearly revealed a French accent. She had a small, pale face with classic features, and she gave them a friendly smile. Then she ushered them into the house, which reinforced the feeling of a bygone era. They first went through a glass veranda with comfortable sofas along both sides. The window ledges were covered with all sorts of odds and ends: ceramic figurines, scented candles, baskets filled with flowers, and lamps in various colours and sizes.

A dark wooden table in the entrance hall served as the check-in desk. On the table stood a brass Strindberg lamp, an old inkwell with fountain pen, and a glass vase with a single rose.

'We call it the Bergman rose,' the Frenchwoman told them. 'It comes from the same rosebush that was planted on his grave.'

Andrea gave a start, not sure whether she thought the rose added to the pleasant atmosphere or not.

The woman gave them the keys to their rooms. Andrea and Sam had been assigned a room upstairs in the main building, while the others were given rooms in the surrounding buildings. They agreed to meet for a drink before the opening ceremonies of the Bergman festival, which would be held in the Fårö church.

'What a . . . picturesque room,' exclaimed Andrea after they huffed and puffed their way up the narrow staircase and opened the door to what was called the 'bridal suite'. She paused in the doorway and looked around in confusion. 'No toilet?'

The room held a double bed with a crocheted coverlet, a small night table, and a chiffonier. It was not a large room, but it was charming and bright. The window was open, facing the flower garden.

'For God's sake, the bathroom is just next door. Remember, this is a bed and breakfast, not some fancy hotel,' said Sam in annoyance as he sank on to the bed. 'We're way out in the country on this little island. What did you expect? A fucking Sheraton?'

Andrea stared at him in surprise.

'What's wrong with you?'

'I'm sorry,' he said, the sharpness gone from his voice. 'It's just that you sounded so whiny. Everything can't be perfect all the time.'

'I know that,' she said, offended. Her cheeks were flushed with indignation. 'Excuse me, but I was just wondering where the toilet was. I thought we were going to have a good time now that you're finally free. And you're the one who wanted to come here. Not me. You should be happy that everybody agreed to do what you wanted.' Disappointment made her voice husky. With one blow he had ruined her joy. How could he? Tears filled her eyes.

'OK. I know.' He sighed. 'I'm sorry. Come here.'

He reached out his arms towards her, and she sank into his embrace. Sam stroked her back. She wrapped her arms around him. The warmth from his body consoled her, and it didn't take long before her mood was restored. She began kissing him on the neck, more and more eagerly, searching for his lips. She wanted to feel close in order to forget about the tiresome exchange they'd just had. They lay down on the bed, and she pressed herself against him, put one leg over his. Gently he pushed her away.

'Now, now, take it easy. We have to meet the others in half an hour. We're going to have a drink before the ceremonies.'

'Oh, is it that late already? I need to fix my hair.'

They gathered in the garden among the apple trees where a table was set with champagne glasses and platters of French cheeses, biscuits and nuts.

'Oh, how marvellous!' exclaimed Beata, beaming at their French hostess, who gave a quick smile and then disappeared after placing two dewy bottles of champagne on the table.

'Time to celebrate!' cried Sam, popping the cork from the first bottle. 'We finished shooting the film yesterday.'

'That's great. Congratulations!' said Håkan. 'It must feel bloody wonderful!'

'You're so clever,' cooed Beata, standing behind Sam. She put her hands on his shoulders and rubbed her curvaceous body against his. 'Simply amazing. You should be proud of your husband, Andrea.'

Andrea managed a strained smile. Sometimes Beata really went overboard.

Stina raised the glass that Sam handed her.

'Cheers, Sam. We'll keep our fingers crossed that the film is a big hit. You deserve it. Right?'

'You better believe it. It's been pure hell. The most difficult and spoiled movie stars that I've ever worked with, not to mention the diva herself: Julia Berger. Good God!'

He rolled his eyes and went on pouring the champagne. When everyone had a glass, Sam cleared his throat, straightened his shoulders, and put on a solemn expression.

'Welcome, dear friends, to our annual holiday together. I've really been looking forward to this trip in particular. You all know why. Bergman was the greatest director and will always remain so. The rest of us mortals try our best, and I'm so happy that today I can also celebrate finally finishing the film, *The Last Commandment*. Thank God it's over. *Skål*, everyone!'

They all raised their glasses as they exchanged glances, glad to be in the company of friends.

The dry champagne tasted perfect.

The church green was crowded with people dressed in their summer best in honour of the evening. The weather was appropriate for the occasion, considering it was Bergman they were celebrating. Dark clouds raced across the sky, forming fantastical shapes at the same time as rays of sunlight sporadically burst through the darkness, creating their own dramatic effect. Light and darkness, which was precisely the speciality of the acclaimed director.

Johan Berg had a few anxious moments as his camerawoman, Pia Lilja, adroitly manoeuvred the TV van through the throng in the car park near the Fårö church. He hadn't been back here since his wedding day.

Two years ago he had stood in this very place on the church green, sweating, with a packed church, a puzzled pastor and a missing bride. It was a real ordeal, especially considering the turbulent relationship that he and Emma had endured. He never knew what sort of ideas would pop into her head. New doubts, new questions. Their first year together had been a real roller coaster. Anything was possible. It would have been typical of their relationship if she hadn't turned up at all. But in the end she did. Thank God. Sometimes when he thought back on everything they had gone through together, he wondered how he'd managed. Love was incomprehensible. Certain relationships couldn't handle the least bit of trouble, while others survived one setback after another. His relationship with Emma belonged to the latter group. That was why he was positive it would last.

Now he looked out at the swarm of people and recognized quite a few famous actors, directors, and others with ties to the film business. There were plenty of figures from the world of culture. He and Pia started walking towards the gravesite, which was a short distance away. Pia was filming.

Ingmar Bergman was buried there alongside his wife in the simple but lovely grave situated high up in one corner of the cemetery, with a view over the fields, meadows and sea.

People had been making pilgrimages there ever since he was laid to rest. There were so many visitors that the cemetery association had been forced to put a flagstone path in the grass leading to the gravesite.

'I can't believe how many celebrities are here today,' exclaimed Pia eagerly as they walked back to the church. 'I'm going to get a few shots before they go inside.'

'Sure,' said Johan as he headed for the actress Pernilla August, who was talking to Jörn Donner, a famous director who had also been Bergman's good friend.

Both of them promised Johan an interview as soon as the opening ceremonies were over.

In the crush he saw the director Sam Dahlberg. He had an open and pleasant face; his sunglasses were pushed up on his head and he had that slightly unshaven look that made him even more handsome. At the moment he was smoking a cigarette with a beautiful, dark-haired woman whom Johan recognized as his wife, Andrea. Johan introduced himself, wanting to know whether he might ask a few questions.

'That's fine. Go ahead,' said Dahlberg enthusiastically.

Johan motioned for Pia to join them. She was busy documenting how Jan Troell was stuffing himself with pastries that the waitresses were serving on big silver trays. The next moment she was at his side, ready to get started.

'What does the Bergman festival mean to you?' asked Johan.

'A tremendous amount. I've been here every year since it started. I think it's important to discuss his work and show his films. And what better place to do that than on Fårö?'

'What are you most looking forward to this week?'

'The bus trip when we ride around to see all of the locations that he used in his films. Four of Bergman's films were shot here on the island. It's going to be especially exciting to see where *Persona* was filmed. Apparently it's very near his house.'

'Bergman's house has stood empty for the past year, and no one seems to know what to do about it. What's your opinion?'

'The nightmare would be if his children think only of the money and sell it to some super-rich Arab prince or a Hollywood millionaire to use as their private summer place. But I also have a hard time imagining it as a museum, with thousands of visitors allowed to tramp through his living room and library. That would seem like an assault on Bergman, since he valued his seclusion here on Fårö so much. But I like the idea of giving out grants to writers and permitting them to spend time here. I think Bergman would have approved of that.'

'What kind of relationship did you – or do you – have with Bergman?'

'Unfortunately, I never met him, but I once talked to him on the phone. He rang after the premiére of my film, *Master*, to say how much he liked it. I thought Andrea was joking when she told me that Ingmar Bergman was on the phone.' Sam Dahlberg laughed, poked his wife in the side, and shook his head.

'So what did he say?'

'He thought the film was important and well done. We talked for quite a while. It was an amazing conversation, and when I put down the phone, I wondered if it had actually taken place. He was calling from here on Fårö. I remember that I imagined where he might be sitting in his house, how it might look.'

'So you've never been there?'

'No, I think hardly anyone has. Its location has always been kept so secret. I know only a few people in the business who ever visited Bergman at his home, and those who have been there of course refuse to say where it's located. Nobody knows. Not even you journalists. Am I right?'

Johan was forced to agree. Where Ingmar Bergman lived was a well-guarded secret. He was fascinated by the loyalty displayed by the residents of Fårö. Whenever a journalist appeared and asked about Bergman's house, the people would shake their heads and seal their lips.

'But maybe all the secrecy will come to an end now that he's no longer alive.'

'I assume so. And I think that's too bad. In our media-fixated society where people's personal lives are exposed right and left, it might be a good thing if some secrets still existed.'

Sam Dahlberg's face took on a distracted expression, and his voice faded. At that moment the church bells began to toll.

It was time.

The man stood a safe distance away and watched the crowd of people outside the church. He was casually dressed in dark-blue chinos and a white shirt. He wore sunglasses, even though it was overcast, and held a cigarette in his hand. Smoking fulfilled a function, since it made him seem occupied. No one noticed that he was focused on only one thing. A single thing that interested him. He was watching her, and from this distance she seemed even more beautiful. Like a madonna with her long hair falling in a mane down her back. Slender and fit, wearing a floral dress in some sort of thin fabric. So thin. He knew what was hidden underneath; he had tasted her fruits, and their sweetness still lingered on his tongue. Like a remembered pain from something that had been lost. Something that would never come back.

No, he shouldn't think like that. It clouded his vision and made his head burn. He had to put out the fire. Take control. Think clearly. Not let anything distract him. He needed to concentrate and focus on his goal. The people around her were nothing but hazy shapes. They were completely superfluous. She was the only one he was interested in. Just her. He didn't let her out of his sight. She thought it was over and done with, but that was only her imagination. She didn't understand what was best for her. He was the one in charge. He tossed his cigarette butt on the ground, grinding it under the sole of his shoe. Then he turned to look at her again. She tossed her head back and laughed. He didn't hear her.

Just watched. Biding his time.

Her flat was at the very top of the building, with a view over Visby's multi-coloured rooftops and the sea beyond. Karin Jacobsson sipped at her evening cup of tea, peering through the dormer window. The usually expansive view was partially obscured right now because the town was swathed in a grey mist after the rain.

Her cockatoo, Vincent, was chattering happily along with the tunes coming from the radio. But Karin was feeling gloomy. She was facing a decisive moment in her life, and she had no idea how to handle it. Time had caught up with her, and she realized that she was going to be forced to deal with the problem. Otherwise she would go mad. It had to do with the daughter she had given up for adoption, the child who was now grown up and probably lived somewhere in Sweden. She would be twenty-five in September. There had been no contact between them in all these years, but now Karin had made up her mind. She had to look for her. Find out who she was.

Karin closed her eyes, summoning up memories from that brief time right after giving birth. The baby at her breast, that warm, sticky creature who was her own flesh and blood. Her little girl. Sometimes she regretted the fact that the midwife had allowed her to hold the baby for those few minutes; it had haunted her ever since. Her parents had decided that the baby would be given up for adoption. There had been no question of doing anything else, and initially Karin had offered no objections. She'd simply wanted to be rid of the evil, to forget that the rape had ever happened.

But the moment she felt the baby's body against her own, she had changed her mind. She had loved her from the first second. In secret she had named the child Lydia.

Karin had no idea what her daughter's real name was. She didn't know where she lived or what sort of work she did or anything else about her. All her life, Karin had kept the secret to herself, refusing to share it with anyone. Her parents never mentioned the subject after that day in the maternity ward when the child was born. And she never saw the baby again. The yearning she had felt since then was like a hole in her heart.

The years had passed, and Karin had moved on with her life. She tried to convince herself that memories of those moments in the dimly lit delivery room would fade with time. She moved to Stockholm, entered secondary school, and made new friends. For many years she had no contact with her parents. What they had done seemed to her a terrible betrayal. They had refused to listen to her. They hadn't told her that she was entitled to take six months to make up her mind, or that she wasn't required to decide before giving birth. They had kept her out of the entire process and got away with it. She would never forgive them.

Then had come the police academy. When she was offered a trainee position in Visby, her first impulse had been to turn it down. She didn't want to return to Gotland or all those memories. But eventually she changed her mind. She decided that it would be better to confront the trauma she'd been through. That was the only way to get beyond it. For the first time in many years she had visited her parents at their house in Tingstäde.

But the memory of Lydia had come back to her even more strongly. Whenever she walked around in Östercentrum, she was reminded of how she had felt when she went there with her ever-expanding stomach. How she'd had coffee with a friend, and how her friend had discovered that she was pregnant. They had been sitting in the Siesta pastry shop. Afterwards Karin had realized that the situation was untenable, that she could no longer conceal her condition. She stopped trying to hide her stomach, but she didn't tell anyone except her parents about being raped. The shame was too much to bear.

At least now she'd made a decision, even though she was filled with dread. She would look for her daughter. Lydia was no longer a minor; she was a grown woman.

Karin could find out who she was without revealing their connection.

Maybe she should speak to the young woman's parents first, find out their view of the matter? One step at a time, she thought.

One step at a time.

It was an unusually warm evening with no wind. After the opening ceremonies, there was a party at Kuten, Fårö's most legendary restaurant, a simple but acclaimed establishment right across from the inn.

The setting for Kuten was unique, to say the least, with a largely fifties feel to it. Originally it had been a petrol station, as evidenced by the red-painted pump that still stood on the forecourt. A Volvo PV was squeezed in between a Chevy Nova and a Cadillac from the same time period. A sign that said 'Kuten's Petrol' hung above the entrance to the rather faded limestone building in which the restaurant was housed. Outside stood a row of rusty oil drums along with an old refrigerator reminiscent of the era when the Swedish welfare state was established. On the building's façade were enamel advertising signs for Esso, Juicy Fruit, and Cuba Cola. The crowning jewel was a sickly green neon sign that said 'Elvis'.

An outdoor bar with a Caribbean theme, decorated with coloured lights, provided a welcome break in style, along with the hard-rock music blaring from the stage.

An American band had been hired for the evening's entertainment.

The group of friends from Terra Nova found seats at a big table outdoors. The enticing aroma of grilled lamb drifted over the crowded restaurant.

'Great,' exclaimed Sam as he sat down. 'What a perfect evening. Don't you think so, sweetheart?' He poked Andrea in the side. No one could avoid hearing the sarcasm in his voice, but Andrea pretended not to notice.

'It certainly is,' she replied, smiling at Sam. 'Absolutely wonderful. And it's so warm.'

'It feels as if we're in Greece or somewhere like that,' said Beata, taking off her shawl, which offered only minimal coverage of her plunging neckline.

She always has to show off, thought Andrea. She just can't help it.

Beata stretched her arms in the air and uttered a little chirping sound.

'Oh, how lovely. But now I want some wine.'

They ordered several bottles and then went to get food from the chef, who stood next to the grill, serving lamb and vegetable gratin and working so hard that he was dripping with sweat.

Soon they were all seated with plates of food in front of them, their glasses filled with red wine. The discussion immediately turned to Bergman.

'Which of his films are your favourites?' asked Sam eagerly, glancing around at everyone.

'I like *The Magician* best,' Beata told him.

'Are you serious?' Sam raised his eyebrows in surprise. *The Magician* was one of Bergman's earlier films, a suggestive drama that was not among his more accessible works. 'Why do you think it's so special?'

Andrea gave Beata a look of distaste. She probably just wanted to draw attention to herself. Beata took another big sip of her wine.

'The eroticism,' she said, casting a mischievous glance at Sam. 'There's so much repressed lust in that movie, and such an erotic undercurrent. And the love scene between Lars Ekborg and Bibi Andersson, in the hamper with the freshly washed linen . . . don't even mention it!'

She laughed with pleasure. Stina and Andrea exchanged looks. John joined the discussion.

'Personally, I like *Summer with Monica* the best, but I'm sure that's mostly because I love the Stockholm archipelago, and I think Harriet Andersson is the most beautiful woman I've ever seen. Well, except for Beata, of course.'

'I thought as much,' laughed Beata, unconcerned. 'You little rascal. Didn't she show her breasts in that movie? Was that what you fell for?' Then she let loose such a peal of laughter that the glasses on the table clattered. Beata was always referring to sex in one way or another. Andrea didn't know why.

An embarrassed silence ensued. Everyone made a show of drinking more wine and praising the food, then talking about the weather and the music.

'To be honest, I've never really understood why Bergman is considered so great,' said Håkan. 'I think he's overrated. He's so strange and difficult. To me, the movies are mostly a hotchpotch, a bunch of disconnected scenes of fear, dark looks, screams and hysterical people.'

His remarks were met with boos.

'You're out of your mind,' exclaimed Beata indignantly. 'Bergman is world famous, for Christ's sake.'

'So what?' countered Håkan. 'He wouldn't be the first person to become famous because of his eccentricities.'

'You're hopeless,' said Stina with a sigh. 'Everybody here should realize that they're listening to a man whose role model is Arnold Schwarzenegger.' She shook her head. 'My favourite, at any rate, is *Persona*. In any category. It beats them all.'

'Why's that?' asked Sam with interest.

Stina leaned forward with an intent expression.

'You remember *Persona*, don't you? With Liv Ullmann as the celebrated actress Elisabeth Vogler who runs away from the spotlight and escapes into silence? She simply stops talking. And Bibi Andersson as her nurse, Alma, who accompanies her to the remote house where she seeks refuge? Alma thinks she's found a soulmate in Elisabeth, even though she doesn't say a single word. Alma gradually opens up more and more to Elisabeth – in fact, she bares herself completely, stripping herself naked, revealing her innermost thoughts and darkest secrets. But in the end it turns out that Elisabeth has just been toying with Alma, that she means nothing to her. Elisabeth utterly betrays her. I don't know, but I think the whole film is one big desperate scream. A cry for help.'

'Exactly,' muttered Håkan. 'That's just what I was saying. They're all about nothing but screaming.'

Sam, on the other hand, seemed impressed by what Stina had said. He opened his mouth to say something, but changed his mind.

The day started off fine. The grey skies had cleared and the sun was shining through the thin curtains. Andrea had slept well all night long, except that just after 3 a.m. she was awakened by the young girls in the next room who giggled as they came stumbling up the stairs in the small inn. The wooden floorboards creaked; there was a thud as one of them dropped something, followed by stifled laughter. In addition to film showings, discussions and lectures about the master director, the Bergman festival included a lot of late-night partying.

She had fallen asleep quickly, only to be awakened this morning by Sam's snoring. He lay in bed with his mouth open, sound asleep. With every inhalation, a gurgling sound issued from deep in his throat and then rose up to his mouth, where it was transformed into a low growl before exploding into a roar that made his chin tremble. She turned over to study his face. With his eyes closed, his dark lashes looked even thicker under his heavy brows. Although he was over forty, his hair was just as thick and dark as when they met twenty years ago. In fact, she thought, he looks even more handsome after all these years. The few wrinkles that he had at the corners of his eyes gave his face character. His nose had a strong curve and sensitive nostrils that quivered whenever he was nervous or upset. At the moment his full lips were open to allow the snoring sounds to escape with a regularity reminiscent of the lapping of the waves outside.

She woke Sam and a short time later they went down to breakfast, which was served in the dining room on the floor below. As soon as Andrea stepped in the door, she was struck by the hushed atmosphere of the room. It was like entering a different century, far from the modern world. And the silence seemed to be affecting everyone. They automatically lowered their voices, breathed more calmly, moved slower. The pace was languid.

Their chairs scraped a bit on the floor as Sam and Andrea sat down.

Although the long room had big windows facing the garden, it seemed dimly lit. Heavy drapes and great quantities of knick-knacks on the window ledges also contributed to keeping out the light. The centre of the room was dominated by a rectangular table made of dark-stained oak, with an assortment of mismatched chairs: one with a high back, another with a plush seat, a third with beautifully curved legs.

Various objects had been placed along the walls: a tiled stove, an Indian elephant made of cloth, an old wind-up gramophone, a shop mannequin draped in a floral-printed dress with a black bowler on its head, a glittery theatre mask, an old sewing machine, a vinyl LP by Maurice Chevalier. The table had been set with care, covered with bowls, platters, and plates – all made of different materials and colours. Next to each place setting was a lovely ornate, stemmed crystal bowl, filled to the brim with vanilla yoghurt, topped with fresh raspberries and a little sprig of mint. There was also a glass plate shaped like a leaf which held fruit salad, a coffee cup decorated with blue flowers, and a silver spoon. In the centre of the table bowls and platters had been lined up, holding bread, cheese, ham, salami, caviar and marmalade. There were eggs in a basket, milk in a silver pitcher, and orange juice in a glass carafe. Almost every centimetre of the table surface was occupied.

From the gramophone came the gentle tones of Bob Dylan as Andrea reached for a piece of freshly baked bread. The inn was so original and so different from the settings she was used to that she found herself letting go of her need to control everything and actually started to relax. While she filled her plate, she glanced around at the others seated at the table.

Across from her sat Håkan, Stina's husband, for whom she'd always harboured particularly warm feelings. He was so endearing, in a subdued sort of way, and his love for Stina was plain to see.

Stina looked small next to her imposing husband. She was so feminine with her petite figure, and her black shiny hair was pulled into a topknot with a girlish pink ribbon. She was dressed in a blouse and skirt. Always attired in a ladylike way; always pretty even without make-up. Stina didn't have to make much of an effort to look good. At the same time she seemed so fragile, like a tiny delicate bird. She was eating slowly, with discreet little movements. She generally ate only meagre portions, and she had a habit of moving the food around on her plate before putting anything in her mouth. The various items would change places with each other several times as she poked and stirred the bits of food every which way before finally deciding to take a bite. And then she would study the food on her fork from different angles before she cautiously put it in her mouth.

Sam used to complain about how odd she was. Her finicky eating habits drove him crazy, but Andrea had persuaded him not to say anything. He could just look the other way.

Soon after they met, Andrea and Stina had started going for walks together to get some exercise, and eventually the walks had become an essential part of their daily routines. That was when they talked about their problems, gossiped about the neighbours, exchanged advice and tips about everything from home decorating to child rearing. But lately Stina had cancelled or declined to come along when invited, offering all sorts of excuses. Andrea couldn't help feeling a bit disappointed. Something was different about her friend, but she didn't know what was wrong. She was hoping they'd have a chance to talk during this holiday trip. She missed their long, intimate conversations.

Next to Stina sat John. He was ten years younger than Beata. They had been the last of the group to move into the development. John was originally from San Diego in California. He and Beata had met in New York when she was working there as a model. John had come into the bar where she and her colleagues hung out every night, and they had started up a romance that ended with him following her back to Sweden. They now had three children, and everything had gone well for them. John had quickly adapted to life in Sweden. He ran a bar in Visby, and he spoke good Swedish, although with a strong American accent. Sometimes he just didn't feel like making the effort and would switch to English. He was nice in a slightly affected way, bordering on pretentious, in Andrea's opinion. It was hard to figure him out. They spent a good deal of time together, of course, and talked about all sorts of things, but it was difficult to know where he stood on many issues.

Beata, on the other hand, was very easy to read – frequently too easy. She suffered from a constant need for attention, which could be terribly annoying. And she was always talking about sex, which was also tiresome. But there were plenty of good sides to her, so Andrea tried to be tolerant. Beata just needed to be seen, as Sam said every time Andrea complained about her friend's behaviour. He ignored Beata's innuendos.

Everyone in the group was used to them. It was a different matter when they had big parties with new arrivals who weren't aware of Beata's idiosyncrasies. She often ended up sitting on the lap of some new neighbour's poor husband, her peals of laughter louder than anyone else's. She was always touching people, especially men, massaging their shoulders, dancing too close. She seemed to lack any sense of boundaries between what was considered decent behaviour and what was inappropriate.

Over the years Andrea had discussed this with Sam many times, but he claimed that Beata was harmless; no one took her seriously. Andrea shouldn't be bad-mouthing their friends. And Beata was a good friend, she really was. She was forthright and honest, always saying what she meant, even if that wasn't the wisest thing to do.

Andrea sipped her coffee and looked out of the window at the apple trees in the garden. A lone man with a beard and straw hat was sitting at a table in the shade, reading. The scene looked so peaceful.

He reminded her of someone, but she couldn't think who that might be. There was just something familiar about him. Maybe she was thinking of an actor or someone else in the film business whom she ought to recognize. She would ask Sam later.

Suddenly the man looked up from his book and stared straight at her. Oddly enough, she felt as if she'd been caught out, as if she'd been surreptitiously studying him. She smiled with embarrassment, stirred her coffee, and turned her gaze to her friends seated around the table.

They all knew that she wasn't particularly talkative first thing in the morning. She preferred silence, at least for her own part. She never wanted to talk to anyone until after breakfast. That was why no one had tried to draw her into the conversation; they left her alone.

Sam, on the other hand, was eagerly conversing as he helped himself liberally to everything on the breakfast table. He kept making the others laugh. He seemed to be in an unusually good mood.

They were sitting across from each other at the kitchen table. On the radio Lisa Syrén was chatting about various topics with people at home all over Sweden. They were having breakfast indoors, in spite of the splendid weather. The children were still asleep. Knutas stole glances at his wife as she read the newspaper. Lina was wearing her reading glasses. Even though she couldn't read anything without her glasses, she was always losing them. Each time she would rope the whole family into looking for them, and by now everyone had grown tired of it. Knutas had suggested that she fasten them to a cord that she could hang around her neck. That would make things easier for all of them. But Lina had retorted: 'Not on your life. That will really make me look like an old lady.'

She does, in fact, look like an old lady, thought Knutas as she sat there in her worn, old bathrobe with her glasses perched on the tip of her nose. She was deeply immersed in reading about personal relationships in the special inside section of *Dagens Nyheter*. She wasn't especially interested in the news or politics. Her attention was most often caught by someone's tragic fate, people's relationship problems, or the diseases they were suffering from. The sort of thing that Knutas found unbelievably upsetting. Absent-mindedly she reached for her tea cup, all the while keeping her eyes fixed on the newspaper. She had eaten only an egg, a slice of ham, and a tomato for breakfast. Every once in a while Lina would go through a weight-loss craze, but it never lasted more than a couple of weeks. During that time she would completely change her diet and start working out. She had tried everything, from power-walking to African dancing, but she never stayed with any programme consistently. During their entire marriage, Lina had always been about 10 kilos overweight, and she periodically managed to lose a few of them. At the moment she didn't seem to care. It had never bothered Knutas. He thought she looked great with her plump curves, her soft white skin, and her freckled arms and legs. She gave a big yawn without covering her mouth.

Lately they hadn't found as much to talk about. They were each so busy with their own jobs. Lina seldom told him about her work any more. In the past she had enthusiastically talked about everything, until it almost became too much for Knutas. Sometimes he would shut her voice out, letting her talk while he settled into his own thoughts and stopped listening. Suddenly it occurred to him that he had no idea how his wife spent her time these days when she wasn't at work.

'I've got to go into the office for a while this morning. What are you going to do today?' he asked.

'What did you say?' she murmured distractedly.

He repeated his question.

'You know very well what I'm doing. I'm taking the eleven o'clock flight to Stockholm.'

Knutas raised his eyebrows.

'I didn't know about that. Why are you going there?'

Lina looked up from the newspaper with a reproachful expression.

'I told you a long time ago. I'm going to see Maria.'

'Maria?'

'Maria Karlsson. The photographer. I'm going to help her with that documentary book about childbirth in various parts of the world. We need to discuss the contents and how to divide up the work.'

In a far corner of his mind Knutas recalled Lina once mentioning this trip to him.

'Oh, right. Of course.'

'What's wrong with you? I'm going to be gone all weekend. Did you forget about that?'

'No, no. Of course I remember. Now that you mention it.'

'Good.'

Lina went back to her article. An uncomfortable silence settled over them. Knutas got up and cleared the table.

He thought about the conversation that he'd had yesterday with his contact at Interpol, who had told him that they'd had some reliable tips that the double murderer Vera Petrov and her husband were in the

Dominican Republic. A Swedish tourist had contacted the Dominican police, claiming that he thought he'd recognized the couple in a restaurant in the town of Puerto Plata. The local police were investigating. Knutas could only hope that the witness was right. The man had managed to photograph the pair, and sometime today the photo would be sent to Sweden.

Knutas really didn't have time to ponder his marital problems. He just wanted to get to the office.

Everyone had high expectations of the bus tour that would take them in Bergman's footsteps. At ten o'clock on Saturday morning, a motley group had assembled outside Fårö's former school, which now served as the information centre during the Bergman festival week. The group consisted primarily of people with ties to the film industry or the cultural world. Stina recognized Jan Troell and his wife, Jörn Donner, with a well-known TV newsreader, the cultural director for the Gotland district, a Swedish author, several actors and a cinema owner from Visby. The bus tour was led by Gotland's own film consultant, a colourful and beautiful woman. With great enthusiasm, she told them about the filming that Bergman had done on Fårö and the various locations that he had used.

Andrea and Stina ended up sitting next to each other. Beata landed next to Sam, and way at the back sat Håkan and John. The bus jolted along the gravel roads, through flocks of sheep, and headed towards the wide expanse of the sea. Film clips were shown on the TV monitor before they arrived at each of the locations where the movies were shot.

'Bergman made a total of four feature films on Fårö – *Through a Glass Darkly*, *Persona*, *Shame* and *The Passion of Anna* – as well as two documentaries,' the guide told them. 'According to some film critics, the windswept and barren landscape here on Fårö supposedly symbolizes the inner life of the main characters. Bergman himself said that the natural setting here suited him perfectly, and it inspired him tremendously.'

Everyone was listening attentively to the guide's lively account.

'Ingmar Bergman came to Fårö for the first time on a stormy April day in the early 1960s. He came here only reluctantly, looking for a location for *Through a Glass Darkly*. In reality, Bergman wanted to shoot the film on the Orkney Islands north of Scotland, but those plans were too expensive for the Swedish film company. The cinematographer Sven Nykvist had shot newsreels on Gotland and Fårö during the war, so he was able to tell his colleague about the barren landscape. Bergman instantly fell in love with the island, built a house here, and became a resident in 1967. He has meant a great deal to the people who live here. He donated money for various construction projects and filmed documentaries about the lives of the islanders. He put Fårö on the world map. That's why the local people, for all these years, have been so loyal to him. No islander would ever tell a visitor where he lived, and in all this time they have respected Bergman's well-known need for solitude.'

'Is the location of his house still a secret, even after his death?' asked Stina.

'Yes. You won't get any of the locals to tell you where it is,' explained the guide with a smile. 'Not even me.'

The tour continued. They found out that Bergman always drove his car down the middle of the road, that the islanders mostly viewed him as a nice man who drove to the shops and bought the newspaper every day, and as someone who was good at finding work for them – many Fårö residents were extras in his films.

While the guide was talking, Andrea poked Stina in the side.

'Look how she's carrying on,' she hissed, motioning behind them. Stina discreetly turned around. Beata was on the other side of the aisle in the row behind them, sitting close to Sam and talking non-stop. She had one hand on his thigh, and he didn't seem to mind.

'What does she think she's doing? Is she out of her mind?' Andrea whispered to Stina. 'She's acting worse than ever. I'm going to say something to her.'

'Wait,' Stina told her. 'Take it easy. You know how she is. Besides, he's moving her hand away.'

Andrea took a quick look back. Beata's hand was gone now, and she could tell that Sam was feeling uncomfortable. He pressed closer to the window. She turned back to Stina.

'I don't understand why she acts like that. Last night she was bloody annoying.'

'She drank too much,' said Stina drily. 'We all do sometimes, don't we?'

Andrea was irritated by Stina's apparent reluctance to bad-mouth a friend. That definitely didn't improve her mood. She wished this damn tour would be over soon so they could go to the beach. She glanced at her watch; they'd been out for an hour and a half. The sun was blazing through the dusty windows, and it was getting hotter with every minute that passed. Sweat ran down her back, and to make matters worse, the bus had no air conditioning.

'I've got a slight hangover myself,' she went on. 'But I noticed you didn't drink much last night.'

Stina smiled.

'No, but that's because I'm on call, you know. They could tell me to come in to work at any time. I didn't want to run the risk of getting drunk. But it looks like there are others suffering from a hangover.'

She motioned towards Håkan and John, who had both fallen asleep at the back of the bus.

Andrea again glanced to the side and gave Beata an angry look.

'On the other hand, she looks quite alert. At the next stop I'm going to change places with her. And that's that.'

The tour ended in Hammars, and everyone realized that they must be very close to Bergman's home. It was common knowledge that Bergman lived somewhere in Hammars.

'In *Through a Glass Darkly* four people come up from the sea at that very spot,' the guide told them, pointing at the shoreline north of Hammars. 'And in the movie there's a slender little tree on a cliff. Most people are very surprised when they see the same tree now, forty years later. It's not so little any more. *Persona* was also shot right here.'

They all got off the bus and clips from the actual shooting of the film were shown on a large movie screen. It was easy to imagine Bergman clambering among the limestone rocks and along the shore, pointing and gesturing as he conversed with the actors. Moving back and forth to get just the right shot with the right light; working with Sven Nykvist, who was always the cinematographer for his films.

They ambled over the rocks, enjoying the view. They noticed that a short distance away, Jörn Donner and the TV newsreader were walking on ahead. They seemed to have a specific destination in mind. They stopped in front of a fence that ran across the middle of the rocks. The field on the other side was nothing more than a wide expanse of stone-covered ground before the low-lying woods began. It seemed completely desolate.

Jörn Donner raised his hand and pointed, but they couldn't hear what he was saying. They could only guess.

The tour ended with a luncheon, and by the time the group returned to the inn, it was already two in the afternoon. She declined to accompany the others to the beach and instead set off on a bicycle ride. She had already decided where to go, but she didn't tell anyone what her plans were. She was going to try to find Bergman's house. She glanced at her watch. She had four hours until she had to be back for the evening film showing. It was at least worth a try. She suspected that they had been very close to his house during the bus tour. She didn't actually remember which way they had gone to get there, but she did know that he had lived somewhere in Hammars.

She decided to take a detour via the ferry dock at Broa in order to get some real exercise. She would bike around the promontory at Ryssudden and then go to the little village of Dämba. From there she would head to Hammars. She set off pedalling towards Fårö church, passed the turn-off for the *rauk* area called Langhammars, and continued down to the ferry dock. Just before reaching the strait between Fårö and Gotland, she turned on to a narrow, asphalt road and went past several limestone farmhouses that sold Fårö potatoes, strawberries and vegetables. What an idyllic country scene, she thought. On one side was the beautiful view of the sea and the houses situated on the shore of Fårösund. On the other side of her were the farms, windmills and small feed barns with high thatched roofs typical of Fårö. She also saw flocks of sheep and windswept heaths where the trees were bent crooked by the wind, never growing taller than a metre high.

As the road meandered upwards, the landscape opened up: flat plains with stone walls in the middle of the barren landscape, juniper bushes, the skeletons of dead trees with white branches, and even more sheep, grazing undisturbed in the poor soil. She kept up a good pace, and it wasn't long before she was drenched with sweat. She enjoyed the exertion and breathed air deep into her lungs. She passed a man standing at the edge of a ditch, staring at her. Without changing expression, he raised his hand in greeting. Otherwise the road was deserted. Most people had probably gone to the beach on such a beautiful day. Fårö had plenty of long sandy beaches.

She passed a big lake. The light-coloured gravel road, dusty with limestone, wound its way onwards, and she saw a cluster of houses up ahead. The secluded village of Dämba consisted of a dozen or so houses, surrounded by low walls. There were also small farms. An old windmill with broken sails stood on a hill a short distance away. Somewhere she'd heard that it belonged to Bergman, and that he'd used it as a guesthouse for people who worked on his films.

After a kilometre, a sign appeared. Hammars. Her pulse quickened. She was now truly in Bergman country. A road, straight as an arrow, led east. On either side were meadows filled with flowers and hectares of oats billowing in the faint breeze. The sun was high overhead, and it had to be over twenty-five degrees centigrade. She passed pastures where well-nourished cows were grazing, and she caught glimpses of the sea. Here and there she saw a summer cottage. All of a sudden she found herself right outside a farm. Too late she discovered that it was private land, and a furious Doberman came rushing towards her as if shot out of a cannon, barking wildly. She froze in terror. The dog would reach her in a matter of seconds. She deeply regretted setting out at all. What business had she being here? At the very moment when she thought the dog was going to take a bite of her bare leg, she heard a sharp whistle. Like a remote-control robot, the dog stopped in mid-air and took off in another direction.

She breathed a sigh of relief. She didn't want to stay here a second longer than necessary, so she pedalled as fast as she could, leaving behind the dog that didn't like strangers. The owner shouted after her, but she pretended not to hear. The road became smaller and smaller, and she jolted over cattle grids, through patches of woodland, and along expanses of shoreline. Several times flocks of sheep blocked the road, but they moved aside, bleating protests as their matchstick legs carried them in all directions. She continued on, even though by this time she had begun to have serious doubts that she was going the right way. Who cares if I'm lost, she thought. At least it's beautiful here.

Suddenly the road split in two, and she ended up in front of a high gate with signs that said: 'Private', 'Beware of the dog', 'Security'. Plus the name and phone number of the security company. Her mouth went dry. Was she in luck? Who else would have this kind of gate on Fårö?

Hesitantly she got off the bicycle, unsure what to do next. She looked around. There was no one in sight. The only sounds were a faint roar from the sea, a few chirping birds in the bushes and her own footsteps on the gravel.

Cautiously she pushed down on the gate's handle. It gave a reluctant creak and seemed to resist, as if it hadn't been used in a long time. She stood on the gravel path, listening intently, but everything seemed calm. Slowly she moved forward, her steps uncertain. Someone might be here, since it was the Bergman festival week and all. But the place seemed completely dead. Desolate and abandoned. With each step, the roar from the sea grew louder.

Then she stopped. Several cars were visible between the trees. Damn it, she thought. Somebody's here after all.

She glanced around, straining to distinguish other sounds besides the roar of the sea, the chirping of the birds, the rustling of the leaves in the trees and bushes. Her own breathing.

She didn't know whether she dared go any further. Frantically she thought about what to say if she got caught. Maybe it would be a good idea to speak English, pretend to be a lost tourist who didn't understand a thing. Or maybe it would be best to tell the truth. Put her cards on the table and confess. 'Yes, I was curious. Who could blame me?' But presumably what she was in the process of doing right now was a punishable offence. Illegal entry.

As she got closer, it became clear that the vehicles parked outside the house were anything but new. Red, dusty old Volvos that looked as if they were at least twenty years old. Probably cars that Bergman had used for his excursions around Fårö, she thought. They didn't look as if they'd been driven in a long time. That gave her renewed courage, and she picked up her pace.

Finally she reached the house itself. A long, narrow wooden structure painted grey with blue window frames. Actually quite modest-looking. To prevent anyone from looking in, a high stone wall ran along both sides of the house. Now she began to feel certain that no one was here. The place looked as if it was locked up.

She paused for a moment to weigh up her next move. Should she make do with this and turn around? She had reached her goal; she had located the house and gone close enough to see it, although she couldn't really make out many details of the property from here. The wall was in the way. It took another minute for her to make up her mind.

Knutas sat in his office, thumbing through the photographs that had arrived from the Dominican police and that presumably showed the woman they were trying to find, along with her husband. But the photos were a big disappointment. They were too blurry to identify the people with any certainty. The techs at the lab had already done everything in their power to enhance the images. Damn it, he thought. Just when he was starting to feel a glimmer of hope. He doubted whether they would ever catch Vera Petrov, who, to the great embarrassment of the police, had managed to slip through their clutches a couple of years ago. With help from Karin, he thought bitterly. What a fine deputy superintendent she was. He gave a start when the object of his ill-humoured thoughts stuck her head in the door.

'Hi. Are you working?'

'Yes. Those photographs from the Dominican Republic came in. You know, the ones that supposedly show Petrov and her husband. But they're totally worthless. See for yourself.'

He handed her the photos.

'That's too bad,' said Karin. 'You can't really see any-thing.'

Her expression was inscrutable. Knutas couldn't tell whether she was relieved or disappointed.

'It looks like we're back at square one. By the way, what are you doing here on a Saturday?'

Karin sighed and sat down in the visitor's chair.

'I'm feeling so restless. I keep thinking about Lydia and what I should do. I'm just too antsy to stay at home. I was thinking of tackling some of the piles of old paperwork that I've got lying around. Just to get my mind on to something else.'

'Sure,' said Knutas, nodding. 'So what are you going to do? About Lydia?'

'I want to find her, and I've done some investigating about how to proceed.' Jacobsson bit her lip and fell silent for a moment. 'It's actually pretty simple. I talked to the Adoption Centre, and to social services here in Visby, and they all say the same thing. Since Lydia is over eighteen, there's nothing to stop me from seek-ing her out. Actually, I could have done it sooner, but they usually recommend that biological parents wait to make contact until the child is no longer a minor. It can be a sensitive issue, and it's not certain that her adop-tive parents would have told her about the situation – I mean, that she was adopted. So essentially, I'm free to make my move, as they say. All I have to do is phone the tax authorities to find out what I need to know. Her name, where she lives, and who her adoptive parents are . . .' Her voice faded away.

'Why are you hesitating?'

'To be quite honest, Anders, I'm scared out of my wits. What if she doesn't want anything to do with me? And as I said, she might not have a clue that she was adopted. Even though the woman at the Adoption Centre and the person at social services said they recommend that adoptive parents do that. Tell the children, I mean. But of course it's their decision. It's different if the child is from China or somewhere like that; then it's a lot more obvious. But Lydia is a hundred per cent Swedish. No one would be able to tell from her appearance, and maybe her parents wanted to protect her from the truth. I mean, she could have contacted me herself, but she never has, even though she's nearly twenty-five. So I'm thinking that she doesn't know. Don't you agree?'

'Maybe. There might be another reason. Maybe she hasn't tried to find you out of concern for her adoptive parents. It's possible that they would be upset.'

Knutas had put down the photos and was studying his colleague intently. He had complete sympathy for the anguish she was going through.

'And I'm wondering what would happen afterwards,' Karin went on. 'If I do find out who she is, what's the next step? Should I just call her up and say: "Hi, it's your mother"? That won't work. Should I write her a letter? Or should I just go over and ring the doorbell? When I think that far, I get terrified, panic-stricken. What if she doesn't want to see me? What if she pushes me away? Asks me why I've turned up now after all these years, when I never cared about her before – at least in her eyes. At the moment I can at least dream about us meeting and having a good relationship.' Karin buried her face in her hands. 'I don't know whether I dare, Anders. But what if I never see her again in my life? That would be the worst of all.'

The forest out here was more dense and impenetrable than he had thought. He had planned to take a short cut to avoid being seen, but it had turned out to be more difficult than he'd counted on. Annoyed, he fought his way through the thickets, pushing branches aside as best he could and trying not to stumble over the uneven ground, the tree roots, the old underbrush and the rabbit holes. He didn't really know what he was expecting. Of course, he hoped to see her. Weeks and months had passed without him giving her a thought. He'd had other things on his mind. But then one day he'd been going through a box of photographs and found all the pictures he'd taken of her, most of them in secret. And everything had come back to him, overwhelming him like an avalanche. Memories crowded in on him, and long-slumbering floods of emotion awoke. He had no defences. It was as if she took over his life again, piece by piece. He hated her because he couldn't help looking at the photos, over and over. He wished he could erase her from his life when she appeared to him in the night and roused him from his dreams, keeping him sleepless. For hours he would lie in bed, wide awake, staring into the dark and picturing her face, which made it impossible for him to drop back off. He couldn't think about anything else. In the past he had been the stronger one; he held the power and could do whatever he liked with her. Then everything had changed. Suddenly she wanted nothing to do with him. Ice cold, she had locked him out, refused any further contact. Never answered his text messages or emails. He had been carrying around such anger.

He looked at her now, between the trees. She was turned away from him, gazing out at the sea. Her hair hung down her back, gleaming in the sunlight. The underbrush rustled beneath his feet. He continued moving forward, not letting her out of his sight. She had kept her trim shape.

Soon it would be his turn again.

He was convinced of that.

With an awkward leap she landed on the other side of the wall. The ground was soft. The property on this side offered nothing more than a meagre amount of grass and a few pitifully stunted pines struggling to survive the wind in such an exposed location. But right now there was only a light breeze. The sea stretched out before her like a blue carpet, glittering in the sun. The road down to the water, a hundred or so metres from the house, was rocky and dry. The shore was strewn with stones, extending as far as the eye could see. Off in the distance a promontory stuck out, blocking the view. Wild and beautiful. It was easy to understand why Bergman had loved this remote spot. Enchanted, she stood there trying to take in the whole scene.

The house didn't really look very impressive. The greyish-brown façade facing the sea bore clear traces of the weather. It was a single-storey structure that seemed to go on and on, with small windows. Typical sixties design. A veranda faced the sea. It was rather worn-looking, with several old deckchairs leaning against the wall. A table with a cement top was fastened to a low, knotty tree trunk growing out of the rocky ground.

Amazing. The gusts must be fierce when the wind really started to blow. She could just imagine it whistling around the corners of the house during an autumn storm. And the darkness. It must be terribly dark out here in the autumn and winter when the daylight disappeared around four in the afternoon.

She wandered slowly along in front of the house; then she went up on to the veranda and peered in through a window. There she saw the kitchen, with simple wooden cupboards and an ordinary pine table. Nothing remarkable at all. A candlestick with a partially burned candle stood on the table. The clock on the wall had stopped.

Suddenly she gave a start. A shadow danced across the floor. The next instant she relaxed when she realized that it was the sun playing through the crowns of the trees. It was just her imagination that someone had appeared. She sat down on the veranda and leaned against the wall with her face lifted towards the sun. The trees surrounding the house whispered in her ears; a seagull shrieked from the water. A man in a rowing boat was fishing out there. Again she closed her eyes, feeling the sun on her face. Here she sat, all alone on Ingmar Bergman's veranda. Almost as if she belonged to the family and had a right to be here. In her mind she pictured him coming out of the house.

Then another thought slipped in. Slowly, as if it didn't really want to announce its presence. No, she thought. That's crazy. Her gaze swept over the warm wooden floor of the veranda, the sheltering trees, the silent house, the cloudless blue sky. Things really couldn't get any better, but that would be the icing on the cake. She glanced at her watch. It was three thirty. There was still time. Eagerly she opened her shoulder bag and took out her mobile. Then she tapped in a text message.

Johan and Pia had finished editing their report about the Bergman festival, and the Stockholm bureau was pleased with it. There were no regional news broadcasts on Saturday, so they had produced the story for *Rapport*, which was going to include it in their main programme. Pia Lilja was thrilled. She was young and ambitious and dreamed of getting a job at one of the big TV stations in Stockholm, so of course she was always eager to show off her talents. Since she was working away from the mainland, that was essential in order to draw the attention of the national news programmes. For some reason they didn't really seem to value anyone who 'only' worked with the local news, treating her almost as if she were less intelligent. A lower-echelon creature in the rigid and inflexible hierarchy of television. Pia was well aware that she'd probably have to spend a number of years struggling before she could hope of getting even a temporary summer position in Stockholm.

The following day Johan's replacement was due to arrive, so the report on the Bergman festival was going to be his last for quite a while. He had a sense of unreality as he gathered up his belongings in the editorial office.

He had never been away from his job for such a long time. Pia sat there with her feet propped up on the desk and watched him from under her straggly black fringe. She had a different coloured gemstone in her nostril today. It was just as black as her hair and the heavy kohl eyeliner she favoured.

'I'm going to miss you, you know,' she muttered.

'Same here.' Johan glanced up from the boxes he was packing and smiled. 'You might not even be here when I get back.'

'Oh, I don't think I'm ever going to escape this place. I'll probably be shooting pictures of herds of sheep, flags on the municipal building and the ring wall until the day I die.'

'Right. If there's anyone who's going to be hanging around here until retirement, it's me. The difference is that I actually wouldn't mind.'

'I know. You silly Mr Mum. We used to be able to go out partying together. But not any more. In that respect, Madeleine Haga is going to be a lot more fun.'

Madeleine had been hired as Johan's replacement. He had worked with her in Stockholm and knew her well. They'd even had a bit of a fling a long time ago. That had happened, too, with several other women who had come and gone at the news bureau over the years. Before he met Emma, he'd lived a very different sort of life.

'By the way, I'm getting hungry. Isn't it about time for our little farewell dinner?'

'Absolutely,' Johan said with a grin. 'The sooner I get out of here, the better.'

Pia had booked a table at a newly opened place on Adelsgatan. The Élite was a first-class restaurant that also had a popular outdoor bar. They walked over there and, as usual, Pia attracted a lot of attention. She was almost six feet tall and slender, with piercings in her nose and navel, which she liked to show off by wearing tops that were much too short. She had unusually large breasts and the biggest eyes that Johan had ever seen. And she used a sooty-coloured eye shadow to enhance the effect. The result was that people stared – both men and women. And Pia enjoyed the attention.

Normally she had a new boyfriend every week, especially during the summer season, but a year ago she had changed completely when it came to that aspect of her life. And her choice of lover was unexpected, to say the least. She had met a sheep farmer on Sudret – a taciturn and morose sort of man, in Johan's opinion. But Pia was more in love than she'd ever been before. When Johan asked her how she was planning to combine a TV career in Stockholm with the life of a sheep farmer, she had merely shrugged, telling him that plenty of people commuted between Stockholm and Gotland.

'I can come home at the weekends. For me, that would be enough, because then we'd have even more fun when we were together. And I wouldn't have to feed those dumb sheep every morning,' she'd said, giving a whoop of laughter.

Johan would never fully understand Pia, but she was the best cameraperson he'd ever worked with, and he enjoyed her company. He really meant it when he said that he would miss her.

They sat down at the table and ordered white wine and seafood pasta.

'*Skål*,' said Johan after filling their glasses. 'This is going to be bloody great. I won't have to work for almost a year.'

'*Skål*.' Pia raised her glass. 'Let's just hope that nothing dramatic happens while you're staying at home and taking care of the kids. How do you think you'll manage?'

'No problem. Once you have children, the world somehow shrinks, and everything starts to revolve around them. Changing nappies, deciding what to have for dinner, what groceries to buy, tending to a sick child, taking his temperature and pampering him, and all sorts of other things. When you're involved in taking care of young children, everything else seems so unimportant.'

'It sounds fucking wonderful,' said Pia drily as she took another sip of her wine and lit a cigarette. 'But can I ring you if I need help?'

'Of course. But Madeleine is a professional, so I don't think you'll have any problems with her.'

'We'll see,' said Pia without much enthusiasm. 'We

might be scratching out each other's eyes before the first week is over.'

'Well, that's not my problem,' replied Johan, grinning. 'But I hope you'll still be here when I get back.'

'I'm not promising anything.'

The cinema in the northern part of Fårö had its premises in a red-painted barn with white trim, located amidst the summer cottages in the holiday community of Sudersand, which had sprouted up around the popular sandy beach. The assembled spectators helped themselves to sparkling wine and hors d'oeuvres as they waited for the evening's programme to begin. They were going to see the film masterpiece *Fanny and Alexander*, with an introduction by the actors Jan Malmsjö and Ewa Fröling, who had played two of the leading roles in the movie.

The group of friends walked around, mingling with the other audience members and enjoying the warm summer evening. Now and then Håkan would look around for Stina. She hadn't turned up yet.

'Where's Stina?' asked Beata, as if she could read his thoughts.

'Apparently she met an old friend while she was out on her bike ride, so she'll be here later. She phoned from Kuten. If I know her, they're probably sitting there talking about childhood memories and drinking wine and have forgotten all about the time,' said Håkan with a smile. 'Apparently the guy she ran into was one of her best friends for several years. He was in her class in middle school, and they haven't seen each other for at least twenty years.'

'Oh. So it's a guy? Maybe you should be worried,' John teased him.

'Ha. Jealousy has never been my thing,' said Håkan, still grinning. 'You of all people should know that.'

'I hope she gets here soon,' said Andrea quickly. 'It'd be a shame for her to miss the introduction.' She turned to look towards the driveway leading up to the cinema.

'It's amazing how you can meet people from all over at this kind of event,' Sam interjected. 'I've run into colleagues that I haven't seen in ages – and Andrea also met an old friend that she hadn't seen in . . . how many years?'

'More than thirty. We were in primary school together,' Andrea laughed. 'Over at the Bergman Centre this afternoon. And the funniest part was that she recognized me at once, even though she hadn't seen me since I was nine.'

'Well, you haven't changed a bit since then,' said Sam drily. '*Skål.*'

He raised his glass but didn't smile. At the same moment they heard the gong ring.

The show was about to start.

When they came out of the cinema four hours later, Stina still hadn't appeared. Håkan switched on his mobile and discovered that he'd missed several calls as well as a text message. *Hi, Sweetheart. Big crisis at work, have to fly to Bangkok 23.05. If we don't catch each other, I'll call tomorrow. Love you. Kisses, Stina.* Håkan sighed in resignation and turned to the others.

'Stina was called in to work.' He looked at his watch. Eleven fifteen. 'Right now she's probably demonstrating the emergency procedures on board the plane to Bangkok.'

'Oh, how disappointing,' exclaimed Andrea. 'I was hoping that she'd slipped in during the film. Now she's going to miss the party.'

'That's really too bad,' Sam agreed sympathetically.

'She's on call, so it's not exactly unexpected,' Håkan replied. 'I'm used to it. We'll just have to have fun without her.'

'Don't worry, we'll take care of you,' Beata consoled him as she came up behind them and took his arm. 'Come on.'

They headed for the chartered buses that were taking

everyone to Kuten. There a light dinner would be served, followed by dancing to the Bo Kasper band.

They were all thirsty and eager to talk after the long film. Sam immediately started waxing poetic about the editing techniques, the acting, the script and the lighting. He talked about the parallels between the film and Bergman's own life, and about how the film ought to be interpreted.

John and Håkan exchanged glances and drank a toast. Sam wore them out with his long monologues about Bergman. Håkan looked worried and picked up his mobile. No answer from Stina. She was probably fully occupied on board the plane, so they wouldn't be able to talk until the next day.

Beata was the only one at the table who showed any interest in what Sam was saying.

'But there's one thing that fascinates me about Bergman,' she managed to say when Sam paused to catch his breath. 'He was so damned insightful when it came to women, their feelings and reactions. Take, for example, *A Lesson in Love*. I think it must be from sometime in the fifties, but there are lines of dialogue that could just as well have been spoken today – half a century later.'

'Like what?' Sam was looking at her with interest.

'Well, like when she talks about her view of women's sexuality.'

'Really? What does she say?'

'That guys are allowed to have as many lovers as they

like, while a woman who amuses herself sexually is considered a slut. It's the same thing today.'

'Is that really true? I don't know whether I agree.'

'No? As soon as women indulge in purely sexual desires, it leads to enormous problems for men. They just can't handle it. They feel lost and frustrated; they lose confidence in themselves and their masculine identity. They can't deal with being challenged in that way. It's true that men may be attracted to sexually liberated women, but in their hearts they would prefer us to be unsullied madonnas. At least the women that they choose for themselves. No matter how much they may pretend otherwise,' she went on, giving John a sharp look. 'It's OK for others to have loose morals, but a man's own woman has to control herself, and be content with only him, the man who chose her to be his mate. And that's regardless of how dissatisfying their sex life might be for her. The man may dream about sexual games, but when it comes right down to it, he can't handle that.'

Sam gave her an inscrutable look.

'It sounds like you speak from experience.'

'You think so?' She gave a little laugh.

The sun had long since disappeared into the sea, and twilight had settled over the remote property in Hammars. It never got truly dark at this time of year. The sea was roaring, and the wind had picked up. Several nocturnal terns shrieked over the waves, finding no peace. The wind whistled angrily around the corners of the house, rattling the roof tiles. Little birds and rabbits sought refuge among the tufts of grass, and the cattle grazing outside headed for the groves of trees where they would find some shelter from the wind.

Suddenly a solitary figure emerged from the shadows and approached the building, seeming to have a definite goal and clearly aware of which way to go. The person didn't climb over the stone wall that surrounded the house but instead went through the gate a short distance away. Moved quickly and deliberately across the grounds, up on to the veranda.

At first glance an outsider might have thought it was the owner of the property who had come home but had forgotten the key, so had to search for the extra key in one of the pots standing on the veranda.

The dark-clad figure was looking for something,

fumbling over the wooden benches, the rough stone table and the surrounding area. Crawling, touching the ground, but apparently not finding what was missing. Then continuing down towards the sea, struggling against the wind that was now tearing at the crowns of the trees as the waves pounded the stony shore. Going through the dilapidated fence and over to the upside-down rowing boat at the water's edge, which was rocking back and forth in an alarming way in the wind.

Then the heavy work began, and it went on for a long time.

The sea grew increasingly angry in the howling wind.

Invisible from the shore, another rowing boat moved further and further away from Fårö.

The passenger ferry M/S *Stora Karlsö* chugged towards Norderhamn where it sailed through an idyllic bay between steep limestone cliffs. After Yellowstone National Park in the United States, Stora Karlsö was the world's oldest protected nature preserve, famous above all for the thousands of common guillemots, but also for the orchids that covered the island in the springtime. It wasn't a big island – just one and half kilometres from north to south, and two kilometres wide.

Stora Karlsö had no year-round inhabitants, but every summer ten thousand tourists visited the island to enjoy its unique flora and fauna.

The group of friends had barely managed to catch the nine-thirty ferry from Klintehamn. They were running late because Håkan had overslept.

Now, as the boat approached the island, Sam and Andrea were standing with John and Beata in the bow, enjoying the view. Håkan had stayed inside, retreating from the others to spend his time intently tapping on his mobile.

Sam watched him through the windows to the

passenger area. Håkan seemed anxious, not his usual friendly and easy-going self. His movements were abrupt and frenzied. There were lines around his mouth that weren't normally there. Last night he had told them that he was worried about his eldest daughter who had moved away from home and now lived alone in Stockholm. Apparently things were even more difficult for her than usual. He was also disappointed that Stina had been forced to go back to work, even though he knew that there was always that risk when she was on call. Håkan seemed nervous and off balance. He had started squinting, which was a sign that things weren't going well; it happened only whenever he was tired or in a bad mood.

The cries of the guillemots were deafening. The steep slopes were black with thousands of birds crowded on to the narrow ledges. The sea below was full of male birds calling to their broods, and the air was whizzing with females, shrieking as they flew back and forth from the ledges to inspire the fledglings to dare to dive. Dust was settling in a protective layer over the limestone rocks where the young birds, who had not yet tried to fly, prepared for the great dive. Twenty days earlier they had hatched on the ledges, and now it was time for them to leave the cliffs and follow their fathers out to sea. There they would make their way to the southern part of the Baltic by swimming. The birds went all the way to the Polish shores to spend the winter there before returning in the spring to the exact same ledges on Stora Karlsö. The diving occurred over a period of one hour. It always began after ten o'clock at night, when it was more or less dark, or at least as dark as it would get in June. At that time of year it was never truly night. The birds waited until evening because their biggest enemy, the gulls, didn't see well in the dark, so they wouldn't be able to take the babies when they dropped like stones towards the ground from a height of thirty or forty metres.

Each year the ornithologists needed help to capture a couple of thousand baby birds that had to be weighed, measured, and marked before they were allowed to disappear out to sea. This required assistance from the public, and about thirty volunteers would show up every evening until the work was done.

After a short briefing meeting near the lighthouse, the group headed for the beach, led by a number of researchers. Everyone was wearing warm sweaters and wellington boots. They followed a winding path along the ridge until they came to a sturdy iron ladder that had been bolted to the slope. It was a lengthy and steep climb down to the shore. The beaches around the island were closed during the spring and summer because of the breeding birds. More than six thousand pairs of guillemots and even more pairs of razor-billed auks bred on the ledges of the steep slopes. The closer to the beach the group of volunteers came, the stronger the din from the thousands of male birds waiting out in the water. The activity was intense, even though the diving itself hadn't yet begun. The shore was rocky and stretched along the full length of the bird cliff. The assistants spread out, while some of the boldest and most nimble in the group made their way out to the big boulders.

Andrea looked up at the steep cliff and could hardly believe her eyes. The ledges were teeming with birds.

She caught a glimpse of some of the fledglings peering fearfully over the edge. Incredible that they dived from such a height even though they hadn't yet begun to fly. The first brave birds hurled themselves off the cliffs and slammed into the ground. One landed right next to her. Terrified, she stared at the baby bird; at first glance it seemed lifeless. But as she went nearer, it shook its head, began peeping, and then dashed for the water. It ran and leaped over the rocks, desperately flapping its embryonic wings.

Andrea managed to catch the bird just as it reached the water's edge. She held its warm, plump body in her hands. Its little black head turned to her, and then it started nipping at her hand with its sharp beak, which really hurt. She was annoyed that no one had told her to wear gloves. She hurried over to one of the tables where four researchers were busy weighing, measuring and taking DNA samples from the birds that were caught, before tagging them. She was told to put the bird into a cage that stood nearby, and then go back for another. More and more baby birds were dropping from the sky, which made Andrea think about the American film *Magnolia*, which she and Sam had seen a few years back. At the end of the movie frogs started raining down from the heavens. She had the same apocalyptic feeling now.

Nearly all the birds survived the fall because of their round shape: their bodies were like little airbags.

It was intense work. Everyone moved frenetically to

catch as many birds as possible, and they soon shed their sweaters and jackets. One bird struck Andrea on the shoulder and another her head. Her friends ran around like lunatics in the dim light. Beata kept uttering little cries whenever tiny balls of fluff thudded down near her slender legs clad in purple-flowered wellingtons. Off in the distance, among the boulders in the most difficult and least accessible places, she glimpsed Sam's tall form. He was crawling around, trying to reach the birds that landed in the crevices. She paused to watch her husband for a while. Tomorrow she was planning to surprise him with the trip she had booked to Florence.

What a wonderful time they were going to have.

Morning dawned over Stora Karlsö, and after a solitary breakfast, Jakob Ekström headed down to the beach near Hienviken. Yesterday he had left his windsurfing gear there, in an outbuilding intended for that purpose. The forecast said the weather was going to deteriorate later in the day, so he wanted to be sure to go out while it was still nice. The sun was shining, and so far the wind conditions were perfect.

Moving quickly and efficiently, he prepared his gear at the water's edge and put on his wetsuit. The water was still so cold that it wasn't wise to stay in for very long.

The bay was quiet and peaceful. Not a soul in sight. The people staying in the nearby cabins were apparently still asleep. He looked at his watch. Nine fifteen. It was high time to get started.

He waded into the water and then hopped up on his board, letting the wind fill the sail. Jakob felt the familiar rush in his stomach as the board picked up speed, racing forward and going faster the further out he went. The speed made his eyes water, and an almost euphoric sense of joy streamed through him. He laughed aloud and hollered into the wind. This is better than anything, he thought.

Clouds were gathering on the horizon, but for now they were staying away.

After an hour of invigorating windsurfing, he was quite a distance out from where he'd started, drifting far from land. His wetsuit felt cold against his body, and his arms were beginning to tire. The weather was rapidly getting worse. It had grown significantly darker, and from far off he heard a thunderclap. It crashed across the sky. He needed to go back. He turned his board and caught sight of the bird mountain. The steep limestone cliffs plunged straight down to the sea, and on the ledges he glimpsed the swarms of black birds. He gave a start and almost lost his grip on the boom when a seal's head popped up from the water right next to him. The seal gave him a surprised look and then disappeared again. He remembered that the chief ranger had said that a porpoise had been sighted off the island a few days ago.

Suddenly he realized that he was getting too close to the rough, inaccessible shore with the huge, jutting boulders that were like barriers, keeping away all unwelcome visitors. He'd heard that the chief ranger kept a sharp eye out for anyone who got too close to the nature preserves, whether it was canoeists or windsurfers, and he always reported them to the police. The darkening clouds looked threatening; the rain might arrive sooner than predicted. He looked up at the sky to try to determine how close the storm was now, but when his gaze reached the top of the cliff, he forgot all about focusing on his surfing. Jakob Ekström stood on his board as if paralysed. He would never forget the sight that met his eyes up there. The gruesome scene happened so quickly, taking little more than a few seconds, but it made such a strong impression on him that it became etched into his memory for the rest of his life.

It was well into the morning by the time the friends from Terra Nova began stirring in their cabins down near the water. The first to appear was Beata, with her hair pulled into an untidy bun and her tall, slender body barely covered by a thin nightgown. She stretched luxuriously, yawned, and gazed out at the bay. The sea was rough and the wind had picked up. Thunderclouds were gathering, but the air was still warm. She made a quick trip to the toilet before walking down to the dock. There was no one around. Swiftly she slipped out of her skimpy garment and dived naked into the water. The cold slammed against her chest. She swam far enough out to be able to see the cliffs of the small island. On the horizon she could just make out the contours of Gotland. How strange to see my home island from this perspective, she thought. She turned around and saw Håkan coming down to the dock.

'Good morning!' she called. 'Or maybe I should say good afternoon?'

Håkan waved and then glanced up at the sky.

'Isn't it cold in the water? It's going to start raining any minute.'

'No, it's great. Come on in and join me.'

Quickly Håkan threw off his clothes, but he kept on his underwear.

'Take it all off. You're not shy, are you?'

A slight hesitation, and then he stripped off his underwear and dived in. A few seconds later his head bobbed up from the water, and he was snorting like a seal.

'Shit, it's cold! You could have warned me!'

'What do you mean?' called Beata innocently. 'There was I thinking you were a real Viking!'

It started raining just as Andrea came down to the dock.

'Good morning,' she called, waving.

'Good morning to you, sleepyhead. It's already past eleven,' shouted Beata.

'I don't know how I could sleep so long. I guess I was worn out from yesterday. I think I caught about thirty baby birds.'

'Where's Sam?' asked Håkan.

'He was gone when I got up. I thought he was out here with you.'

'No, we haven't seen him,' said Håkan.

'His painting gear is gone, so he must have gone out to paint. Not exactly great weather for it.' She looked up at the sky. 'Maybe it was better earlier. He's probably sitting somewhere doing his artwork. But I don't think he'll be long. The storm is already here.'

Beata and Håkan quickly got out of the water, and then all three of them ran for the cabins, hunching over as the rain suddenly came pouring down.

John joined them as they were making breakfast in the kitchen of one of the cabins. Then they dashed over to the big common room in the old hunting lodge, which had been built in the late 1800s as a gathering place for the members of an aristocratic club dedicated to hunting hares on the island.

They settled in front of the fireplace.

'Oh, how cosy,' sighed Beata contentedly, sipping at her cup of strong, hot coffee. 'By the way, I have to tell you what happened yesterday after you'd all gone to bed. John and I decided to stay up for a while. It was hours after the last baby had dived off the ledges, and all the birds in the water had disappeared. But suddenly we heard a peeping sound coming from the bushes, and there was a lost guillemot hopping about right below the veranda. Every once in a while it would peep, and it seemed so forlorn. It must have gone astray, and instead of going down to the water, it got lost on the beach and headed up to the woods.'

'Oh . . .' murmured Andrea, amused.

'We chased it down to the water, and it finally went in and began swimming away. We could see its head and a little wake left behind in the water as it headed out to sea. And we thought that little baby was done for. But guess what happened.'

Andrea didn't answer. She was looking out at the white horses through the rain-streaked window and seemed lost in thought.

'Hello. Are you listening?' Beata sounded offended.

'Sure. Of course I am.'

'Don't worry about Sam,' said Håkan. 'He'll be back soon.'

'When the baby bird had swum out a short distance, it began peeping again,' Beata went on. 'And you know what? It wasn't long before it got an answer, and we saw a male bird coming from far away, from the other side of the bird mountain. And it was peeping nonstop so that the baby would hear. They swam until they reached each other and then disappeared together out to sea. Cute, huh?' Beata clapped her hands.

Sometimes she's such a child, thought Andrea.

'That's amazing. Really.'

'Yeah, a real Walt Disney ending to the day. It was unbelievable. I think that's the one thing I'll remember most from out here.' Beata sighed happily.

Andrea drank the rest of her coffee.

'What time is it?' she asked.

'Twelve forty-five,' replied Håkan.

'Can that be right?' Andrea frowned, and then turned again to look out of the window.

'Sam will be fine,' said Håkan, trying to reassure her. 'He probably sought shelter from the storm. He'll be back as soon as it stops raining.'

Karin Jacobsson had closed the door to her office in police headquarters so she could make the phone call in peace. It was the most important call of her life, so far. She had decided to start by finding out more about the adoption procedure and how it had been accomplished before she did any more digging into the past. She tapped in the number for the tax office and supplied her national insurance number. Ten minutes later all the information arrived by fax. Her heart was pounding when the fax machine beeped to announce that the printout was ready. She stared at the machine that stood in a corner of her office. The pages were neatly stacked up in the tray. They represented the only thing of importance in her life, the only thing that had any real meaning: the information about her daughter – her name and where she lived. It was incomprehensible and made her feel dizzy. Karin's mouth went dry, and she longed for a cigarette. Slowly she got up from her chair with her eyes fixed on the fax machine. Her hand shook as she reached for the pages. Without looking at them, she picked them all up and went back to her desk to sit down. She took a deep breath before she began to read. Her eyes immediately stopped on a date and a name.

Born 14 September 1983 at 7.16 a.m. in Visby hospital. Hanna Elisabeth von Schwerin. Karin stopped breathing and just stared at the name: von Schwerin. Of all the God-awful names.

Karin was a confirmed supporter of left-wing politics; she detested everything that had to do with ultra-conservative and right-wing beliefs. But her own daughter, Lydia, had the ultimate aristocratic surname. The room slowly began to spin. It couldn't be true. There was nothing worse. She pictured a blonde young woman with a pageboy hairstyle and pearl necklace, her blouse tucked into a straight black skirt, wearing nylon stockings and pumps. Pink lipstick. Living in a big flat in the Östermalm district of Stockholm. Right-wing opinions, a manor house in Skåne and skeet shooting. She couldn't imagine anything more terrible. The class difference alone would create an insurmountable barrier between them.

She pictured herself ringing the doorbell of her daughter's place, wearing her tracksuit jacket, jeans and Converse trainers. Her daughter's supercilious expression. You're supposed to be my mother? Ha!

Karin stared at the name for a long time, speechless as thoughts whirled through her mind.

The rain pattered on the roof. Beata, Andrea, John and Håkan were playing cards and reading in the lodge's common room as they waited for Sam to return.

'Where the hell can he be?' Andrea gathered up the cards after the second round and peered out of the window, even though the visibility was non-existent. It was impossible to see down to the shore any more. 'OK, that's enough. I'm going to go look for him.'

'You can't go out in this weather. Isn't he answering his mobile?' said Beata, not taking her eyes off the page of the paperback book that she was reading.

'No, the coverage out here is really lousy,' complained Andrea. 'I tried to phone the kids too, but it's not working.'

'Same with me,' said Håkan. 'I haven't been able to contact Stina. She hasn't texted me or answered her mobile since we got here. The kids haven't either,' he muttered.

'The chief ranger said that the coverage is erratic on the island. So while we're here we apparently can't count on getting in touch with the outside world. That's what he told us as soon as we came ashore,' said John. 'It's no use even trying our mobiles. And I think that's just as well, by the way. It feels damn great to be free of those wretched things for a while.'

'I agree in principle, but I have to admit that it would have been nice if they were working at the moment. It seems strange that Sam has been gone so long. And in this horrible weather. Did he take anything with him to eat? He must be hungry by now.'

'Maybe he met somebody with a big lunch box,' Beata joked, rolling her eyes and poking Andrea in the side. 'Maybe he's having his fill right now, of one thing and another.'

'Very funny.' Andrea gave her an annoyed look. 'As soon as the rain stops, I'm going out to look for him. It's not a big island, after all.'

'I'll go with you,' said Beata amiably. 'The rain is already letting up. While we're waiting, we can get changed.'

At decisive moments, Beata always came through. Andrea smiled gratefully, reminded why they were such good friends, in spite of everything.

They went over to their respective cabins and changed into outdoor gear and wellingtons. As if on command, the rain stopped and the clouds dispersed so they were able to set off. The path around the island was hilly, and the ground was uneven. The rocks were slippery, and it was muddy after the day's downpour.

'How long do you think it takes to get round the

whole island?' asked Andrea as they walked towards the restaurant and café.

'I read in the brochure that it's six kilometres in circumference, but I'm sure it's much shorter if we stick to the walking path. It'll probably take us an hour, tops. He must have taken shelter from the rain somewhere. There are tons of caves on the island. He's probably sitting inside of one of them, moping. I think we should search along the shore. But we can't actually go out on the beaches, because they're all closed to tourists.'

'There's no real reason to think that he'd be down near the water,' Andrea objected. 'He could just as well have gone to a valley in the centre of the island.'

'In any case, Sam is fully capable of taking care of himself. And besides, he's only been missing since this morning.'

'You're right.' Andrea laughed, feeling a bit embarrassed. 'I know it's probably ridiculous to get so worried. But I'm thinking about his diabetes. He's not good about eating regular meals, and sometimes he forgets to take his insulin with him. I'm afraid that he might have passed out. But I'm the nervous type, as you well know. Sam is always teasing me for acting like such a mother hen with the children. And whenever he doesn't come home at the time he promised, I can't help imagining the worst.'

They went into the restaurant and asked around, but no one had seen Sam since the previous evening. As they came back outside, the sun broke through the clouds.

After that, the temperature quickly rose. They checked the pirate cave, which the guide had shown them during the sightseeing tour they'd taken the day before. Then they continued along the walking path, calling Sam's name and searching the bushes and thickets. They looked for him among the boulders along the sea, at the bird mountain, and in the valleys. They even went all the way out to the lighthouse. Sam was nowhere to be found. And not one of the people they asked had seen him. In the meantime, the afternoon ferry had left the island. Many of those who had spent the past day on Stora Karlsö had now gone back to Gotland, while new tourists had arrived to take their place.

They sat down on the lighthouse steps.

'What should we do? I'm really starting to get worried now,' said Andrea. Her voice quavered a bit.

Beata looked concerned. She took a big gulp of water from the bottle that they'd brought along and glanced at her watch.

'Three fifty. Where could he be?' She took out her mobile. 'I'm going to ring John and find out if Sam has turned up there.'

'But do you think it will really—'

That was all Andrea managed to say before Beata angrily stuffed her mobile back in her belt bag.

'Dead as a doornail, of course. Shit. Come on, let's make another round. We haven't checked the other bird mountain way over there.'

'What other bird mountain?'

'The one that's beyond the others. There's another cliff back there. With lots of guillemots, but it's not as accessible, so nobody makes an effort to go there. It wouldn't surprise me to find him hunched over his easel and painting away. He probably forgot all about the time.'

Andrea's face lit up. 'That would be so typical of Sam. He always wants whatever is unobtainable. Anything that feels exclusive.' She patted Beata's arm. 'Thanks for coming with me, Beata. You're a real friend.'

They started walking along the road but didn't meet a single other person. Steam rose up from the damp ground. Up ahead towered the other bird mountain, but so far they could see no guillemots on the slope.

They stepped off the path and continued towards the cliff. They heard sounds that told them of the birds' presence; their shrieks rose up to the sky. They rounded a promontory and suddenly the whole scene opened before them. Row upon row of black female guillemots were crowded together, their tiny chicks barely visible beneath their protective wings. Beata pointed to the top.

'Look at that. There's something up there,' she shouted eagerly.

'Where?' Andrea turned to look at her friend.

'There. On the other side of the slope, just below the crest. Do you see it?'

'That looks like Sam's backpack.'

They ran back to the path and followed it up the other

side of the bird mountain. The backpack was lying in the grass just below the plateau.

Both women began yelling Sam's name in unison.

They turned to look in every direction. Beata went as close to the edge of the cliff as she dared and looked down. The drop was so steep that it took her breath away. Birds were everywhere. All those birds and the terrible din they were making added to her dizziness, and she had to step back. She sank down on to a rock. Now a trace of annoyance was apparent in her voice.

'Where the hell can he be?'

Andrea shook her head.

'I don't understand.'

Beata gave her a solemn look.

'We need to ring the police. What if he fell into the sea?'

Knutas had just left police headquarters and started to walk home when Karin Jacobsson called him.

'Two people have disappeared on Stora Karlsö. One of them is the film director Sam Dahlberg. He's been missing since this morning, and no one knows where he might have gone. His wife is worried sick.'

'What happened?'

'Apparently there's a whole group out there. They arrived yesterday morning and are staying in cabins. When his wife woke up this morning, Sam Dahlberg wasn't in bed, and she couldn't find him anywhere. Then she noticed his backpack with his painting gear was missing. He's an artist too, you know. She assumed that Sam had gone out somewhere to paint, but by afternoon he still hadn't turned up even though a storm had moved in. So she started getting worried. That was when she and a friend went out to look for him.'

'And?'

'They found his backpack and a portable easel near the top of a cliff. Evidently there are several slopes that serve as breeding grounds for the guillemots, and not just where the tourists tend to go. This was a rather remote area, beyond the famous bird mountains. It looks like Dahlberg was planning to paint, but then something happened. Maybe he fell off the cliff. Or he might have his own reasons for staying away. What do I know?'

'Has anyone checked out the beach?'

'No, they've just started doing a systematic search for him. The thing is that he's diabetic, so his wife is very worried that he hasn't taken his insulin.'

'And there's no chance that he might have left the island?'

'First of all, we have to ask why he would do that when he's on a holiday trip with good friends. But if, against all odds, he did leave, it wasn't by taking the regular boat. The ferry made two separate departures from the island during the day, and Dahlberg wasn't on board either time. The captain knows him well, and he swears that he would have noticed.'

'You said that two people were missing, is that right?'

'Yes. A windsurfer also seems to have disappeared. A twenty-six-year-old man from Stockholm named Jakob Ekström. He arrived yesterday and rented a room in a hostel in the village. He's supposed to be there for three days. The last time the people staying in the next room saw him was last night, but a witness from the hostel saw him surfing off Hienviken this morning. Nobody has seen him since. The manager of the hostel phoned and sounded worried.'

'You and Wittberg will have to go out to the island. How fast can you get there?'

'I talked to the coastguard, and they can get us there in an hour. We leave from Klintehamn.'

Berg leaned back against the sofa cushions in the living room at home in Roma. He was bored. Elin was at the day nursery, and Anton was having his afternoon nap. Emma had gone to see a friend in Visby.

Listlessly he looked around the messy room. He really ought to tidy things up and vacuum, but he couldn't make himself get up from the sofa. He switched on the TV and aimlessly surfed through the channels. Reluctantly he was forced to admit that the life of a stay-at-home dad was already starting to wear on him. He was unbearably tired of dust balls, dirty dishes and unmade beds. His life seemed to revolve entirely around feeding Anton, changing his nappy and getting him to take a nap, as well as taking him out in the pram, comforting him when he cried, feeding him again, changing him again, and finally putting him to bed for the night. That meant that he and Emma had a maximum of one or two hours to themselves before, dead tired, they fell into bed around 10 p.m.

Johan took an apple out of the fruit bowl and apathetically looked through the selection of news-papers on the table before settling on *Gotlands Allehanda*.

He found himself looking at the obituaries, and one name in particular caught his interest. Erik Berg. The same name as his father, who had died of cancer a few years back. Johan still missed him terribly and thought about him every single day. He had been very close to his father, maybe because he was the oldest son. He was sad that his father hadn't lived long enough to see the birth of his children, Elin and Anton.

As the eldest of five brothers, Johan had been forced to take on a great deal of responsibility when his father died; in a sense he'd taken over the role of family patriarch. His mother had been devastated, and Johan had had to handle all the practical matters. He was also expected to be available whenever his mother needed consoling. No one had thought about Johan's own needs. He hadn't either. Now his mother had a new man in her life, and everything had been going well lately, considering the circumstances. But Johan still missed his father.

He leafed backwards through the newspaper. For some strange reason he had started reading the papers from back to front ever since going on paternity leave. Maybe it's a sign that I'm living in an upside-down world these days, he thought.

A double-page spread was devoted to the question of what was going to happen to Ingmar Bergman's home on Fårö now that the director had passed away. There had been all sorts of speculation during the past year. Apparently a Gotland entrepreneur was now prepared to invest in the project in order to transform the property into an artists' retreat – primarily for screenwriters and authors who could stay there for short periods and find inspiration for their writing. At the same time, the abandoned school near the Fårö church would be turned into a Bergman Centre, with exhibitions about the acclaimed director's life. The article included a number of theories and assumptions as to what would become of Bergman's property, which was estimated to be worth millions.

Johan's newspaper reading was interrupted by a brief cry from the baby's room. He was painfully aware that the sound would shortly erupt into loud wails. Daily life was calling. As usual.

It was late afternoon by the time the coastguard boat approached Stora Karlsö. Those on board saw at once that something was happening. Members of the Home Guard and a host of volunteers had gone out in their own boats to help look for Sam Dahlberg and Jakob Ekström. A search on land had also been organized, and everyone staying on the island had joined in. The shore of the small harbour below the island's only restaurant was teeming with people. It was a matter of making full use of the time before it got dark. They still had a few hours.

The fact that Sam Dahlberg suffered from diabetes and might have forgotten his insulin provided a possible explanation for his disappearance. He might have simply passed out somewhere.

But the police were puzzled to hear that a windsurfer had gone missing at the same time.

The boat pulled into dock, and Wittberg and Jacobsson were immediately greeted by a guide who was going to direct the coastguard vessel to the beach below the bird mountain where Dahlberg's backpack had been found. Everyone feared the worst: that he had fallen from the cliff and landed on the rocks below. The chances of surviving that sort of fall were infinitesimal.

Jacobsson asked the coastguard crew to wait for her. Then she and Wittberg disembarked and headed for the building that housed an information desk and restaurant. A group of people had gathered there to listen to instructions from the island's chief ranger. When he was finished, everyone moved off in different directions, and he motioned to the two police officers.

'Hi. I'm glad you're here. Things are a bit chaotic.'

They shook hands.

'Is Andrea Dahlberg around?' asked Jacobsson. 'Could we talk to her?'

'Of course. I think she's in the restaurant. Come with me.'

They followed the chief ranger, who headed for the entrance, taking long strides as if he didn't want to be stopped by anyone. The restaurant was empty except for two people sitting at a table in the far corner of the room. The woman had her face buried in her hands. The tall man was patting her arm, trying to console her.

'I'm sorry to disturb you,' said Jacobsson. She introduced herself and her colleague Wittberg. 'Could we talk to you for a moment?'

The man excused himself and left. Andrea Dahlberg was trembling. She hugged her torso, rocking gently back and forth.

'I'm terribly worried.'

'I understand,' said Jacobsson sympathetically. 'But

please try to answer our questions. It's important. We want to find Sam as quickly as possible.'

'Of course,' whispered his wife. 'I'll try,' she added and cleared her throat.

'When did you last see your husband?'

'Yesterday when we went to bed.'

'What did you do in the evening?'

'We had been out catching baby birds with a group of friends, and after that we were all so wired that nobody wanted to go to bed. We sat outdoors in front of one of the cabins where we're staying and drank wine while we looked at the sea.'

'Did you and your husband go to bed at the same time?'

Andrea nodded.

'When was that?'

'Around three in the morning, I think.'

'Did you both fall asleep at once?'

'Yes, I think so. At least I did.'

'Is it possible that Sam got up after you were asleep?'

Andrea looked bewildered.

'Sure, yes. I suppose so.'

'Would you have noticed?'

'No, I don't think so. I'm a very sound sleeper.'

'So it's possible that he might have disappeared some-time in the middle of the night?'

'Well, maybe, but why would he . . . ?' Confused, she shifted her glance from one officer to the other.

'I don't know,' said Jacobsson. 'But maybe he couldn't

sleep and went out to get some fresh air. And then decided to take a walk. Or maybe he met someone.'

'But why would he take along his backpack with all his paintbrushes? And leave in the middle of the night?'

'What happened when you woke up?'

'I noticed at once that he wasn't in the room. I got dressed and then went out to have a look around. I thought he might be sitting on the dock or on a deck-chair somewhere outside. Or he might be taking a morning dip. But I didn't find him anywhere.'

'What time was this?'

'I don't know . . . Nine thirty. Maybe ten. I didn't look at my watch.'

'Did you check his belongings? To see what he might have taken with him?'

'Yes, I saw that his painting gear was gone. That's why I wasn't really worried. But then the weather got bad and the rain came pouring down. When he still hadn't come back by late afternoon, I really started to wonder what could have happened to him. Sam is diabetic, and it's very important for him to eat at regular intervals.'

'What did you do next?'

'Beata and I went out to look for him. The island isn't very big, and we were sure that we'd find him. I was afraid that his blood sugar might have dropped drastically, and that can be life-threatening if he doesn't get help.'

'And had anyone you talked to seen him?'

'No, not a single person. I can't understand where he could have gone.'

'What about his mobile phone?'

'He took it with him. That's not so strange, even though the coverage is awful here on the island. Sam never goes anywhere without his mobile. He even takes it with him to the toilet.' A fleeting smile passed over her face. Then her expression turned serious again. 'What do you think could have happened to him?'

'It wouldn't be wise to speculate at this point,' said Jacobsson. 'We don't really know anything yet. Our first priority is to locate your husband. Is it possible that he left the island without telling you?'

Andrea Dahlberg looked genuinely surprised.

'Why would he do that?'

'At this stage we can't rule out any possibility. You have children, don't you? When did he last speak to them?'

'I don't know.'

'Have you told them that their father has gone missing?'

'No. I didn't want to upset them,' said Andrea in a stifled voice. For a moment she hid her face in her hands.

'Where are the children?'

'They're staying with my mother and her husband on Mjölkö in the Stockholm archipelago.'

'It might be a good idea to phone them.'

'You're right . . . I'll do it soon.'

'We're done here for the moment. Just one last question. How is your relationship with Sam?'

Andrea gave them a resolute look as she replied.

'It's great. Couldn't be better. We love each other. We always have.'

'OK.' Jacobsson stood up and shook Andrea's hand. 'That's all for now. I think you should ring your children right away. If you find out that your husband contacted them or your mother, you need to notify us at once. Any information is important. Try to think about how Sam has acted lately. How has he behaved? Have you noticed anything out of the ordinary? Has anything new come into your lives? A new person? A new situation? Think about these things, and we'll come back to see you again later.'

She gave the anxious wife a friendly pat on the shoulder before leaving the room.

Jacobsson went with the coastguard crew to search the shore beneath the bird mountain where Dahlberg's backpack had been found. Wittberg stayed behind at the cabin area to coordinate the search efforts.

The inflatable boat puttered quietly along the shore-line. The beach was rocky and inaccessible. From the water it was difficult, if not impossible, to tell whether there might be a body on shore. One of the coastguard officers steered the boat towards a strip of land at the foot of the cliffs. The boat careened as it struck several big rocks on the approach to shore. They had to get out and wade the last few metres. Jacobsson was grateful that she'd had the good sense to wear wellington boots. The group consisted of five people: four beefy guys from the coastguard service, and Jacobsson. As they reached shore, the birds seemed to get alarmed and their shriek-ing grew even louder.

Out in the water the male birds had already started to gather. In a few hours the diving would begin. In spite of the situation, Jacobsson couldn't help being fascinated by the birds. She raised her head and looked up. They were everywhere, and here and there she caught a glimpse of several fledglings. Birds were flying back and forth through the air, reminding her of Alfred Hitchcock's classic horror film *The Birds*. Her stomach turned over at the thought that they might suddenly go on the attack.

She and the officers spread out to begin their search, with the angry protests of the birds continuing overhead. The whole time big auks and gulls glided along the slopes, hoping to catch a baby bird. They posed an ever-present threat.

After only a few minutes one of the men waved from the edge of the beach and everyone else hurried over to him. Jacobsson felt a rush of relief. It must mean that Sam was still alive.

But behind a boulder they found the windsurfer Jakob Ekström.

'Thank God you came,' he said.

'How are you?' asked Jacobsson, leaning down to take his pulse. The young man was suffering from hypothermia and exhaustion. He was bleeding from a cut on his forehead, and his right leg was bent at a strange angle. It was probably broken.

'He's in much worse shape than me,' muttered Ekström. 'That other guy.'

'What do you mean?'

He raised his hand to point at several boulders further away.

Jacobsson and two of the men ran off in that direction.

They stopped abruptly when they caught sight of Sam Dahlberg. Or what was left of him.

With growing surprise Knutas had listened to Jacobsson's report from Stora Karlsö when she called from the island ranger station.

Knutas organized the efforts from police headquarters and did what he could to handle the press without saying too much. The police spokesperson, Lars Norrby, had gone home long ago. It was past 9 p.m. when Jacobsson rang to relay the news. Journalists are like vultures, Knutas thought. They're hovering at the door before the police have even gathered all the information.

The dead man's mangled body had been taken by police helicopter to the mortuary in Visby. The windsurfer Jakob Ekström ended up in the building right next door, in the emergency ward of Visby hospital. X-rays showed that his leg was broken, just as Jacobsson had assumed, and it needed to be put in a cast. Knutas had managed to get the attending physician, whom he'd actually known since primary school, to agree to allow the police to have a few words with Ekström that same evening. According to Jacobsson, when they found the young man on the beach, he'd reported that he'd witnessed a murder. But at the time he was in such bad shape that it had been hard to get too many details out of him.

A meeting of the investigative team was postponed until 11 p.m. Jacobsson and Wittberg were expected to be back by then.

Knutas cast a glance at his watch as he hurried to the hospital entrance. He had a little less than an hour.

Jakob Ekström was in a private room on the third floor.

Knutas grabbed a chair and brought it over to the bed.

'How are you feeling?'

'Not so good. My leg hurts like hell. I broke it when I tried to go ashore.'

'Can you tell me what happened? Start from the very beginning.'

Knutas took out his notebook and a ballpoint pen. He gave a nod of encouragement to Ekström, who grimaced with pain when he tried to sit up straighter.

'I went out early this morning. It was only nine or nine thirty. I'd been surfing for about an hour when I saw what happened . . . up there on the bird mountain.' He fidgeted and looked away. 'It was . . . it was horrible.'

'I understand,' said Knutas, patting his arm sympathetically. 'Take your time. Just tell me as many details as you can. The smallest thing might be important.'

The young man reached for the glass of water on the table next to his bed. He took several sips. Then he looked out of the window for a moment before going on.

'Well, first I saw two people way up there on top of the cliff.'

Knutas studied his face.

'Try to remember exactly what you saw.'

'They were standing at the very edge and quite close to each other. I was holding onto the boom and had to keep my eye on the waves because the wind had started to gust, and right about then it began to rain. I couldn't have been watching those people up there for more than a few seconds when suddenly one of them took a couple of steps forward and gave the other person a big shove so that he was thrown off the cliff. It was terrible . . . He fell straight down. His body ricocheted off several rocks before it hit the ground. And the birds were flying in all directions.'

'Are you positive that it was a deliberate push? Could it have been an accident? Or could he have jumped on purpose?'

'I'm a hundred per cent sure. There's no doubt in my mind. The other person ruthlessly pushed him over the edge.'

'Could you tell that it was a man who fell?'

Ekström shuddered, as if to get rid of the image that appeared in his mind.

'No, I couldn't tell from so far away. But now I know that it was a man. The director, Sam Dahlberg. At the time I had no idea. I couldn't tell whether the people on top of the slope were men or women.'

'Could you make out any details? Their height? Body shape? Clothing? Did you notice anything else?'

Ekström slowly shook his head.

'No. It all happened so fast.'

'So when the person fell, what did you do then?'

'I looked up at the top again, and I shouldn't have done that. Because that's when I rammed into a boulder and broke my leg.' He grimaced again and looked at his right leg, which was elevated in a metal contraption attached to the bed.

'What happened then?'

'I guess I passed out for a while because all I remember is an awful bang and then everything went black. When I came to, I was lying in the water and my leg hurt like hell. My board was next to me. The mast had come off, but I managed to make my way to shore. It was touch and go. I had to fight like crazy out there. For a while I really didn't think I was going to make it . . .' His voice broke, and he stared blankly into space.

'All right,' said Knutas. 'That's enough for now. We can talk more in the morning.'

There was a knock on the door, and a nurse stuck her head in.

'Your mother and father are here, Jakob.'

Knutas stood up.

'Thank you. Your testimony is very important. Good luck with your leg. We'll be in touch later on.'

Jakob Ekström nodded but didn't say a word.

That evening a strained atmosphere reigned on board the extra ferry that had been brought in to take everyone back to Klintehamn. They had all been looking forward to this holiday with such anticipation, but now it had ended in tragedy. And the police had told them very little, refusing to say whether they thought Sam had died as the result of an accident or because of foul play. The coastguard vessel had taken Andrea back to Gotland where she was transported to Visby hospital. After she'd been asked to identify Sam on the beach, she had collapsed completely.

Håkan was sitting inside the ferry with Beata and John. Beata had been crying for hours, but now she seemed to have used up all her tears. John was silent and withdrawn. Håkan was nervously fidgeting with his mobile. He hadn't been able to tell Stina about the terrible thing that had happened. There was still no connection. His mobile had been dead the entire time they were on Stora Karlsö. He'd been able to phone the children from the ranger station, but he hadn't managed to reach Stina. They had sent text messages back and forth across the ocean as long as his mobile was functioning. But they kept missing each other, and there was never an opportunity to talk on the phone. And now he was getting no answer at all. He was terrified that she'd find out about Sam's death from someone else. It won't be long before the press reveals his identity, he thought.

As soon as Håkan disembarked in Klintehamn and his mobile had coverage, he tried again to get through to his wife, but without success. Frustrated, he tapped in the number for her boss. Luckily, he had her home phone number.

'Elisabeth Ljungdahl.'

'Hi, Elisabeth. This is Håkan Ek, Stina's husband. I'm sorry to be phoning so late, but I really need to get hold of Stina.'

'Is something wrong?'

'Something terrible has happened, and I'm trying to reach her, but I can't get through. She's in Bangkok, and I'm wondering whether you have the number of her hotel or for one of her colleagues. It's really urgent.'

'Now you're worrying me. Has something happened to you or the children?'

'No, but a good friend of ours has died. Unfortunately.'

'You said she's in Bangkok? Are you sure?'

'Yes, she was called in on short notice on Saturday and had to rush off. Apparently some sort of emergency.'

There was silence on the other end of the line. Then

Elisabeth spoke again, this time sounding hesitant.

'Are you absolutely sure about that?'

'Yes, of course I am. She left on Saturday night. We were out on Fårö, and she sent me a text message saying that she had to step in at the last minute for someone who was sick. She flew to Bangkok. I think the plane left Stockholm at five past eleven that night.'

'Could I call you back? I need to check on something.'

'Sure.'

He ended the call and then waited, his concern growing.

A few minutes later Elisabeth rang him back.

'Håkan . . .' she began, seeming at a loss for words. 'There must be some sort of misunderstanding. Stina wasn't called in and she didn't fly to Bangkok. She's expected back on the job tomorrow at five a.m. I don't understand . . .'

'What are you saying?'

'Well, I've checked the schedule and talked to my colleagues, and it seems that . . .'

Her voice faded into nothingness. The words formed a jumble of incomprehensible syllables: echoes of a melody that he couldn't be bothered to listen to. He stood there in bewilderment, holding the mobile pressed to his ear, and his mind was completely blank. The sound of Elisabeth's nervous voice disappeared.

Without thinking, he flung his mobile as hard as he could into the water. Slowly he sank on to the asphalt.

He tried to gather all the disparate thoughts as images raced before his eyes. Sam dead. Stina missing.

At the very back of his mind a warning began to sound, ringing monotonously, reverberating louder and louder.

Knutas got back to police headquarters just in time for the meeting of the investigative team. It's been a while since we've all had occasion to gather, he thought as he took his customary place at the head of the table and looked at his colleagues.

Karin Jacobsson and Thomas Wittberg sat on one side of the table. Crime technician Erik Sohlman and Chief Prosecutor Birger Smittenberg were seated on the other side, along with the police spokesperson, Lars Norrby.

Knutas began by telling them about the events that had occurred on Stora Karlsö over the past twenty-four hours, which had subsequently led to the discovery of the dead man and the injured windsurfer.

'So it's almost certain that what we're dealing with is the murder of Sam Dahlberg. And by the way, his body was identified this evening by his wife Andrea. In this case, we have an unusual circumstance since there was an eyewitness to the murder: the windsurfer saw someone push Dahlberg off the cliff. I met with him at the hospital a short time ago, and he seems completely reliable.'

Knutas summarized what he'd learned from his interview with Jakob Ekström.

'Good Lord,' exclaimed Smittenberg. 'You mean he actually saw it? The very second it happened? That's amazing.'

'Unfortunately, he wasn't able to tell whether it was a woman or a man who pushed Dahlberg. Nor can he say anything about the person's appearance, but that's understandable. He was so far away, and it happened so fast. At any rate, he described watching the body bounce down the mountainside. Bloody awful.' Knutas shook his head. 'The preliminary post-mortem report will take a few days. The body will be transported to the pathology lab tomorrow, although we already know the cause of death. And what happened. The question is: Who could be so damned cold-blooded?'

'Have you done any other interviews yet?' asked Smittenberg.

'So far we've only had time to speak briefly with a few people who work on the island and the group of friends that Sam Dahlberg was travelling with,' said Jacobsson. 'All of them will come in for official interviews tomorrow. Dahlberg was on the island with these friends, neighbours of his in Terra Nova – several couples who spend a lot of time together and usually take a trip every summer. They left on Friday and spent the first two days on Fårö before continuing on to Stora Karlsö.'

'What have they said so far?'

'Not much. They all gave more or less the same story about what happened. When they left Fårö everything was hunky-dory. Sam was his usual self, although maybe a bit more cheerful than normal. They arrived at Stora Karlsö on the nine thirty ferry yesterday morning. During the day they took the sightseeing tour around the island, then went swimming and relaxed. All without incident. They were together the whole time. In the evening they helped catch baby birds until close to midnight. Then they sat on the dock at Hienviken near their cabins and drank wine until late – between two and three a.m.'

'OK. Then what?' asked Smittenberg. 'Who was the last to see Dahlberg?'

Jacobsson looked down at her notes.

'His wife said that she's a very sound sleeper. When she woke up, Sam was gone. She assumed that he was somewhere outside, close by. A couple of their friends were out swimming, but he wasn't with them. Since his painting gear was missing, she thought that he must have gone off to paint. She joined the others in the group for a late breakfast.'

'Paint?' asked Norrby in confusion.

'Sam Dahlberg was quite a respected artist. Don't you know that?' said Jacobsson a bit snidely. She couldn't stand Norrby, and the feeling was mutual. Their relationship had been strained ever since she was promoted a few years back – overtaking him to become Knutas's deputy. 'He'd had several exhibitions of his work, including one here in Visby,' she went on. 'He painted landscapes. Watercolours. That's why it took a while before his wife started to worry. But when the storm moved in and he still hadn't returned a few hours later, she and a friend went out to look for him.' Jacobsson again glanced at her notes. 'Beata Dunmar, married to an American named John Dunmar. She was the one who went along with Andrea, but they didn't find him, of course. Though they did find his backpack up on the bird mountain. The same one where someone pushed him off.'

'What time was that?' asked Knutas.

'It must have been about five p.m., because shortly after that they rang the police. The officer on duty took the call at five seventeen.'

Knutas rubbed the tip of his nose.

'OK. They found his belongings at five o'clock. According to the windsurfer, Jakob, he saw Sam Dahlberg get pushed off the cliff around ten or ten thirty in the morning. That's just an estimate, because he wasn't wearing a watch. When was Dahlberg last seen? And by whom? What did he do on Sunday morning? His wife said that she didn't wake up in the night. Is she positive that he slept in their bed at all?'

'Yes. At least that's what I gathered when we talked to her,' said Jacobsson. She cast a glance at Wittberg, who nodded agreement.

'OK. That means we have no idea what Dahlberg was doing during the night or in the morning up until ten or eleven o'clock,' Knutas concluded. He turned to crime tech Erik Sohlman. 'What sort of evidence do we have?'

'Not much,' Sohlman admitted, ruffling his red hair, which looked even more dishevelled than usual. 'But we still have several techs out there, working on site. The crime scene itself is very rocky, and it's unlikely that we'll find many traces. Plus that damn rainstorm swept in at just the wrong time and presumably erased any potential evidence. But we did find a few things.'

He stood up and switched off the light. Then he clicked on a picture of Stora Karlsö that appeared on the screen at the front of the room.

'Here's the bird mountain,' said Sohlman, pointing his ballpoint pen at the image. 'This is the spot where the backpack was found on the slope, just below the crest. We found three cigarette butts there. Gold Blend. And guess who smoked that brand? I'll give you three guesses.'

'Sam Dahlberg,' said Jacobsson.

'Gold Blend?' Wittberg frowned. 'Does that brand still exist? I haven't seen it for ages.'

'Yes, it does. So we can assume that he was on the mountain and stayed for a while. Otherwise, we haven't found a thing at the crime scene. Any footprints or other marks on the ground were washed away by the rain. Since it started to rain before the murder occurred, there weren't many people out and about. Plus the bird mountain is off the beaten path. And the beach below can only be reached from the water – it's completely cut off from any land access. Ideal for a murder, in other words. The body was in bad shape when we found it. The birds had been there, having a feast. Feel free not to look,' Sohlman warned his colleagues, specifically looking at Jacobsson. 'These photos require a strong stomach.'

Pictures appeared on the screen, showing the victim from several different angles. The body was ripped to shreds and lay in an unnatural position. Parts of the skeleton jutted out, and several organs lay outside the body. The skull had been crushed. Only two dark holes remained where the eyes should have been. Silence descended on the room as everyone studied the horrible images.

Knutas surreptitiously glanced at Jacobsson. She was prepared, since she'd seen the actual body, but her face had gone pale under her suntan, and she was partially shading her eyes with one hand. He motioned to Sohlman to stop.

'I think we've seen enough for the moment. The perpetrator is most likely one of the visitors to the island or a staff member on Stora Karlsö. Unless the killer arrived by boat, that is. I can't even venture a guess as to how many people were on the island at the time of the murder.'

'Approximately one hundred,' said Jacobsson. 'We have the names, addresses, and phone numbers of the ones that we didn't talk to personally. Tomorrow we have to start bringing people in.'

'What the hell could the motive be?' interjected Wittberg. 'It doesn't seem credible that it was an accident, does it?'

'I assume that the killer is probably one of his friends from that group,' said Norrby.

'Maybe we should mention that one person who was with the others on Fårö left the group the day before yesterday,' said Jacobsson. 'Her name is Stina Ek, and she's married to Håkan Ek, who was also with the group. She's a flight attendant, and she was called in to work at the last minute.'

'OK,' said Norrby, looking from Jacobsson to Knutas. 'So what do we know about Sam Dahlberg?'

'Not very much. He was a film director, of course,' replied Knutas. 'As far as I know, he's never been involved in any criminal activity or trouble.'

'Wasn't he once an item with that actress, the one who was so great?' exclaimed Wittberg. 'Damned cute too. What was her name? Miranda Mollberger?'

'That was ages ago,' said Jacobsson. 'Back in the eighties.'

'I remember her in that movie when she had her first big role. What was it called? *Prima Vera* – that's it. She played Vera. My mates and I practically drooled over her. But she hasn't been in any films since then, has she?'

'Good Lord. Cut it out. We're talking about Sam Dahlberg here,' said Jacobsson with a sigh.

'So he's been married for a long time?' asked Norrby.

'Yes. And his wife claims that they had the world's best relationship,' said Jacobsson. 'She says they're still mad about each other after twenty years together and that everyone who meets them thinks they're newly in love.' She rolled her eyes before going on. 'But Sam Dahlberg was clearly a real ladies' man. That was obvious. Thick, wavy hair, sunglasses, his shirt unbuttoned, muscular arms, a charming smile that he fired off every fifteen minutes, and bedroom eyes. Sort of like you,' she teased, looking at Wittberg.

To his great embarrassment, he could feel himself blushing.

'Oh, right. Well, if I'm part of this choice circle of friends, then who are you?'

'Stina Ek. She had the good sense to leave for work before the whole circus got started.'

'Yeah, that sounds just like you. Retreat to your job as soon as anything gets personal.'

'That's enough.' Knutas slapped his hands on the table. 'It's much too early to be throwing around a lot of disjointed speculations. And we have better things to do than sit here and listen to your sodding banter. Let's get to work. We need to ask the chief ranger on the island, as well as the coastguard, what boats have been seen in the area over the past twenty-four hours. We also need to check with the ferry terminal at Klintehamn and anywhere else that people can buy tickets to Stora Karlsö. Karin and Thomas, I want you to find out the names of everyone who was on the island at the time in question. Get whatever help you need from the department. We also have to contact the National Criminal Police. Karin, could you ring Kihlgård? I'm sure he'll be more amenable if you're the one who makes the call.'

Johan was warming up some baby formula in a saucepan on the stove when he heard the news on the local radio station. A man had been found dead on the beach of Stora Karlsö. He had apparently fallen from a cliff and died at the scene. But it was the last part of the story that surprised Johan most: 'The police are saying very little about the circumstances, but they are not ruling out that the man may have been the victim of a crime.'

He jumped so hard that the hot formula splashed all over.

'Bloody hell!'

As he stuck his burned hand under the cold water tap, the newsreader moved on to the weather forecast.

Emma was always teasing Johan because he insisted on heating up the formula the old-fashioned way, in a pot on the stove. She thought he could just as well have used the microwave. Right now he could definitely see her point.

He dashed into the living room and turned on the TV to see if the national news programme had anything to say about the story. Regional news didn't have any morning broadcasts during the summer. He sat down on the sofa holding Anton in his arms. The baby greedily sucked on the bottle of formula, as usual. Both *Rapport* and *Nyheterna* on TV4 had a short piece, but neither offered any more details than what he'd already heard on the radio.

It was a little past nine in the morning. There probably wasn't anyone in the editorial office this early. When Anton fell asleep, Johan carefully laid him in his cot and then rang Pia on her mobile. He could hear at once by the excitement in her voice that she was in her element.

'Hi! Things are crazy here,' she told him, out of breath.

It sounded as if she was outdoors, walking. Or rather, running.

'I heard on the radio about the incident on Stora Karlsö. I just had to ring,' he told her apologetically. 'What's going on?'

'You won't believe it. The dead guy isn't just anybody. It's Sam Dahlberg.'

'What? Are you sure? He's the one who fell?'

'Of course I'm sure. Although I wouldn't exactly use the word "fell".'

'They said on the radio that the police suspect foul play.'

'More than suspect. But you know what? I really don't have time to talk right now. Maddie and I have to catch the ferry to Stora Karlsö. It's the story of the year!'

'Just a couple more minutes,' Johan pleaded. 'Can't you tell me anything?'

'Sam Dahlberg was murdered. Somebody pushed him off a cliff that's about forty metres high. He must have died instantly.'

'How can you be so sure that it was murder?'

'Because there was an eyewitness,' Pia told him triumphantly. 'A windsurfer saw the whole thing. With his own eyes!'

'How do you know all this?' asked Johan, sounding sceptical.

'I have a friend who works at the restaurant on Stora Karlsö. Her parents own the place. She told me that when the police found the body, there was a young guy out there who was injured. At the same spot on the beach, I mean. He'd been out windsurfing and saw everything. It's incredible. There are a bunch of cops over there interviewing everybody. We're on our way out there now. Everybody wants a report, as you can imagine.'

'Do you need my help? Emma's not home, but I could get a babysitter.'

'No. Thanks, anyway. But that's not necessary. Stockholm is sending over reinforcements, so we'll be fine. We're doing a live report. Sorry, but I can't talk any more. Have to run. Bye.'

Johan sat there for a long time, holding the mute mobile in his hand.

The task of charting the last days of Sam Dahlberg's life began at once. Everyone who was on Stora Karlsö during the relevant time period had to be interviewed. Jacobsson rang her old friend Martin Kihlgård at the NCP.

'Hi there, Karin,' he bellowed into the phone.

After the usual opening remarks about life in general, he asked her what was on her mind.

'Did you hear about the man who was found dead on Stora Karlsö?' she asked.

'You mean the director, Sam Dahlberg? Someone here at the office mentioned that he was found dead. What happened?'

'According to an eyewitness, we're talking about murder. A windsurfer saw with his own eyes how someone deliberately pushed Dahlberg off the cliff. But he was too far away to tell whether it was a man or a woman, much less identify the perpetrator.' She fell silent for a moment. 'What are you doing? Are you eating something?'

Her question was justified. She could hardly understand what her colleague in Stockholm was saying, since his mouth seemed to be full.

'Sorry, but we're up to our ears in work over here, so there's no time to go out and grab some food. But you said it's murder? Are you sure?'

'Well, the witness seems very reliable.'

'Good Lord. Do you have any suspects?'

'Far from it, I'm afraid. To be perfectly honest, we don't really know anything at this stage. But I was hoping to get some help from the NCP, especially with all of the interviews. But if you're that busy, I assume we can't expect any assistance from Stockholm.'

'I always have time for you,' Kihlgård protested between bites. 'Why don't you at least tell me what you need?'

Jacobsson briefly ran through the situation.

'I can hear that you've got a lot on your hands. But to be honest, I don't know whether we can let anyone go just now. We're dealing with those race-track murders right now.'

'Right.' Jacobsson knew all about the case of the unexplained murders of several harness-racing trainers that had taken place over the past few months and alarmed everyone involved in harness racing in Sweden. The latest had occurred only a week ago, and the police didn't have much to go on.

'But let me give it some thought. OK?'

'Absolutely. Do that. I'll keep my fingers crossed.'

The call came through just as Knutas stepped into his office in the morning. Stina Ek, who was also part of Sam Dahlberg's circle of friends from Terra Nova, had gone missing. No one had seen her since she left on a bicycle ride on Fårö. Her husband, Håkan Ek, who had rung the police to report his wife as missing, had been summoned to headquarters for an interview. Several minutes later Knutas and Jacobsson entered the room together.

Sitting on a chair in the middle of the room was a hollow-eyed and visibly nervous man in his fifties. Sweat was running down his forehead, and he kept on wiping it off with a handkerchief.

The heat was oppressive, and there was no air conditioning. A pitcher of iced water stood on the table. Håkan Ek kept taking sips from his glass. He was squinting. Knutas switched on the tape recorder; then he leaned back and studied the man on the other side of the table.

'When did you last hear from your wife?'

'Yesterday morning. I got a text message from her.'

'What did it say?'

'That it was damn hot and she was longing for home.'

'This whole thing about her job definitely seems surprising. Can you tell us exactly what happened when you found out that she had to cut short her holiday and go back to work?'

Håkan shook his head.

'I can't believe I was stupid enough to throw away my mobile.'

Knutas blanched.

'What did you say?'

'My mobile. I got so mad when I realized that she'd been lying to me that I threw it in the water.'

'Where?'

'At the harbour in Klintehamn, when we arrived by boat last night.'

Knutas and Jacobsson exchanged glances.

'I know it was idiotic. Everything was on it. The time when she sent the message, everything. But I saw red when I heard that she wasn't expected at work after all. That none of it was true.'

'Try to think back,' Knutas admonished him, speaking in a gentler voice. Jacobsson sat in the background, studying Håkan Ek in silence.

'OK. Let me see. Right. We were on Fårö, and Stina was on call, so we knew that she might have to go in to work at any time—' As he said these words, he broke off. 'What am I saying? Maybe she wasn't on call. Or . . . I forgot to ask her. Maybe she wasn't. Maybe it was all a lie. Did she make up the whole story?' He gave the two police officers a pleading look.

'Let's move on for a moment,' said Knutas. 'Just tell us your version of what happened, what your response was, based on the information you had at the time.'

Håkan moved restlessly on his chair, nervously picking at a scab on his hand. He took several more gulps of water. His gaze swept over the cold white walls – there was nothing on which to fix his eyes. Nothing that might interrupt the conversation. He stopped picking at his hand and seemed to gather his thoughts.

'We left on Friday and got there in time for the opening ceremonies of the Bergman festival, which were held at Fårö church. It was a really splendid event, with a lot of people and plenty of celebrities among the guests. Afterwards a film was shown, and then there was a rock concert at Kuten. We had a great time. I think everybody would agree with that.'

'And how did Stina seem?'

'In a good mood, I think. She hasn't been that happy and relaxed in a long time. I think both Stina and I were glad to get away from home and have some time off, without any kids or obligations.'

'Why's that? Was there any special reason why you needed to get away?'

'Not really. But this spring has been hard for both of us. Stina has had to do a lot of overtime. There always seems to be a shortage of staff at the airline. And I've had a lot on my plate too. For one thing, my daughter from a previous marriage has been having problems. I've been running back and forth between Stockholm and Gotland.'

'OK. So you and your wife have been busy lately. How has that affected your relationship?'

'Hmm . . . I suppose it's been sort of a stalemate lately. We haven't had any fights, but not much contact either. Not like usual.'

'Any other problems in your marriage?'

'I don't think you could say that. Although Stina is not an easy person to live with. It doesn't take much for her to feel off balance.'

'Let's go back to Fårö and what happened there. Try to remember everything you can. The slightest detail could be important. When was the last time you saw Stina?'

'On Saturday when we took a bus tour, following in Bergman's footsteps. The tour ended with lunch at Lauters restaurant, and later we were supposed to go swimming, but Stina didn't want to come along. Instead she decided to go for a bike ride.'

'And that was the last time you saw her?'

'Yes.'

'Did she say where she was going?'

'No, she just wanted to ride around the island.'

'Did you see which direction she headed?'

'Only that she turned left up on the main road.'

'Left? From where?'

'We were staying in one of the cabins down by the sea, so she was heading back towards Fårö church and the ferry dock.'

'Could she have left the island at that time?'

A shadow passed over Håkan Ek's face. Apparently that thought hadn't occurred to him.

'Left the island? Why would she do that? We were on holiday.'

'Maybe she didn't leave voluntarily.'

'You mean she was abducted?' he said, sounding angry. 'Kidnapped?'

'We can't rule out anything at this point,' said Knutas. 'We need to keep all avenues open.'

'Now wait a minute,' Håkan objected. 'I got a phone call and text messages from her.'

'When was this?'

'Several times during the evening. First around five o'clock, when she rang to say that she would be late because she'd run into an old schoolfriend and they were having a glass of wine at Kuten. I was supposed to save her a seat.'

'I see,' said Knutas with a new spark of interest in his eyes. 'Did she tell you who this person was?'

'No, actually she didn't. But she referred to this schoolfriend as "he", so it had to be a man.'

'How did she sound?'

'The same as usual. Cheerful.'

'OK. What happened next?'

'I had to switch off my mobile during the film. First

there was a discussion with some of the actors, and then the movie lasted over three hours.'

'So during what time was your mobile switched off?'

'Between about seven and eleven o'clock, I think. I turned it on as soon as we came out of the cinema, and I saw that there was a new message. Something about the fact that she'd been called in to work and had to leave immediately for Arlanda. So she took a taxi to the airport and managed to catch the last plane to Stockholm. From there she was going to Bangkok on a flight that left at eleven, so she couldn't get in touch with me until she landed in Bangkok.'

'And you didn't think any of this was odd?'

'No. It's not unusual for her to have to go to work when she's on call. We knew that it might happen. And it wasn't strange that she'd have to catch a long-distance flight, either. She's always taking those kinds of flights – to Bangkok, New York, Tokyo, and places like that.'

'What about this male childhood friend that she met?'

'In hindsight it does seem like a strange coincidence, that he would turn up at the very moment that she disappeared. But at the time I didn't react. The Bergman festival is the kind of event that attracts people from all over. Several of us have run into people that we haven't seen in a long time. For example, I know that Andrea also met an old classmate.'

'Also a man?'

'No, it was a woman, actually. Whatever that has to do with things.'

'Presumably nothing. But I can't help wondering about this man. Did Stina say anything else about him?'

'No. I was standing in the middle of the crowd before the film started. There were so many people around me that we just talked very briefly.'

'Do you remember reacting to anything when you read her text message? Anything about the wording, I mean. How she expressed herself?'

Håkan looked pensive.

'No, I don't think so.'

Knutas leaned forward and fixed his eyes on the man, who seemed to have shrunk more and more as the conversation progressed.

'Could you try to recall the text messages that you got? What did the messages say, and when did you receive them?'

Silence filled the room. Håkan wrung his hands as he stared mutely at the floor.

'I don't really know. They were short. Nothing special. I don't understand any of this. None of it makes any sense.'

The next day Knutas arrived at work even earlier than usual. It wasn't even seven o'clock when he stepped through the door of police headquarters and said hello to the duty officer. He wanted to have an hour to himself in order to gather his thoughts and go over everything they'd done in the investigation so far. He couldn't really think at home; he needed the quiet of his office.

He opened the window and sank down on his old, worn desk chair, setting a cup of coffee in front of him. He pulled out the top desk drawer, got out his pipe, and then carefully filled it as he gazed out of the window. Even though it was early in the morning, people were walking or cycling past on the street. Cars with baggage tied to the roof also drove by, presumably headed for the ferry.

It was the height of the tourist season. The economic crisis of recent months meant that many more Swedes had decided to be tourists in their own country. The tourist bureau predicted that the number of visitors, which was normally between two and three hundred thousand during the summer, would increase by another hundred thousand, as far as Gotland was concerned. Those were enormous numbers, considering that the permanent residents barely totalled sixty thousand.

The flood of tourists also made the crime statistics rise. The question was whether the murder that had been committed on Stora Karlsö had anything to do with summer tourism. It was certainly possible, even though most of the tourists who visited Stora Karlsö were middle-aged people interested in nature, and they neither littered nor started brawls. The police had interviewed the chief ranger, as well as the other employees, but no one had noticed anything out of the ordinary about any of the visitors who were on the island during the relevant time period. No incidents. No jealous fights. Not the slightest hint of any discord. On the surface, everything had appeared calm and harmonious.

The police had their hands full trying to track down all the visitors, but they hadn't yet located everyone. Then there was the matter of the people who had come to the island just for the day – those who arrived on the morning ferry and went home in the afternoon. Their names were not registered anywhere.

Another possibility was that the murderer had spent the night in a tent or maybe under open skies. The summer heat meant that it was quite pleasant to sleep outdoors at night. Maybe Sam Dahlberg had acquired some enemies over the years; he was a relatively controversial director.

Knutas recalled one of his films from a few years back that contained explicit sexual scenes that dealt with issues of religion and prejudice against homosexuals. It had aroused strong reactions all over the country, especially among the nonconformist religious circles. Particularly because one of Sweden's most famous Pentecostal pastors was portrayed as a perverted fascist in the film. No name was ever mentioned, but no one who saw the movie could have had any doubts as to who the character was intended to be.

One theory was that someone had taken their own boat to Stora Karlsö, killed Dahlberg, and then escaped unnoticed.

Knutas went over to the window with his unlit pipe between his lips and looked out over the ring wall which surrounded the town. If someone had deliberately wanted to kill Dahlberg in cold blood, why go to so much trouble? Why follow him out to Stora Karlsö?

Unless the murder was committed by a member of the group that was spending the holiday together. How reliable was the information that his wife Andrea had given the police? Could the perpetrator be one of the neighbours? Who knows what might be hidden under the friendly surface? thought Knutas. A person's best friend, somebody that he thought he knew inside and out, could turn out to be someone else entirely. That was something he'd learned from bitter personal experience. Leif Almlöv had been dead and buried for a long time now, but that didn't stop Knutas from thinking about him – almost every day. And where the hell was Stina Ek? Did she have something to do with the murder? Had she pushed Dahlberg off the cliff and then bolted? The question was what her motive could be. According to everyone else in the group, she and Sam got along well and had never had any quarrels. The police needed to dig deeper into this group. Find out everything about their lives, their habits, their pasts.

He was interrupted by someone knocking on the door. Karin Jacobsson stuck her head in.

'Hey, we've got something. Stina Ek's handbag was found in a ditch on Fårö.'

They took Knutas's old Mercedes so as not to attract too much attention and drove to Fårösund.

'The bag was discovered a few hours ago by a man taking a walk along the road between north and south Sudersand,' said Jacobsson. 'There's a tractor path that goes out to several summer cottages, almost right across from the pizzeria – you know, the place that has such good pizzas, baked in a wood oven. What's it called? Oh, right. Carlssons.'

'I know exactly the place you mean,' said Knutas. 'We spent a lot of time up there after the murder of . . . you know.'

'Peter Bovide.'

Knutas gave Jacobsson a quick glance. It was Bovide's killer who was still on the loose along with her husband somewhere in the world.

'That's one case we're never going to forget.'

'Thanks for reminding me,' said Jacobsson tonelessly.

They continued on in silence. At Fårösund they encountered a winding queue of cars long before they reached the ferry dock. People were patiently waiting in the heat, hoping to get on board. Knutas looked at his watch. It was nine fifty-five.

They drove past the entire queue and stopped at the front of the line for Fårö. A short while later the ferry pulled up to the dock, and in five minutes they were on the other side. The change in the natural setting was instantly noticeable. More stone fences, more sheep, and more windmills. A more barren landscape. Here the dwarf pines were even more bent, and the coastline was closer. The shores were covered with stones, areas of *raukar*, and scattered expanses of sandy beach – all of which was reminiscent of islands in the South Pacific. So far the island was free of any big hotel complexes, and most of it was relatively unexploited. No wonder that so many people took refuge there.

The most developed area was the one they were on their way to see: Sudersand, which had cabins, camp-sites and restaurants near the long sandy shore. It was full of hustle and bustle. Families with small children headed to the beach, loaded down with picnic baskets, beach games and towels. There were large groups of teenagers on bicycles, and tourists as far as the eye could see. Knutas parked near the Carlsson pizzeria, where every outdoor table under the trees was fully occupied.

The path where the handbag had been found led through the area over to the main road. Police tape was now keeping out the public. Even though there was no proof that Stina Ek had met with foul play, it was not a good sign that her bag had been found. At the same time, it was possible that she was the killer. In either case, the discovery of her handbag represented important evidence in the on-going homicide investigation.

The ditch was on the side of the road and barely visible through the bushes and thickets. An excellent place to hide something, especially if someone was in a hurry, thought Knutas as they walked towards the site. The ditch was hidden by the thick vegetation, consisting of various types of reeds, shrubs and brush. The man who found the handbag had rather sheepishly admitted to the police that he'd gone over to have a pee and then caught sight of something shiny in the grass. Thinking that it might be something valuable, he had dug out the handbag, which lay underneath a lot of leaves and grass. Inside he found a purse containing cash and ID, along with the usual things that most women kept in their bags: tissues, lipstick, a pocket mirror, keys, a small hairbrush and a pocket diary. Erik Sohlman had confirmed that the ID belonged to Stina Ek.

Four days had passed since anyone had seen her.

Knutas squatted down and stared at the ditch.

'So what the hell do you think?'

'There are lots of possibilities,' said Jacobsson. 'Stina might have fallen victim to the murderer, and if so, it seems reasonable to assume that it was the same perpetrator who killed Sam. Or she could be the one behind everything, and she got rid of her bag to try and throw us off the track.'

'OK, but let's consider the second option. Would she

have left behind her cash, ID and keys, both to her house and car?'

'No, you're right. That doesn't seem likely. The question is: What happened to her bicycle? I wonder if that part was a lie too.'

'If so, she would have had to get a cab. They left their car at home because they got a lift with Sam and Andrea.'

'Has anyone contacted the cab company?'

'I haven't, at any rate,' said Jacobsson grimly. And she got out her mobile.

It turned out that no taxi had picked up a customer on Fårö during that specific time period. And no one by the name of Stina Ek had checked in for a flight from the Visby airport.

'It's damn unlucky that we don't have Håkan Ek's mobile,' grumbled Knutas.

'But we can still find out a lot about his calls and texts from the mobile service,' said Jacobsson.

'Of course we can find out who sent a text message, and who it was sent to and at what time, but we can't find out what the texts said. It's strange that all of Stina's valuables were still in her bag, except for her mobile.'

'All of these facts are based on Håkan Ek's testimony. Who's to say that any of it is true? For instance, did Stina really tell him that she had to work? Håkan is the only one who can confirm that; nobody else received a text. Wouldn't she have texted her children, or her best friend, Andrea?'

'And Håkan Ek threw his mobile into the sea,' muttered Knutas. 'I think we need to have another talk with him.'

They got in the car and drove over to the Slow Train Inn, where the group of friends had stayed.

Jacobsson pulled into the small car park outside the garden. Everything seemed calm and peaceful. There was no one in sight.

They went up on to the porch and knocked on the front door. When no one came, they went in. They could hear music from a radio coming from the kitchen, and a pale woman with beautiful long hair appeared at once in the doorway. She spoke with a strong French accent when she asked: 'Can I help you with something?'

Knutas introduced himself and his colleague and then explained the reason for their visit.

'You had a group of people staying here for a couple of nights over the weekend. I'm sure that you've heard that one of them, Sam Dahlberg, was found dead on Stora Karlsö.'

The woman nodded.

'It now turns out that another person from the group is missing. A woman with Asian roots. Stina Ek. Do you remember her?'

'Yes. She was staying with her husband in one of the cabins down by the water. She was very nice.'

'Well, she has been missing for several days now. In fact, she hasn't been seen since Saturday afternoon here on Fårö when she set off for a bike ride from the inn.'

'Is that right? Would you mind if we sat down?'

'Not at all.'

They followed her into the dining room, where they sat down at a long table.

'Did you notice anything special about these guests? Or about Stina Ek, for that matter?'

'No, they were all so happy and nice. They talked a lot and they got pretty loud. But they were very pleasant.'

'And nothing special happened while they were here?'

'No, nothing.'

'When did you last see Stina Ek?'

The woman paused to think.

'It must have been when they ate breakfast here. On Saturday morning.'

'And everything seemed perfectly normal?'

'Yes.'

'And you didn't see her again after that?'

'No.'

'Has anyone stayed in the cabin after she and her husband left?'

'Yes. This is our busy season, so we're fully booked. We have guests staying there right now.'

'Could we have a look at the place?'

'Of course. I'll take you there.'

They followed the woman, who gracefully led the

way across the road and down to the water on the other side. She seems almost unreal, thought Knutas. Like some sort of ethereal being.

The cabin was locked when they arrived. The owner knocked several times, but no one answered. She turned to Knutas.

'They're probably down at the beach. But I'll let you in.'

She unlocked the door and they peered inside. It was a small, charming space with a bed and a dining table. Clothes and other belongings were strewn everywhere.

'Have other people stayed here since then?' asked Jacobsson.

'Yes, a couple of other people before these guests.'

'If there was any evidence, it's gone by now,' sighed Knutas. 'But thanks anyway.'

He handed the woman his card.

'Phone me if you happen to think of anything at all that might be important.'

'Of course.'

They walked back to the car. When Knutas turned around at the road, the Frenchwoman was still standing near the cabin. She had turned to gaze out at the sea.

He had been sitting among the trees at a safe distance, studying her for quite a while now. He could see her clearly through the big picture window of the house. He had never grasped why people would choose to have that much glass, reaching all the way down to the floor. They must be exhibitionists, harbouring a secret longing to be observed, seen. He'd never had such a need. He liked to melt into the crowd, to become erased and merge with all the others. He'd never understood people who wanted to stand out. On the other hand, it allowed him to admire them in secret with a combination of horror and delight. Like her. She had been like that. She loved having others look at her, admire her. And they did. She was just as alive inside of him now as she had been back then. Even though they'd managed to enjoy each other only a few times, her scent still lingered in his nostrils, her voice echoed in his head, and her lips still burned against his. Time could not wash away those memories. They were etched into him for all eternity. For him there had been nobody after her. Of course he'd met others; he'd had superficial relationships, but only for sex. He used to amuse himself by comparing all the others to her. The length of their hair, their fingers, nails, shoulders and collarbone. No one had a collarbone to match hers. As if created by God Himself. He recalled how he would run his fingertips along it, lightly, so lightly. Infinitely gentle. He could bring goose bumps to her skin. He felt sick at the thought of someone else touching her. Couldn't bring himself to picture it.

Then had come the death blow. One day she suddenly told him that he had to stop contacting her. Cold as ice, she cut the bond between them. Betrayed, that was how he felt. Betrayed. And he wasn't going to take it any longer. He had lived with his loneliness. Carried his longing like a throbbing abscess in his chest.

But at last he'd been given a sign. And it kept getting clearer. Soon it would be his turn. Again.

Several days had now passed since Sam Dahlberg's body was found on Stora Karlsö, and the police still had no lead on a possible suspect. The tech team had meticulously examined the cabin that the Dahlbergs had rented. Everyone in the group from Terra Nova had been interviewed again, and the police were now in the process of checking on their backgrounds. So far nothing out of the ordinary had surfaced. Nothing in their pasts had produced any leads that might help solve the case.

Håkan Ek was the one who seemed the least emotionally stable, but that wasn't really so strange. It was only natural for him to be worried about his wife, who still hadn't returned. He'd been grilled several times by Knutas and Jacobsson, without result. Like a mantra, he just kept repeating what he'd told them before, over and over again. Finally they were forced to give up and let him go. It turned out that he'd been married twice before and had a child with each ex-wife. Knutas couldn't figure the man out. He was evasive and difficult to pin down.

It had been a huge undertaking to interview all the tourists who were on the island at the time the murder was committed. The local police had been assisted by two officers from the NCP, but Kihlgård had not yet found time to come over to Gotland himself. Not a single person who had been interviewed provided any information of value. Nobody had noticed anything suspicious. The homes of both couples in Terra Nova had been searched, and their neighbours, relatives and work colleagues had all been questioned. No one was able to give the police any leads.

Knutas, Jacobsson and Wittberg were sitting dejectedly in Knutas's office on Thursday morning, trying to come up with a new angle.

'What if we focus solely on the murder of Dahlberg for a moment, and consider exactly what happened,' suggested Jacobsson. 'The fact that he was pushed off a cliff on Stora Karlsö. What does that indicate? What does it say about the perpetrator?'

'First and foremost, it seems likely that they knew each other, or at least had been talking to each other before it happened,' Knutas said.

'And presumably it was not premeditated,' interjected Wittberg. 'If someone was planning a murder, would they really choose a place like that? First of all, somebody might have seen them at the site, or as they walked there. It's really unfortunate that no one did, especially considering the fact that there were so many tourists on the island at the time.'

'But it's a fairly easy way of killing someone, don't you think?' replied Jacobsson. 'No weapon is required, and there wouldn't be any evidence left behind. And at such an inaccessible spot, the risk of being seen would be extremely small.'

'So how likely does it seem that the killer was someone he didn't know?' asked Knutas. 'Do you think he got into an argument with a stranger, who happened to have a murderous bent and who got so worked up that he threw Sam off the cliff?'

'Not really. So the only option left is that it was someone he knew,' said Jacobsson. 'Could the killer be a woman?'

'Yes. I have no doubt about that,' said Wittberg. 'Especially if he didn't have any warning. Maybe he'd turned his back.'

'What about his wife, Andrea? Could someone as small as Stina Ek have done it? Or someone else in that circle of friends?'

'Håkan doesn't have an alibi, since he was sleeping alone,' said Knutas. 'And Andrea was too, actually. While Stina wasn't even there.'

'Maybe she has a specific reason for staying away. Or else she may have fallen and her dead body is lying out there somewhere,' Wittberg speculated.

'OK. We really have no idea about that. But what about the motive? Who had a reason for wanting Sam Dahlberg dead?'

For a moment none of them said a word. Finally Jacobsson spoke.

'Maybe we're on the wrong track. We're locked into the idea that it had to be someone in the group. What if the site itself is the reason for the murder – the fact that they were on Stora Karlsö? Had Sam ever been there before? Did he have a connection to any of the employees? Or has he ever worked there in the past? Have we checked on that?'

Knutas shook his head.

'Not as far as I know. Could you follow up on that?'

'Of course,' said Jacobsson. 'But it's only a suggestion. It seems so strange that Stina has disappeared. What exactly do we know about her?'

'Not much. She was adopted from Vietnam, and she's generally well liked. A close friend of both Andrea and Sam. Her parents weren't able to tell us much. Her colleagues couldn't either. She's always been conscientious, both at home and on the job. Apparently she has never drawn attention to herself. Everyone describes her as pleasant and nice, but somewhat reserved. A bit hard to get to know.'

'I still think that the group of friends holds the answer to this case,' said Wittberg. 'One thing that has struck me with this whole investigation is that those people from Terra Nova seem to have a slightly unhealthy sort of friendship. I mean, good Lord, they do everything together. They live only a few metres from each other, the kids are in the same classes, they work out together, they have all their celebrations together, they help each other repair their houses and cars. They do their Christmas baking together, spend Midsummer with each other, and hold their annual crayfish parties and New Year's Eve celebrations together. Some of them have summer cabins in the same area near Sudret. It's unbelievable. They can't even take holidays on their own! The ones who like to ski go to the mountains every year; the women take "girl holidays" together, and some of them even get together to do major grocery shopping. Can you imagine that? Every week they make lists and then take turns driving to the ICA Supermarket to shop. It almost seems like some sort of cult. It wouldn't surprise me if they even fucked together!'

'I don't think there's anything wrong with helping each other out and offering support,' Jacobsson objected. 'It seems only natural, especially since they have children the same age.'

'But shopping for groceries together? And spending holidays together? Doesn't that seem a bit extreme? For me it sounds like a real Knutby situation, the way they've put up such a united front. I wouldn't be surprised if we find out that one of them is the killer. Somebody who wanted Sam out of the way.'

'But why?'

'I have no idea. Maybe someone has been getting it on with Andrea.'

'So according to your theory, his wife, Andrea, made

friends with someone and it went so far that she and her lover decided to get rid of Sam?' said Knutas. 'Why not just get a divorce if that was the case?'

A brief silence ensued. Then there was a knock on the door. Erik Sohlman stuck his head in.

'They've found a sleeping bag and some other things hidden in a grove of trees on Stora Karlsö. It seems that our killer spent the night there.'

Johan Berg was filled with anticipation as he pulled up outside the Swedish Radio and TV building in Visby and parked his car. It was going to be great to have some adult conversation for a change, talking shop with his colleagues and hearing the latest scuttlebutt from TV headquarters in Stockholm. He'd missed the annual summer party, which was always a huge bash, with alcohol flowing in rivers. And once in a while some of the party-goers would really let loose. It would be fun to hear who had gone home together at the end of the evening.

As he approached the front door, he really felt how much he had missed his job. He said hello to a few of his radio colleagues who were standing outside, having a smoke in the sunshine. Then he bounded up the stairs to the editorial office. He had made arrangements with Pia and Madeleine, his replacement, to drop by and have a cup of coffee, since he was in town anyway. He'd stopped at the pastry shop on Norrgatt on the way in and bought a coffee cake.

Both women were on the phone when he came in. He could tell at once that something had happened.

Madeleine quickly ended her call and jumped to her feet when she caught sight of Johan in the doorway.

'Hi. It's so great to see you.' She gave him a big, warm hug, which made him happy. He'd always had a soft spot for Madeleine. She was dark-haired and petite, radiating a charisma that could make even a horse feel weak at the knees.

'Looks like you've put on a little weight, haven't you?' She pinched his stomach affectionately.

'That's life with little kids, you know.' He laughed. 'Everything revolves around eating and sleeping.' He flopped down on to his favourite chair. 'It's so good to see both of you. So what's happening?'

'We'll get to that in a moment,' said Madeleine, indicating Pia, who was sitting with her back to them and seemed deeply engrossed in her phone conversation. She looked at Johan with amusement. 'So what about you? Are you enjoying being a home-body?'

'It's fantastic, glorious, just amazing,' he said emphatically. 'I love it. I couldn't ask for anything better. I can't even describe how wonderful it is to be a father.'

'And how's the baby? What's the little one's name? Is it a boy or a girl?'

'A boy. Anton. He'll be seven months soon.'

'Ah. How sweet.'

Pia put down the phone and turned towards Johan.

'Did you know that somebody has gone missing from the group that Sam Dahlberg belonged to?'

'What do you mean?'

'Some friends went on holiday together – first to the Bergman festival on Fårö, and then on to Stora Karlsö. All of them live in Terra Nova, and it seems to be a really tight crowd. Just before you arrived, I talked to one of my brother's friends who works on the Fårö ferry. He told me that the police have made several trips over there this week, and yesterday they went up to Kuten and the inn where the whole group of friends had stayed, the Slow Train. They were asking about Stina Ek, who was also part of the gang. And now she's gone missing.'

'Missing?' Johan foolishly repeated, but at the same time he felt the familiar churning inside his stomach.

'Apparently she disappeared on Fårö. On Saturday afternoon. She took off on a bicycle, and nobody has seen her since.'

'Oh shit. What if she was murdered too?'

'Or maybe she's actually the killer,' Madeleine interjected. 'You never know.'

'So what are you doing now?'

Pia glanced at her watch.

'It's eleven ten. If we leave now, we can catch the twelve o'clock ferry.' She began gathering up her equipment.

'Have you got an interview lined up?'

'Yup. The guy who owns Kuten is willing to talk to us, and there won't be any problem finding someone to interview on the ferry. Then we'll talk to folks at the scene, of course. You know how it's done.' She smiled broadly. Pia was a wizard at getting people to open up, and she knew it.

'What about the police?'

'We'll catch them later. On the way back.'

'Can I help with anything? I could stay here and hold the fort. Emma is home with the kids, so it's no problem. Or do we have any extra cameras here? If so, I could go over to police headquarters and do an interview. I can stay and edit it too, so all you'll have to do is insert it in the story later on.'

While he was talking, Madeleine and Pia had finished packing up their gear, and now they were headed for the door.

'Thanks for the offer,' said Pia, 'but isn't that overdoing it a little? We'll manage on our own. Gotta go now. See you later!'

And before he could say another word, they were gone.

The fresh cinnamon coffee cake was still in the bag on the table.

The chief ranger, who had discovered the items in the woods, had been sensible enough not to touch them, and instead waited for the police to arrive. He had asked one of his colleagues to stop anyone from approaching the site. When Knutas and Jacobsson, accompanied by Thomas Wittberg, disembarked from the boat at Stora Karlsö, the chief ranger was waiting for them on the dock. They went at once to the discovery site, which was a little less than a kilometre from the lighthouse, but in an area that was off-limits during the summer. For that reason, it was a good place for someone to spend the night undisturbed.

'We can't possibly keep track of everyone who comes over here on the day boats,' the chief ranger told them as they made their way through the brush-covered terrain. 'A lot of people pay cash for a ticket at the ferry terminal in Klintehamn. They come over to spend a few hours here and then go back home. It's impossible to know when people arrive or depart. There are also those who spend the night, and we have a little more contact with them, or at least some of them. But not everyone, by any means. Ten thousand people come through here in the summertime, so I can't remember all of them.'

'When did you discover these things?' asked Knutas, who was panting in the heat. He noticed to his dismay that he wasn't in as good physical condition as he used to be. He'd been lazy about working out lately.

'I was out taking a morning walk and thought I'd go over to the most distant bird mountain to try and find out how many baby birds still haven't left. So I took a short cut through that area; it takes half the time, compared to following the road. The first thing I saw was something pink fluttering from a bush. That's what made me go down into the clearing. I never would have done it otherwise. I don't like to disturb the wildlife here unless it's really necessary.'

Knutas raised his eyebrows.

'Something pink?'

'Yes. It turned out to be a hair ribbon. The old-fashioned kind that little girls used to wear when I was at school. Very wide and sort of silky. You'll see for yourselves. I left it where it was. I didn't touch anything,' he added with a trace of pride in his voice.

Smart dude, thought Jacobsson crossly. You've probably watched crime shows on TV, even though you don't seem like the type. She was already annoyed by the chief ranger's pedantic attitude. He was close to her own age, but he acted like an old man.

They turned off on to a smaller path that headed down towards the sea. The ground was dry and covered with stones. They had to hunch over so as not to run into the dense network of tree branches. Soon a clearing opened before them, with soft grass surrounded by protective thickets. A perfect hiding place.

The next moment they caught sight of the ribbon. It was hanging on a thorny bush. Jacobsson gave a start. She'd seen photos of the missing Stina Ek, and she recalled seeing the woman wearing a similar ribbon in her hair.

'There it is,' said the chief ranger, pointing.

Silently they all stopped next to the bush to study the ribbon. It looked out of place in this remote natural setting. And somehow ominous. Are we going to find her now? Jacobsson asked herself. Is she dead or alive?

The chief ranger continued on through the trees.

'Look over there. In that crevice.'

And there it was: a light-blue sleeping bag. Jacobsson felt her mouth go dry. This could very well be the murderer's hiding place. Instinctively she glanced around, as if the perpetrator might be lurking in the thickets. But all she saw was a water bottle lying in the grass. Knutas ordered everyone back.

'Not another step closer. We need to cordon off the area.'

Wittberg immediately began putting up police tape.

Everyone felt a spark of hope. Finally they had a lead.

But what does that pink ribbon mean? thought Jacobsson. Then the same question that had been bugging her lately popped up again. Stina Ek: was she a victim or the perpetrator?

She turned around and let her gaze sweep over the scene. It was a perfect hiding place, well protected from the wind and any prying eyes.

'If these things belong to the killer, why didn't he take them with him? He should have been terrified about leaving any evidence behind.'

'Maybe something unexpected happened. If the murder was not premeditated, it's not so strange that he would be panic-stricken and decide to leave in a hurry. But where the hell did that ribbon come from?'

Knutas leaned forward to study the gleaming strip of fabric. 'Very strange. Almost as if it were a signal, asking to be noticed.'

'Or else it got caught there by mistake,' said Jacobsson. 'I mean if the murderer is a woman who wore a ribbon in her hair. Or maybe Stina was here, along with the killer.'

She looked out at the sea. Where on earth was Stina Ek?

On the surface everything looked the same as usual in the residential area of Terra Nova. But inside Håkan Ek's home, everything had changed. His parents were looking after his daughters for a few days, while he went around like a zombie, unable to sleep or eat. Beata and John refused to leave him for long; at the moment they were sitting on the terrace. Andrea was there too. It was as if they were seeking solace from each other. Håkan had poured strong mojitos for all of them. The alcohol helped – at least for the first few drinks.

'The police came over to our place today. I've stopped counting how many times they've come to see us,' sighed Beata. 'I don't know what they're looking for any more. They ask the same questions, over and over.'

'Well, what else can they do?' said John. 'If this was the United States, we'd all be sitting in jail.'

'There are probably some people who think that's where we belong,' said Andrea tonelessly.

'What do you mean?' asked Beata.

Andrea shrugged. She took a big gulp of her drink and lit a cigarette.

'I don't know. But I bet some people think one of us is the murderer.'

'You mean because people have been avoiding us? They probably just don't know what to say,' replied Håkan. 'I feel that way myself.'

'I think the majority opinion is the exact opposite,' said Beata. 'People have been talking to me, at any rate, but I suppose it's not as sensitive an issue with me. I ran into Eva-Britt and Göran today. They hinted that there are rumours going around that Stina was the one who pushed Sam. And that's why she's staying away.'

'Are they crazy?' raged Håkan. 'They think Stina would . . . ? How can they possibly accuse her of something like that?'

Beata gave Håkan a searching look.

'You shouldn't think that everybody regards Stina as the sweetheart you think she is. Stina can actually be quite snobbish. And a lot of people think she's been acting strangely lately. She has really retreated, not wanting to go for walks any more and turning down invitations to have dinner with the girls. She usually goes grocery shopping with Andrea, but she has stopped doing that too. Right?' She turned to Andrea for support.

'Yes, but there might be some other reason for that,' said Andrea wearily. She was leaning back in her chair. Now she rubbed her forehead and closed her eyes. 'Actually, there's something I've been meaning to ask you, Håkan,' she said suddenly.

'What's that?' Håkan's tone was aggressive, and he kept taking sips of his drink.

'I've also noticed that Stina has changed. Quite drastically, as a matter of fact. How have things been between the two of you?'

'What do you mean?'

Andrea opened her eyes and looked at him.

'You always used to be so affectionate with each other. Really paying attention to each other. Holding hands and hugging. But I don't recall you doing that sort of thing lately.'

'In the past, Stina was always sitting on your lap,' Beata added. 'I haven't seen her do that for at least a year.'

Håkan spat out his words. 'There's nothing wrong in our marriage. Things are great between Stina and me. Of course we have our ups and downs, just like everybody else. That's how it goes when you've been together for a long time – you both know that as well as I do. And Stina and I have been faithful to each other, not sleeping with anyone else – unlike certain other people!'

The last remark was clearly aimed at Beata and John. It was well known that they had an open relationship when it came to sex.

'Calm down, damn it,' snapped John, joining the conversation for the first time. 'Everyone makes their own choices about how to live. It's none of your business.'

'That's OK as long as you stick to people outside of the immediate circle. And if you're *discreet* about it. But that's certainly not something I could ever accuse you of being. I've seen how you've tried to make a play for Stina. You've always been hot for her. We all know that. And I'm not even going to talk about you,' Håkan screamed at Beata. 'You'll open your legs for anybody who's got balls. It's disgusting!' He stood up furiously, downed his drink in one gulp, and stomped off into the house.

The others sat there as if turned to stone, holding their mojitos in their hands.

On the other side of the hedge, where the neighbours were having a dinner party, it was suddenly very, very quiet.

During the afternoon, the suspicion grew that Stina Ek was behind the murder of Sam Dahlberg. One of the crew members on the ferry thought he recognized her from the photos the police had shown him. He was almost positive that she had taken the Karlsö boat from Klintehamn on the evening before the others arrived on the island. He distinctly remembered that the rest of the group caught the nine thirty boat on Sunday morning. The famous director Sam Dahlberg was with them, and that fact had not escaped notice. He was a well-known figure on the island.

At the same time that Knutas wanted to devote all his energies to the investigation, he was also struggling with personal problems. For one thing, he was concerned about Karin Jacobsson and her search for her daughter. Karin had been looking so pale lately, and she seemed even thinner than usual. He noticed that she was frequently lost in her own thoughts. He thought she was so lovely, and on a few occasions he had felt an inexplicable tension between them when they happened to be alone together outside of work. There was *something*, which he couldn't understand or control. But he quickly dismissed the feeling. He'd been in love with Lina for so many years that his feelings for his wife overshadowed everything else that had to do with the opposite sex. It worried him that Karin often haunted his thoughts. That was so unlike him. He had to see to it that he and Lina spent more time together. They needed to find their way back to each other. When he suddenly recalled that she'd mentioned something about taking a trip with a girlfriend at the end of the summer, he felt an immediate urge to talk to her. They could do something together instead. Just the two of them. Impatiently he tapped in her number on his mobile. She picked up after it rang four rings, sounding just as happy and cheerful as usual. He found that reassuring.

'Hi. What are you doing?'

'I'm lying in the sun in the garden, feeling lazy. It's such beautiful weather.'

Knutas looked out of the window. The summer was turning out to be marvellous after all the rain they'd had earlier in June.

'Why don't you come with me and the kids out to the country after we get back from Italy the third week of August?'

For several seconds there was only silence on the other end of the line. He could hear her breathing. What was she doing? Trying to think of something to say? Knutas felt his temper rising.

'But, Anders, we've already discussed this. You know that I'm going on a trip with Maria to make the documentary.'

'What documentary?'

'Come on. I've told you all about it. We're going to Cape Verde to do a report on childbirth. It's for the book that Maria is writing.'

Knutas frowned. Cape Verde? Didn't that sound awfully far away? An image of the football player Henke Larsson flashed through his mind. Wasn't his father from there? Why on earth were they going there, of all places? He'd barely even heard of the country. At the same time Knutas remembered that Lina had told him something about the trip. But he hadn't realized that the plans had been finalized.

'Yes, but do you really have to go there during the summer holidays?'

'Yes, we do. What's so strange about that?'

'And why do you have to be the one to help her with this book?' he continued stubbornly. 'Is she paying you anything?'

'Cut it out. I don't want to listen to this.'

When Lina got angry or upset, her Danish accent was stronger than usual.

'But why do you have to go there in August? Isn't that the rainy season – loads of storms? Won't it be miserable?'

'Good God, Anders, we're not off on holiday. We're

going to work, not lie on the beach. And by the way, I think the weather is good all year round. It's in Africa, you know.'

'But I still don't understand why you have to go.' Knutas couldn't help hearing how plaintive he sounded.

Lina sighed.

'Have you listened to anything I've said? The book is about childbirth in various parts of the world. I'm going along to help the author gather factual information and then make comparisons with the situation in Sweden. I'm really looking forward to the trip. End of discussion. Bye.'

She cut off the conversation with a click that echoed in his ears.

Early morning. He parked over by the gardener's shed and set off on foot. The asphalt under the soles of his shoes was level and dry. His footsteps made no sound and left no prints. He was wearing shorts and a T-shirt, exactly like ninety per cent of the men who lived in the area. In a few hours they would wake in their comfortable beds and get up to have coffee. Then they would sit under the apple trees in the well-kept gardens or on the verandas that they'd built themselves. Everyone had seen enough of Martin Timell or Ernst Kirchsteiger promoting home carpentry projects on TV. They're the manly role models who reign in a place like this, he thought with a snort. The people were entrenched in their lives here. The cars were parked in the drives with the morning sun reflecting off the windscreens. He passed house after house, noting that the people who lived there were either asleep or away. It was the summer holidays, after all. But for him no such concept existed. For him, the time of year didn't matter; he lived outside the normal world. He'd left it behind long ago, although no one could tell just by looking at him.

The house was at the very end of the street, near the little turning circle. A double garage, a gravel path that led to the somewhat ostentatious entrance with the pillars on either side and curving steps. Blue-painted clay pots planted with flowers that draped perfectly over the sides. A neatly mown lawn. First he merely walked past the house, pretending not to show any interest. A car was parked in the drive. A newspaper was sticking out of the letterbox. So the newspaper boy had already been there. Good. Nice and quiet. He glanced at his watch. Six fifteen. He took a quick look around before he slipped unnoticed on to the well-maintained property and crept around the corner of the house to the back, which faced the woods. Swiftly he surveyed the garden. A greenhouse that occupied the middle of the lawn revealed that football was not a priority here, but a trampoline stood in the far corner. A shed for gardening equipment, a covered bicycle rack, a group of patio furniture on the lawn, with more chairs up on the deck.

A low wooden fence surrounded the property, easy to climb over. He cautiously stepped on to the deck. It creaked loudly under his feet. At one end of the house a trellis had been put up to keep anyone from looking in. No neighbours from that direction would be able to see him. And, fortunately, the family that lived on the other side seemed to be away. There hadn't been a car in the drive for several days. He would not be disturbed.

He moved forward and grasped the handle of the deck

door. Locked, of course. He hadn't expected anything different. He peered inside. The kitchen was modern and typically designed with an open floor plan facing the living room. The refrigerator and freezer and cooker hood were all made of stainless steel. Tiles on the floor. Shiny white kitchen cupboards. Hardly anything on the counters except for a gleaming coffee maker, kettle and mixer. No curtains or rugs; everything bright and shiny. Attractive but impersonal. Almost like in a furniture shop. Did these people spend as much time cleaning up after themselves as they did living? He discovered that he was breathing so hard on the windowpane that it had clouded up. He knew exactly what he had to do. He took off his backpack and got out his gloves and picklocks.

Then he set to work.

Ventspils, Latvia

The darkness of night had faded, giving way to a hesitant morning light. A haze covered the sun. Janis Ullmanis was cycling as fast as he could over the bumpy cobblestone street lined with low, dilapidated brick houses on either side. The cramped inner court-yards were hidden behind tall wooden fences. The boy stopped so abruptly at the last house that his tyres shrieked. Then he knocked on the double window on the corner. The secret signal. Three quick raps, two slow, again three quick ones. He waited for thirty seconds as he caught his breath, then he repeated the same sequence. He'd barely finished the final rap before the door in the fence opened with a loud squeak. A pale boy's face appeared. Two dark eyes under close-cropped hair. Bruno Lesinski was Janis's best friend, and they were in the same class at school. But right now it was the summer holidays, with all that entailed, and school seemed far away.

'Are you ready?' asked Janis.

Bruno held his index finger to his lips and whispered,

'Shh. My mother is such a light sleeper.' Then he cast a glance over his shoulder before grabbing his bicycle, which was parked just inside the fence.

The next second they were on their way. They pedalled hard, riding along side by side since there were no cars on the road. Two skinny thirteen-year-olds with scraped knees, filled with anticipation. They'd fastened their nets and buckets to the bike panniers. They headed to the shore just beyond the harbour. But it wasn't fish that they were going to catch.

Ventspils was a run-down little town about 160 kilometres west of the capital of Riga, but its harbour was one of the biggest in Latvia. It was considerably oversized in comparison to the modest town with only fifty thousand inhabitants, but it was strategically located, close to both Sweden and Finland and right on the mouth of the Venta River, in the direct path of the Russian natural gas pipeline. For that reason it had expanded rapidly and become one of the largest ports on the Baltic Sea. The town hadn't kept up with its growth.

The boys passed the two piers that extended into the outer harbour like protective arms, breaking the waves and embracing visitors from the sea. At the end of each pier stood a lighthouse guarding the entrance. To the south a promenade had been built and it was very popular because it also provided a vantage point with an impressive view. At the moment nobody was there.

The long sandy beach began just beyond the south

pier and stretched for several kilometres. The sand was coarse and the water quite murky. Rubbish was scattered about: ice-cream wrappers, plastic bottles and pieces of rusty old junk. But it was still a popular place for people to sunbathe in the summertime. The people who lived in Ventspils were not very particular.

When the boys reached the beach, they found it deserted except for a few seagulls strutting about in search of something to eat. The strong winds of the night had subsided, and the hesitant rays of the sun were growing stronger. It was just past seven o'clock, and the fishing boats that were usually moored at the dock had already gone out to sea.

Janis and Bruno knew that they had to get an early start if they were to have any luck at all. A few days earlier a woman from the area had found a piece of amber that weighed over a kilo at this very spot on the beach. And interest in looking for the amber had increased considerably.

They flung their bicycles down on the sand, picked up their buckets and nets, and squelched along the water's edge in their ungainly sea boots. Sometimes it was possible to find several hectograms of amber in one day after a strong wind. The amber was torn away from the sea floor or seaweed and tossed on to shore by the surging waves.

Eagerly the two boys searched the beach. Hunched over and with their eyes fixed on the ground, they scanned the shore, centimetre by centimetre. Every once in a while they talked about how they would spend the money they were going to get for the amber. If they were lucky.

A little later Bruno called to Janis, who assumed that he must have found some amber. He turned around expectantly to look at his friend, who had stopped some distance away. Bruno was pointing out towards the water.

'Look at that!' he yelled.

An empty rowing boat was bobbing on the waves. It looked old and leaky, with a rusty motor at the stern. The rowlocks were empty. It had obviously been drifting about, probably after the high winds of the night had torn it from its mooring.

'Let's bring it in,' suggested Bruno. 'Maybe we can keep it.'

'It'd be great to have our own boat! Then we could go out fishing and put out nets,' exclaimed Janis. He pictured the two of them setting out to sea. If they were lucky, nobody would lay claim to the boat. It had probably come from far away, drifting out of Riga Bay and continuing south along the coast. It looked so decrepit that the owner might not make much of an effort to track it down.

Bruno waded out into the water until it reached way over the tops of his boots. He reached for the prow and pulled on the boat. Janis hurried forward to help, but then stopped abruptly. Bruno heard his friend breathing hard.

In the bottom of the boat lay a gaunt old man, curled up in a foetal position. He was wearing a dark-blue woollen pullover and black trousers. His head was half hidden under one arm, but it was clear that he was badly injured. A huge gash was visible on his forehead, crusted with blood.

The man wasn't moving.

Detective Inspector Martin Kihlgård of the National Criminal Police arrived early the following morning. Kihlgård had assisted the Visby police on several previous occasions, and it was obvious from the reception he received at police headquarters that he was more than welcome. Everyone seemed aware that the boisterous and popular colleague from Stockholm had arrived, because more and more people poured out of their offices to greet him. Knutas couldn't help being impressed by the sheer number of friendships that Kihlgård had managed to make among the police during the time he'd spent on Gotland. He seemed to know more people than Knutas did, which was admittedly a bit annoying. He'd always felt slightly competitive towards Kihlgård, even though he tried to hide it. He actually found the effusive welcome rather pathetic, since it was exactly what was expected whenever NCP officers arrived in an out-of-the-way town to offer assistance. In spite of the island's sixty thousand inhabitants, their district was small potatoes compared to Stockholm. But there was no denying that Kihlgård was a nice guy. In addition to his fun-loving personality and good humour, he was energetic, tenacious and fearless. He also possessed a sensitivity and empathy for others that he put to good use in his job as police interrogator. One of Kihlgård's most distinguishing traits was his tremendous love of food. There was never any risk of too much time passing between meals whenever he was around. Knutas noted that a large basket of fresh cinnamon rolls had been ordered for their usual morning coffee, just so that Kihlgård would feel at home.

He'd brought along two colleagues, and as soon as the introductions were over, everyone sat down for the meeting.

Knutas began by giving a brief summary of the case and reporting on the latest developments.

'Right now we're putting all of our efforts into finding the woman who disappeared a week ago. Stina Ek.'

Kihlgård pushed his glasses up on to his forehead and leaned back in his chair.

'As I understand it, you consider her a prime suspect. Is that right?'

'Yes, at least the way things stand at the moment. But we're not locking ourselves into any particular theory.'

'That's good. She could just as well be a victim. How are you going about searching for this Stina Ek? And by the way, do you have a photograph of her?'

'Of course.'

Erik Sohlman got up and clicked on his computer to

produce a picture on the screen at the front of the room. It was a photo of Stina Ek. She was a beautiful woman. Her hair was pulled back into a ponytail. She wore a white blouse, a pink cardigan and jeans.

Kihlgård studied the photo thoughtfully.

'And you said that she's thirty-seven years old? Christ, she doesn't look more than twenty.'

'The picture is a couple of years old,' muttered Sohlman. 'But she does look awfully young.'

'Nobody has seen her since she left for a bicycle ride on Fårö, except for a crew member on the Stora Karlsö ferry,' said Jacobsson. 'He thinks that he saw her, but he's not sure.'

Kihlgård shook his head, but didn't take his eyes off the photo.

'We did find a few traces of her,' Knutas reminded the others. 'Her bag, plus what was found on Stora Karlsö.'

'The last person to see Stina Ek was her husband Håkan. On Fårö, on the afternoon of Saturday, the twenty-eighth of June. Just before she left for her bike ride. After that no one has seen either her or her bicycle. In my opinion, that's where we need to start. Where did Stina go? Who did she meet? What happened? Who is the man that she claimed to have met, the old classmate of hers?' Kihlgård gave Knutas an enquiring glance. 'Have you talked to him?'

'No,' sighed Knutas. 'We don't know who he is. Or what his name is.'

'When were they in school together? In primary

school? Middle school? Secondary school? Or even nursery school?'

'Håkan Ek says that he thinks it was in middle school.'

'But you haven't checked up on that?'

The colour of Knutas's face had grown significantly redder under Kihlgård's cross-examination.

'No,' he exclaimed. 'We haven't done that yet because we didn't think it was particularly urgent. We suspect that Stina Ek was lying about that too.'

'But what if it's true? What if she really did meet this old classmate? And then disappeared.'

'She said on the phone that they were sitting in a restaurant called Kuten on Fårö,' Knutas went on, annoyed. 'And of course we investigated this thoroughly, since it was the last phone call she made, meaning that it was the last time anyone had direct contact with Stina. None of the employees remember seeing an Asian-looking woman in the restaurant on that Saturday afternoon. Right now all indications are that the purported meeting was nothing but a lie. It seems more and more likely that she is the perpetrator. The ribbon that was found in the hiding place on Stora Karlsö belongs to Stina. Then there's her mysterious disappearance and the fabricated text messages. It all adds up.'

'So what's the motive?'

Knutas threw out his hands.

'I have no idea! The gods only know what sort of intrigues have been going on with that group of people.

They almost seem like a cult – the perfect scenario for bloodshed and revenge.'

Kihlgård reached for what had to be his third cinnamon roll, took a bite, and then swallowed before saying, 'To sum up, we can conclude that we don't know a fucking thing. We have no facts to go on. In other words, it's an open question as to who's the killer and who's the victim. I suggest that my NCP colleagues and I get started at once on searching for Stina.'

'Considering that a murder has actually been committed, shouldn't we put out an APB on Stina Ek?' said Wittberg. 'I mean, to the general public? Since so many people have been in the area, both on Fårö and on Stora Karlsö, we might get some tips if we make use of the media.'

Silence fell over the room. Everyone was considering this suggestion.

'You're probably right,' Knutas said at last. 'That's exactly what we should do.'

He fixed his eyes once again on the smiling woman in the photograph on the screen.

After the meeting Knutas went to his office and closed the door. The room seemed stuffy and stifling. He opened a window. For once he felt in great need of a smoke. He usually just filled his pipe without lighting it, but right now he was feeling very irritated.

Lina had phoned to say that she was thinking of going to Stockholm for a couple of days now that the children were away at a music festival in Roskilde. She had time off from her job, and she didn't feel like sitting at home, waiting for him to get off work.

He pushed away all thoughts of Lina and puffed on his pipe. In his mind's eye he saw the mangled body of Sam Dahlberg. They were getting nowhere with the case. All of the interviews that they'd done had proved more or less useless. They had turned the Dahlberg family home on Norra Glasmästargatan in Terra Nova upside down but found nothing of interest. Outwardly everything seemed perfect: their marriage, the planned surprise trip to Florence, the fancy house. At the same time, Andrea Dahlberg was the last person to see her husband alive. It was entirely possible that she had gone up to the bird mountain with him and pushed him off. We've got to get to the bottom of things with her, thought Knutas. With that whole Terra Nova crowd.

The reinforcements from the NCP were definitely needed, even though he couldn't help feeling irritated with Kihlgård. He asked questions and generally behaved as if he was the one in charge.

Knutas's thoughts were interrupted by the phone ringing. It was the duty officer.

'We had a call while you were in the meeting, but I didn't want to disturb you.'

'What's it about?'

'A woman rang from Fårö. A Märta Gardell. She wanted to file a missing person report.'

'And?'

'Her brother Valter Olsson has been missing for several days. Maybe a whole week.'

'Where does he live?'

'He lives alone in a house in Hammars. He's actually the closest neighbour to Ingmar Bergman's house.'

Knutas immediately rang Karin Jacobsson. She and Kihlgård were scheduled to go out to Fårö on the following day, so they could begin by paying a visit to Märta Gardell to talk about her brother's disappearance. Knutas asked Karin to find out everything she could about the missing man, and try to see if there was some connection with the murder of Sam Dahlberg. Yet he knew from experience that most people who were reported missing usually turned up. People simply didn't keep in very good touch with each other.

Feeling dejected, Knutas left police headquarters around lunchtime on Friday. He regretted that he was not going out to Fårö with Karin. Then he would at least have a sense of doing something constructive. Right now he seemed to be merely sitting in his office like some sodding administrator, ordering people around. He longed to be doing ordinary, respectable police footwork.

He was going to spend the weekend at home alone, and he wasn't looking forward to it. He closed the glass door of the Criminal Division with a sigh of relief. He was planning to have lunch and then spend the rest of the afternoon working at home. He wanted to go through the transcripts from the latest interviews, and that was something he preferred to do at home. He would have the whole house to himself all weekend, so there was no risk of being interrupted.

Knutas felt anything but at ease with himself and his life in general. On top of his personal problems, the murder investigation seemed to be going nowhere. It felt as if they were simply treading water. I need to have some time for myself, he thought as he crossed the car park outside police headquarters. Time to think.

He stopped at the little pizzeria on his way home. By now the lunchtime rush was over, and the place was empty. He ordered a calzone and a strong beer. He needed it. He exchanged a few words with the owner, but no more than necessary. After all these years, they knew each other well enough so that the pizzeria owner recognized when Knutas wanted to talk and when he didn't.

Knutas found a secluded table next to the window at the back of the restaurant. He took a big gulp of the cold beer. That helped. He suddenly noticed that he smelled of sweat and glanced down at his shirt. Big damp patches had appeared under his arms. The heat was taking its toll on him. At least here in the restaurant it was cooler than outdoors. Listlessly he stared out of the window. Was he getting depressed? Was he overworked? In fact, there were several indications that he was burned out. That was the term usually used, although he didn't much care for it. What did it actually mean? But he'd been suffering from insomnia for weeks, and his sexual desire was completely gone. Not that he and Lina had been feeling particularly passionate lately, but they usually managed to have sex at least a few times a month. And normally it was great. But it had been a long time now. Neither of them felt like taking the initiative. Could it be so bad that they'd actually grown tired of each other? He would never have believed that. Lina had been the love of his life. Good Lord, am I already thinking in the past tense? he realized with alarm. He took another swallow of beer. He was definitely feeling out of sorts; maybe that was part of it. He was having a hard time sleeping, a hard time concentrating. Earlier in the week he'd gone to the ICA Supermarket to buy groceries. When he came out with a full shopping cart, he couldn't for the life of him remember where he'd parked the car. It took him a good fifteen minutes to find it, but he still couldn't recall parking it in that particular spot less than an hour earlier. He needed to pull himself together. He was like a spider in the web of the homicide investigation, expected to contribute a majority of the input. But right now he didn't even have enough energy to deal with the pile of bills and other important papers he should be reading. He ignored them all, almost as if hoping that they'd simply disappear on their own. Friends and acquaintances phoned to ask if he'd like to get together, but their invitations felt burdensome, so he frequently declined, which only made the situation with Lina even worse. She thought he was being negative and boring. Every time the phone rang at home, he would jump. The phone had become a device that meant stress, and he wanted it to remain silent so he could retreat from everything and everyone. He wanted peace and quiet. He wanted to push away all the problems and decisions that needed to be dealt with. Put them in the deep-freeze and take them out later, when he felt better.

He had finished his beer by the time the fragrant, hot pizza arrived. He ordered another one. That was exactly what he needed.

After he had finished eating and had downed the last of his second beer, he noticed that he was feeling tipsy. He cursed himself. Here he was drinking strong beer in the middle of the day. What an idiot. What if someone saw him? Fortunately, he was still alone in the little restaurant. Probably no one would want to sit inside eating pizza in this heat. The front door stood open to let in some air. Fatigue suddenly overwhelmed him. He hadn't slept properly for weeks. He ordered coffee and asked for the bill.

When he left the restaurant, he was a bit unsteady on his feet. And the contempt that he felt for himself grew.

Johan Berg was cooking dinner. He was itching to get back to his job. He sighed heavily, hoping that the feeling would pass. He couldn't go around like this for the next six months. He thought with admiration of all the women who stayed at home with their children year after year. He was amazed they could stand it.

For the moment peace reigned in the house. Elin was watching a TV programme for kids while Anton sat on the floor, waving a rattle. Johan had showered and shaved and was sipping a glass of red wine that he'd placed within reach. Emma was at the gym and would be home soon.

The phone rang. He picked it up as he continued stirring the chicken casserole, redolent with garlic. It was Emma's favourite dish.

He didn't recognize the voice of the man on the phone.

'Uh, hello, I'm sorry to bother you. This is Arne Gustavsson, and I live on Fårö. I'm a good friend of Emma's parents. They gave me your number.'

'Oh. Hello.'

Emma's parents had lived for many years in the northern part of Fårö.

'I'm calling about the pictures they've published on the Internet. You know, the ones of the missing woman.'

The missing woman? Johan had no idea what the man was talking about.

'Yes?'

'Well, I know that you're a journalist and so I talked to Sture, Emma's father. We've been friends for a long time. Here on Fårö everybody knows everyone else, more or less. There aren't that many of us living here, after all. And I thought that I should ring you. I've talked to the police too, of course, but Sture said that you'd definitely be interested.'

Johan took his eyes off the stove for a moment, picked up his glass of wine, and sat down on a chair at the kitchen table. What in the world was this guy babbling about?

'What's this about?'

'Well, the thing is, a week ago I saw the missing woman – Stina Ek, whose picture is in all the papers – right outside where I live. She came cycling past, and my dog ran after her. I called out to her, but she just kept on going. I wanted to stop her because she was headed for some private land, and I didn't know who she was.'

'Private land?'

'Yes, I live next to Ingmar Bergman's property out here in Hammars. And it looked like she was headed in that direction.'

Johan slowly lowered his hand, still holding the glass.

He was trying to gather his thoughts. He'd spent the whole day without listening to a single news broadcast, and he hadn't turned on his computer since morning. He had no idea what the man was trying to tell him.

'I'm sorry if I seem a bit confused,' he apologized. 'I'm in the middle of taking care of the kids and cooking dinner, so I haven't a clue what happened today. Could you tell me what this is all about?'

'Sure.' The man on the phone cleared his throat. 'The police are looking for a woman named Stina Ek. She was apparently part of the same group as Sam Dahlberg, who was found dead on Stora Karlsö. A bunch of friends from Visby had come over for the Bergman festival and then continued on to Stora Karlsö. One of the women, whose name is Stina Ek, disappeared from Fårö a week ago. Now the police want to find out any information they can about her, and I seem to have been the last person to see her before she vanished.'

'When was that?'

'Last Saturday. She came cycling past in the afternoon.'

'I see.'

Johan was beginning to understand. At that moment Elin came in from the living room, sobbing. She wasn't wearing a nappy, and she had wet herself. At the same time, Anton began crying.

'Maybe it would be best for us to meet so you could explain things in more detail. Would that be OK?'

'Sure, that's no problem.'

'How about tomorrow morning? Around eleven? I can come out to your place.'

'All right. My wife and I will be home.'

Johan asked for directions, which he quickly jotted down while the sound of the children crying rose to a deafening level in the background.

He put down the phone and dealt with the chaos while thoughts whirled through his mind.

Fifteen minutes later calm was once again restored. He had just enough time to ring Pia before Emma came home.

He picked up the phone and tapped in her home number.

Maybe now she'd have time to talk.

Exhausted, Andrea sank down on to the sofa. It was past midnight before the children had finally fallen asleep. They had been sad, bewildered, and on edge ever since she'd been forced to tell them that their father was dead. Pontus worried that he was going to die too, while Oliver had closed off his emotions and declined to speak at all. The youngest child, Mathilda, was convinced that her mother was also going to disappear, so she clung to Andrea, refusing to let go. In reality, the kids hadn't had a particularly close or strong relationship with their father. Andrea was always the one who had taken most of the responsibility. She was the one who was at home, cleaning, doing the laundry, baking apple cakes and helping the children with their homework. She was the one who drove them to football and hockey practice and to their riding lessons. She was the one who attended the parent-teacher meetings. Sam could always blame his absence on his job. Pappa had to go out of town. Pappa had to work on a screenplay. Don't bother Pappa because he's reading through script changes; he needs his sleep because he's shooting a film.

Andrea tried to find some solace in these kinds of thoughts. At least the children still had her. If it weren't for the kids, she would have preferred to lie down and die. In fact, she had actually toyed with that idea. She would go out to Sandviken on the east coast of Gotland, since she had such fond memories of that place. There she'd take off all her clothes except for a white cotton dress that was her favourite. She'd put on bright-red lipstick, the kind that wouldn't come off in the water. Paint her toenails the same colour, and then in the evening walk barefoot straight out into the water. Let the sea envelop her; let the water rush into all the nooks and crannies of her body, capturing her life's breath and extinguishing it. She would be a lovely corpse, no question about that.

She yawned without feeling sleepy, shivering with cold even though it was still warm outside. She switched on the TV and tried to concentrate on a Spanish film by Almodóvar. She and Sam both liked the Spanish director very much, and they'd seen all his films. Tonight it was *Women on the Verge of a Nervous Breakdown*. The perfect movie for me, she thought ironically. She was wearing only her bathrobe. She spread a blanket over her legs, turned on a light, and poured herself another glass of wine. It wouldn't matter if she got a bit drunk before going to bed. She'd done that every night since Sam was found dead, out there on Stora Karlsö. She was filled with nausea at the thought of how he'd looked. His body completely ravaged. She'd been forced to identify him, but she'd hardly recognized her own husband. The father of her children.

A sob rose in her throat but no tears fell. Even though she'd lost everything, she still hadn't been able to cry. She felt dried up, shrivelled up, stunned. Thoughts whirled through her mind without meaning or purpose. Disconnected. Nothing made any sense. She had no idea how long she might remain in these hellish depths. Everything she'd had was now gone. She was floating about in a void, a no man's land, a limbo. She took some more sips of wine.

Suddenly she gave a start. She thought she saw a shadow race past outside the window. The big windows facing the back garden reached from floor to ceiling. That was one thing that Sam had insisted on when the house was built. Andrea had been less convinced; it seemed so exposed. 'Who's going to look in?' Sam had protested. 'Both the living room and kitchen face the woods. Nobody is going to be walking past.' She could hear his voice so clearly, echoing inside her head. She froze, the wine glass halfway to her lips, and stared into the darkness. She could just make out the apple trees in the garden, the lilac arbour in the distance. The edge of the woods. The silhouette of a bird was visible against the darkening sky. It never got pitch dark at this time of year. Probably a blackbird, she thought. It sat very still. Quiet and motionless.

What had she seen? The next second she heard a clattering sound. Someone or something was definitely out there. Keeping her eyes fixed on the window, she slowly set her glass on the coffee table and turned off the lamp. Darkness settled over the room. Reflected in the windowpanes she saw only the fading embers in the fireplace. Now it would be much harder to see her from outside. Cautiously she got up from the sofa and crept over to the far wall, pressing herself against the surface to hide.

It was quiet outside. Nothing moved. Her heart was pounding hard, but she tried to reason with herself. It was probably just a bird. Or a cat. Or a hedgehog, now that the heat of the day lingered into the night. One evening, when she'd turned off the outside lights before going to bed, she'd seen dark little shapes dotting the lawn. A hideous sight. As if they were sitting there, biding their time. Just waiting to come towards her.

The shrill sound of the phone suddenly broke the silence. She jumped. Who could be calling so late? It was almost 1 a.m. None of their friends would ever ring in the middle of the night. Her first thought was that it must be the police. Had something happened? Had they found Stina? Her whole being urged her to answer the phone, but she wasn't sure that she dared. What if somebody was still out there? She assumed that she couldn't be seen from where she was standing, but if she picked up the phone, she'd give herself away. All she had to do was turn her head towards the window to sense the threat lurking outside. It couldn't be just her imagination; the feeling was too strong.

The phone stopped ringing. Then it started up again. The caller was trying again, so it must be important. She strained to see something in the dark, but in vain. Nothing moved. What should she do? She cursed herself for not switching on the security system. Anybody could get inside the house without being noticed. She took a deep breath, and then rushed from her hiding place and grabbed the phone on the wall between the living room and kitchen.

'Hello?'

She heard someone breathing.

'Hello?' she repeated. 'Who is this?'

Silence. Breathing. A faint wheezing sound.

Fear flashed through her body, but she also felt her anger growing. Who had the right to terrorize her like this in the middle of the night?

'Who is this?' she said, harshly.

Finally a voice. Sounding horribly hollow.

'I can see you. I'm out here. You look so lovely in your robe. Shall I come in and take it off?'

'Tell me who you are,' she pleaded.

'Shall I come in and . . . ?'

Whispering in her ear. Sexual. Very close. She held her breath, turned towards the dark window. Someone was out there. Someone was watching her. Someone knew what she had done. Her hand was shaking as she put down the phone.

It was only eight o'clock when Jacobsson picked up Kihlgård outside his hotel on Saturday morning. They had a lot to do that day. Their first topic of conversation was the request for information about Stina Ek, which had appeared in the media and had already resulted in numerous calls from the public.

'The most interesting tip is from a man on Fårö named Arne Gustavsson,' Karin told Martin. 'He lives in Hammars, and Stina rode past him on her bike the day that she disappeared. She was heading straight for Bergman's property.'

'Really?'

'At least it confirms that she was cycling in that area. Whether she disappeared from that part of the island is another matter. At any rate, he tried to stop her since she was approaching private land, but she just kept on going.'

Kihlgård whistled.

'Interesting. He may have been the last one to see her. Do we have time to talk to him?'

'Of course. But it'll have to be after lunch. He couldn't meet with us until then. Something else has happened that we need to check out. Andrea Dahlberg rang the duty officer in the middle of the night to say that some idiot was making nuisance phone calls.'

'What? What do you mean?'

'It started with her hearing strange noises outside late at night. The children were asleep upstairs, and she was sitting on the sofa in the living room watching TV. Several times she thought she saw someone moving about the property, but she decided it was just her imagination. Then the phone rang. By then it was really late, around one a.m. At first she heard only someone breathing, but then a man started making sexual remarks.'

'What did he say?'

'Something about how he could see she was wearing only a robe, and then he suggested that he could come in and take it off her.'

'Then what happened?'

'She rang the police. She was so upset that the duty officer sent out a patrol car. They checked outside the house but found nothing. Then they stayed to talk to her until she calmed down.'

'What in Christ's name could that be about? Did she recognize the voice?'

'I don't think so. But I haven't talked to her. Wittberg was the one who went out there to see her.'

'The guy must have been right outside her window. Have you checked with the neighbours? Asked them if anybody suspicious was seen outside the Dahlberg house, I mean?'

'Of course we have,' said Jacobsson impatiently. 'No one noticed anything unusual. At least they said they didn't. I'm starting to have serious doubts about whether this group can be trusted.'

They passed the little village of Tingstäde.

'Isn't this where your parents live?' asked Kihlgård.

'Yes.'

'Whereabouts?'

'You can't see their house from the road.'

Kihlgård fell silent. It was obvious that Karin didn't want to talk about her parents.

'Would you like one?' He held out a bag of sugar doughnuts. Jacobsson couldn't help smiling.

'Didn't you have time for breakfast?'

'Yes, but there's a bakery right next door to the hotel, and every morning when I open the window, I can smell the fresh doughnuts. I couldn't resist. Coffee?' Kihlgård pulled out a thermos and two paper cups.

'And where did you get those?'

'Well, I've made friends with the waiter who serves breakfast, and I told him we were driving all the way to Fårö and wondered whether we could get some coffee to take along. He said it was no problem.'

Jacobsson gratefully accepted a cup of coffee. They soon reached the dock at Fårösund, just in time to catch the ferry. At this hour on a Saturday morning, only a few cars were on board.

They were going to start by driving over to the home of the woman that Knutas had spoken to yesterday, the one who had reported her brother missing. Märta Gardell lived just outside the village of Dämba, which consisted of a cluster of houses crowded in between sheep pastures. She lived in a small, low limestone house, and she'd set the table in the garden for coffee. All three of them sat down in the shade. Kihlgård helped himself to the homemade saffron pancakes.

'So tell us what happened,' said Jacobsson. 'You said your brother has disappeared. Is that right?'

'Yes,' replied Märta. 'I haven't heard from him all week, and that's not like him. He usually comes by at least every other day to have a meal with me. We both live alone now. My husband passed away last year, almost the same time as Ingmar Bergman, just a week later. And Valter has never married. He has lived over there in that cabin of his all these years. The only people he ever sees are me and my family, plus Ingmar. They were neighbours, you know. Valter helped him out a lot, taking care of the house when Ingmar was in Stockholm or travelling.'

'When did you last see your brother?'

'A week ago. He came over and we had dinner together. He'd brought me several flounders.'

'Did you notice anything different about him?'

'Not at all. He was just the same as usual. Very quiet. My brother doesn't talk much. Not like me.'

'How long did he stay?'

'He must have been here a couple of hours. He helped me with some digging in the garden and then chopped some wood for me. My arms aren't as strong as they used to be.'

'So this was a week ago? And you haven't heard from him since?'

'No, not a word. I haven't seen him, and nobody else has either. I've asked all the neighbours, everyone we know, in the shops and down by the ferry. Not a single person has seen hide nor hair of him for a whole week.'

'And you said that he lives alone?'

'That's right. He always has, though I don't know why. But I've never asked. That's his own business.' She sighed.

'Does he usually keep to himself?'

'I suppose he's somewhat of a loner, but we've always got along well. We enjoy each other's company. And after the children moved away and my husband died, he doesn't mind coming over here. In the past there was always so much commotion in the house, and he doesn't do well in noisy situations. So he didn't come around much. But as I said, I started to think something was wrong, and he's not answering his phone. He does spend a lot of time outdoors, but still. I've tried phoning early in the morning and late in the evening. Yesterday I went over there because I was getting really worried. That's when I discovered that his boat was missing.

'His boat?' queried Jacobsson.

'Yes, the rowing boat he always uses when he goes out fishing. It's not there.'

'Did you notice anything out of the ordinary inside his house?'

'The coffee thermos wasn't in its usual place on the counter. I looked everywhere, but I couldn't find it. He always takes it with him when he goes fishing. That's what made me really worried, the fact that the boat and the thermos were gone. Something must have happened out at sea. There was a strong wind all week. I'm afraid that something bad has happened to him. We only have each other, Valter and I. Everyone else is gone. There's nothing else left.' Tears filled the old woman's eyes. 'I also went down to his fishing shack, and it looks like he took his nets along. And the binoculars were gone too. They weren't hanging on the hook.'

'Could we borrow the key to Valter's house?' asked Jacobsson. 'We'd like to have a look around.'

It took Knutas less time than he expected to plough his way through the interview transcripts that he'd brought home over the weekend. But reading through the material hadn't produced any new leads. He felt discouraged when he awoke in the empty house on Saturday morning. To take his mind off things, he decided to drive up to the family's summer cottage in Lickershamn. He needed to get away and have a change of scene. Why should he stay home alone in Visby when he'd finished the work he needed to do and the weather was so nice? Lina and the children were all away. Besides, he needed to repair the roof of the cottage. Several roof tiles had blown off during a spring storm. He'd been meaning to replace them for a long time, but so far nothing had come of his good intentions. If nothing special happened in the investigation, he planned to stay overnight.

He drove north, relieved to be leaving the city behind. Even though it wasn't a long drive, only twenty-five kilometres, he always had a feeling of liberation upon arriving at the cottage, located on the rocky shore in north-west Gotland. There was no phone and only a few neighbours, so he would be undisturbed. And he wouldn't have to talk to a soul.

A warm, happy sensation came over him when the grey plastered limestone house appeared a kilometre beyond the picturesque harbour area. It was surrounded by a stone wall, isolated, and with no neighbours within sight. Bright-red poppies gleamed against the fence. He noted that the grass had sprouted up to an unacceptable height. It was going to be a tough job for their halting old lawnmower, which he should have replaced long ago. He parked in front of the cottage and got out of the car. There he stood for a moment, filling his lungs with fresh air that smelled of the salt water and seaweed. He got out the bags of groceries and then unlocked the front door, breathing in the usual smell of damp stone. He loved the smell that always lingered inside until he threw open all the windows to air the place. Slightly stuffy, with a hint of indolence and a sense of anticipation. A longing for something else.

He put the groceries in the fridge and pantry. He was planning to cook himself a steak for supper. With potato wedges and red wine. For lunch he would have sliced meatballs and pickled beets on the famous flat bread that his parents made at their farm just a little further north, in Kappelshamn. He realized that it had been a while since he'd visited them. So he decided to drop by and have coffee with them tomorrow before he went back to town. But first he needed to get busy with the tedious task of repairing the roof. He made coffee and poured himself a cup. Then he set the transistor radio on the table outside so he could listen to the programme *Melodikrysset* while he was working.

He went out to the tool shed to fetch a hammer and nails, as well as the roof tiles that he'd bought some time ago. He leaned the ladder against the eaves, but then realized it was too hot for the clothes he was wearing. He went back inside to change his jeans and shirt for a pair of shorts and a polo shirt. He glanced at the thermometer in the kitchen window. Already twenty-four degrees centigrade, even though it wasn't even ten o'clock. An area of high pressure was on its way from Russia, and it would probably park itself over Gotland and stay for weeks. He was hoping that would happen. Not so much for his own sake, since he didn't enjoy really hot weather, but Lina and the kids did. Not to mention all the tourists, of course.

He put on the carpenter's belt that Lina had given him for his birthday a few years back. He'd taken the hint, realizing that if he had the tools handy, he could just as well do the work himself instead of hiring someone. Several years ago he'd helped a good friend put on a tile roof, so he should be able to manage. He put the tiles on his shoulder and climbed up the ladder just as the theme song of *Melodikrysset* started playing. The next second he heard the familiar voice of Anders Eldeman giving the correct answers from the previous week's show.

When Knutas had climbed high enough up, he lifted

off the tiles and set them on the roof. Then he nervously took a step away from the ladder. He'd always been a bit scared of heights. On trembling legs he carried the tiles up to the place on the ridge where the old tiles had blown away. He carefully knelt down, placing the tiles next to him. Only then could he enjoy the view. He looked out over the sea, glittering with sunlight, and the rocky shore; way off in the distance, near the harbour, he could see the *rauk* called Jungfrun, which was a landmark for Lickershamn. Suddenly he heard a clattering sound next to him. In a flash he saw that the tiles had started sliding down the roof. He reached out to grab them, but at that moment he lost his balance.

He didn't even have time to think before he found himself tumbling down off the roof.

Valter Olsson's home was located in the middle of the woods. A blue gate near the narrow road was the only indication that someone lived in the vicinity. They parked outside the gate, struck by the silence that enveloped them. The only sound was the constant, soothing roar of the sea. Karin took a deep breath. How fresh the air was.

A one-storey wooden house painted brown stood in a clearing right above the water. A storage shed and an outdoor privy also stood nearby. Nothing fancy. A small piece of ground surrounded the cabin; a broom leaned against the front wall. No porch. Another small blue gate faced the sea.

Jacobsson lifted the hasp and stepped inside the gate; then she stopped among the trees to look down at the rocky shore. There she saw an old rotting boathouse that looked as if it might collapse at any minute. An upside-down rowing boat lay near the water's edge; it was in disrepair and bleached from the sun. It clearly hadn't been used for a long time. According to Märta Gardell, her brother kept his fishing boat inside the boathouse. Right now it was empty.

A few terns glided over the surface of the water. Jacobsson turned to peer with curiosity in the direction where she assumed Ingmar Bergman had lived. Cliffs; barbed wire ending out in the sea. The house must be beyond the next bend.

The cabin seemed deserted. A rusty old bicycle was parked outside. A few dirty and dented plastic containers lay on the grass. There was no real garden to speak of. The ground was barren, covered with stones, the only vegetation a few juniper shrubs clustered together inside the stone wall that surrounded the property.

The door opened with a creak. Quietly Kihlgård pushed it further open so they could go inside. They were instantly struck by the view of the water. Straight ahead, at the other end of the cabin, was a row of windows. The small, cramped kitchen faced the other direction. There they saw a table and two chairs with floral-patterned cushions. Jacobsson guessed that it was Valter's sister who had made them. The curtains had the same pattern. She felt a lump settle in her stomach. Life was so strange. Would it really finish in this lonely way? Was this all that was left at the end? Thoughts of Lydia flitted through her mind. She was interrupted when Kihlgård shouted from the bedroom.

'Look at this.'

Kihlgård was standing next to the bed, holding a photograph in his hand. Jacobsson stood on tiptoe to peer at an old black-and-white photo, probably taken sometime in the 1960s. Bergman, wearing a beret and polo-neck sweater, was standing on a rock near the sea with his arm around a lean-looking man clad in a vest and peaked cap. Both were suntanned and smiling at the camera.

'This must be him,' said Kihlgård. 'Valter Olsson. They certainly look like they were good friends.'

'They certainly do.'

'The bed seems to have been recently made. But it's impossible to tell when it was last used.'

Jacobsson sat down on the edge of the bed with a sigh, feeling discouraged.

'What should we do?'

'First we'll search the cabin, and then we'll have a look at the boathouse down by the water. I'm afraid that since his boat is gone and he hasn't been seen for a whole week, we have to expect the worst. He may have drowned when he was out fishing.' Kihlgård got out his mobile. 'I'll ask the others to find out if a rowing boat has come ashore anywhere along the coast. If so, we'll soon have our answer.'

Jacobsson stared up at her colleague from under her fringe.

'Don't you think this is all a bit strange? First Sam Dahlberg is found dead on Stora Karlsö a couple of days after he's been here on Fårö to attend the Bergman festival. Then Stina Ek disappears from the island during the same week while taking a bicycle ride. And now another man is missing. And who does he happen to be? Bergman's closest neighbour. I don't think it's just a coincidence. There must be a connection.'

Kihlgård nodded pensively.

'I'm sure you're right. The question is: What on earth does Ingmar Bergman have to do with all of this?'

Knutas looked around the room. The hospital smells prickled his nose. Cautiously he turned his wrist, grimacing with pain.

Fortunately his neighbour had been able to take him to accident and emergency after he fell off the roof. He was feeling dazed and gratefully accepted a painkiller and a glass of water from a nurse who came into the room. She gave him a smile.

'So how's it going?'

'I'm not sure,' said Knutas. 'I feel sick. My wrist hurts. My head does too.'

'You have a bad concussion, and your wrist is broken. It was a nasty fall. Considering the circumstances, you're doing well.'

'What time is it?'

'Twelve ten. We've phoned Lina, and she's on her way.'

Everyone knew Lina. She'd worked at the hospital for fifteen years.

'We need to put a cast on your wrist. We'll do that later this afternoon.'

'Will I be able to go to work?' asked Knutas worriedly.

'That's for the doctor to decide, but I think you'll probably need to stay home for a week at least. A serious concussion is nothing to muck around with. There can be complications if you don't take it easy. But it was lucky that it was your left hand. You're right-handed, aren't you?'

'Yes. Could I make a phone call?'

'Of course. Would you like your mobile?'

'Yes, please. But first I've got to use the toilet.'

'Let me help you.'

With great effort he sat up and put his feet on the floor. At that moment his head started to spin, as if someone had struck him.

'How are you doing?' asked the nurse, holding him by the arm.

Knutas sighed. It seemed very unlikely that he'd be back at work on Monday.

The flat was situated in a row of dilapidated buildings with external walkways built sometime in the 1960s.

At the moment no lights were on in any of the windows. No one seemed to be at home. That suited him perfectly.

He unlocked the front door and entered the hall. Since he had just stepped in from outside, he noticed how stuffy it smelled. He walked through the living room, which was furnished with a white leather sofa, a coffee table with smoked glass and gilded feet, and a bookcase made of cherry. A porcelain Dalmatian adorned one corner of the room. The blinds were drawn, hanging drearily in front of the window and blocking the view of the building on the other side of the street. Just the way he liked it. He didn't want to be aware of the world outside. Not now. He needed to concentrate on what was ahead. He had to prepare. He went into the bedroom, where the bed was still unmade, and pulled out the drawer of the nightstand to get the key to the locked room. In addition to the kitchen the flat consisted of three rooms, but he used only two of them on a daily basis. The empty room was intended for special purposes. He turned the key in the lock. It was pitch dark inside, with a faint aroma of incense. The fragrance called up memories for him, and if he stayed inside for any length of time, he almost felt dizzy – from both desire and yearning. He had meticulously furnished what he called the Red Room – although it had nothing to do with Strindberg's novel of the same name.

He switched on the ceiling light and went in. The purple-coloured carpet was soft under his feet; the walls were inviting with their warm, rust-red colour. It was the biggest room in the flat, and was most likely intended to be the living room. He had placed the water bed in the centre, and the ceiling was covered with mirrors. In each corner stood a pillar sprayed gold and topped with a scented candle and incense burner. The opposite wall was papered with photos of her. Naked on the bed, semi-nude in the garden on the other side of the hedge, fully dressed with the children outside the Coop Forum.

He was going to bring her here, and they would re-experience what they'd once had. It would be even better than before. If only he could manage to persuade her, if only she would allow him near her again, then she would realize it was here she belonged. In the Red Room. With him and no one else. And now he had taken a definite step closer to his goal. A very important step. Pleased and filled with confidence, he opened his bag and took out another stack of photos.

Then he began tacking them up on the wall, one after the other.

Jacobsson and Kihlgård decided to have lunch at the Kuten restaurant, which was right across from where the ill-fated Terra Nova group had stayed.

Kihlgård looked astounded as Jacobsson pulled into the small car park near the road and stopped next to an old American Ford Falcon. They could hear fifties rock music as soon as they got out of the car. Playing on the restaurant jukebox was Little Gerhard's big hit, 'Buona Sera'.

'What a place!' he exclaimed. 'It takes me right back to the fifties.' He pointed at a sign above the entrance. 'What an original name for a restaurant. *Kuten*,' he said. 'Doesn't that mean seal pup?'

Jacobsson shrugged.

'I have no idea.'

Inside the restaurant a genuine French chef was busy making crêpes. Kihlgård exchanged a few words with him in his native tongue. They ordered lunch and managed to find a free table. It was stifling inside, and Jacobsson felt a band of pressure on her forehead.

'I can tell we're in for a thunderstorm before tonight.'

As soon as the food appeared, they both fell silent.

Kihlgård was so preoccupied with his fragrant crêpe filled with salmon that he couldn't talk. Only when his plate was empty did he feel like conversing.

'That was fantastic,' he said. 'Don't you agree? So crisp. And what flavour! You can tell that the chef is a real expert.'

'Yes, but it's incredibly rich.' Jacobsson put down her fork. She'd eaten only half of her crêpe.

'A real Frenchman, too,' Kihlgård went on with satisfaction. 'You can always tell when something is genuinely French.'

Kihlgård's weakness for France was well known, and a couple of years earlier he had told his colleagues that he had a French boyfriend. Jacobsson assumed that they were still together. She and Kihlgård liked each other on a professional basis, but they almost never talked about anything personal.

She studied her colleague, unable to ignore his hungry glances. Swiftly she shoved her plate over to his side of the table.

'I'm done. Have the rest if you like.'

Kihlgård looked like a child on Christmas Eve.

'Really? Thanks.'

After lunch they found their way out to Arne Gustavsson's place. He ran a farm in Hammars and lived close to Valter Olsson's cabin. They declined the offer of coffee since they were starting to run out of time. A dog barked from an enclosed dog run. They sat down in the yard, and Gustavsson told them how Stina had ridden past on her bicycle a week ago, on Saturday afternoon.

'Do you recall what time it was when you saw her?'

'It was sometime after three o'clock, but no later than four. I'm afraid I can't be more exact than that.'

'How did she seem?' asked Jacobsson.

'I didn't see much because she was going so fast. She rode past my house, with my dog barking after her. I think she wanted to get away as quickly as possible. My dog can seem a bit scary.'

'Then what happened?'

'I called after her, trying to get her to stop, but she just kept going. Then she disappeared.'

'And you didn't see her again?'

'No, I didn't.'

'Did you notice anyone following her?'

'No. Although I didn't stand there to watch. I was busy with my own things. There's always work to do here on the farm.'

'Do you remember seeing any other traffic on that day? Cars or bicycles, people walking past?'

'Not many people come by here. Most stay away because they realize that they'll have to cross our property if they want to keep going. And the rest of the promontory is private. It all belongs to Bergman. There's no reason for anyone to come here.'

'So you didn't see anyone else pass by?'

'Not that day. But there was someone in the night.'

Jacobsson was suddenly alert.

'When was that?'

'Later, after I'd gone to bed on Saturday. I woke up in the middle of the night. Being a farmer, I'm a light sleeper, because of the livestock, you know.'

Jacobsson nodded even though she didn't really understand what the man meant by that. She was waiting impatiently for him to go on.

'Anyway, I was woken by the sound of a car. I wondered who would be driving around at that ungodly hour, so I got out of bed to look outside. The bedroom window faces the road.' He turned around to point at an upstairs window of his house. 'I managed to see a car driving down the road, but I couldn't tell what kind it was. Or who was driving.'

'Could you tell if there was more than one person in the car?' asked Kihlgård.

'I'm afraid not. It happened so fast.'

'Do you know what time it was?'

'As a matter of fact, I checked to see the time. It was almost morning. Ten past four.'

'And you're sure of that?'

'A hundred per cent sure. I looked at the alarm clock that I keep next to the bed. And it keeps good time.'

'Did you see what colour the car was?' asked Jacobsson.

'No. I think it was a very dark colour, but it's difficult

to say. It was just before dawn, so the morning fog had come in and made it hard to see. I couldn't really make it out properly; I just heard the sound.'

'And can you tell us anything about that? Did it sound like an old car?'

'No, I don't think so. There was nothing special about it. Just a droning sound.'

'And that's the last you saw of it?'

'Well, I went back to bed but I couldn't sleep. So I got up and made coffee. Then I went out to the barn. And that's when I heard the car again. When I was inside.' The farmer shook his head.

'What time was it then?'

'That must have been almost an hour later. About five.'

Jacobsson and Kihlgård exchanged glances.

'Do you know whether anyone else here in Hammars noticed that car?'

'No, but I haven't really asked anyone. I happened to think about it when I saw the pictures of the woman who's gone missing. I recognized her at once and then I thought maybe the car had something to do with her disappearance, since it was headed in the same direction. And the road goes only to Bergman's place. And to his neighbour's house, of course. Valter.'

After their expedition to Fårö, Jacobsson went into her office and closed the door. She turned on her computer and checked the flights to Stockholm on the following day. There were still seats on the 10.30 departure, and she could return at 5.30. That would give her six hours in the city. She couldn't wait any longer. At the same time as she was busy with the investigation, the name Hanna von Schwerin kept buzzing in the back of her mind. At this point Jacobsson wasn't planning to contact her daughter's adoptive family; she just wanted to see Hanna. Nor did she intend to announce her presence right now. Just have a look. It should be possible on a Sunday. She booked a return ticket to Stockholm. She hoped that Hanna wasn't away on holiday, but that was a risk she'd have to take. At least she would see the house where her daughter lived. That was always a start.

Kihlgård and Knutas would have to hold the fort while she was away. Pleased that she'd finally made a decision, Jacobsson leaned back in her chair and clasped her hands behind her head. She tried to imagine what her daughter might look like. Almost twenty-five. Her name didn't necessarily mean anything. Maybe she was a completely ordinary young woman.

Her musings were interrupted when the phone rang. It was a call from the police in the Latvian town of Ventspils. Surprisingly enough, the officer spoke Swedish. Before she could ask, he explained that his mother was Swedish.

'I'm calling because we discovered a dead man in a rowing boat south of the harbour here in Ventspils. Two boys found it when they were searching for amber along the beach. It's possible that the victim is Swedish.'

'What makes you think that?'

'We've spent the whole day trying to match the description of the dead man with any missing persons in Latvia. Without success. The next step is to contact our neighbouring countries. And when it comes to Sweden, I decided to start with the police in Visby, since it's most likely that the boat would have drifted across from Gotland. It's a pretty direct route.'

Jacobsson felt her interest growing.

'How old is the man?'

'I'd say he's in his seventies. He looks weatherbeaten, like an old fisherman. He also had a lot of fishing gear in the boat.'

'Did he suffer any injuries?'

'Yes. The ME hasn't been here yet, but according to our technical officer, the man probably died from a violent blow to the head. He was obviously assaulted and has numerous contusions. He has clearly been in that boat for a while. Our crime tech thinks that he must have been dead at least a week.'

'Can you give me a more detailed description?'

'Five foot ten, dark hair with hardly any grey. A thin, wiry body. No moustache or beard. He was wearing dark trousers, sandals and a blue shirt. He had a key in his pocket. A pair of binoculars and a thermos of coffee were in the boat along with some fishing gear. That's all.'

Jacobsson swallowed hard. The description was an exact match.

Knutas could tell from the footsteps approaching the door that Lina was on her way. His wrist was now in a cast, he'd slept for a few hours, and he'd had something to eat. He was feeling better.

When his wife appeared, Knutas felt a warmth spread through his body. He was glad to see her. She was holding a bag and a big bouquet of flowers.

'Hi, sweetheart.' She smiled and gave him a big hug. Knutas felt tears come to his eyes, but he managed not to cry.

'Hi.'

She'd brought one of the hospital's stainless-steel vases, which she filled with water at the sink. She put the flowers in the vase and opened the bag, which contained grapes, a chocolate cake and a stack of newspapers.

Then she sat down on the edge of the bed and took his hand.

'How are you feeling?'

She looked worried. All of a sudden he noticed that she seemed thinner. He hadn't noticed that before.

'Have you lost weight?'

She laughed.

'What sort of question is that?'

'Have you?'

'I've lost a few kilos,' she admitted. 'Haven't you noticed? But it doesn't matter. How are you?'

'I'm OK. My wrist hurts a little, but that's all.'

'The doctor told me that you also have a concussion. I was so worried when they called me. It could have been a lot worse. You're not allowed to go up on the roof ever again. We'll hire a handyman from now on. And the doctor said you can't go back to work for at least a week.'

'But we're in the middle of an investigation.'

'That's not important. Concussion is a serious matter, and it's not worth taking any risks. You'll have to stay at home and take it easy.'

'Does Karin know?'

'I haven't called her yet. But I'm sure they'll manage without you.'

As if on cue, Knutas's mobile rang, and Jacobsson's name appeared on the display.

'You need to come over to the office as soon as possible. There's a lot happening here.'

'Like what?'

'I'll tell you when you get here,' said Jacobsson impatiently. 'Hurry up.'

Knutas could only sigh.

The aroma of grilled meat hovered over the neighbourhood. Those who hadn't gone away on holiday were holding the obligatory outdoor barbecues this evening. On nearly every terrace and balcony, in almost every back garden, smoke was rising up from some sort of grill. Children were laughing as they played around the hedges and flowerbeds. The grown-ups were sipping wine as they sat on patio chairs, enjoying the warm summer night.

Andrea was smoking a cigarette as she sat alone on her veranda, which was shielded from view. The children were again staying with her mother. Beata had just phoned again. She was constantly calling Andrea. Of course it was because she was concerned, but she came over so often that Andrea was starting to get annoyed. Even so, she had accepted the invitation when Beata had suggested that she and John could come over to make her dinner. It wasn't good for Andrea to be alone, Beata had insisted. As if she had a clue. Håkan would come too. He was a nervous wreck, out of his mind with worry about Stina. It was lucky that his children were also staying with relatives. His nervous state was hard on the kids, and he didn't have the energy to deal with their unhappiness on top of his own. It was the same for Andrea. She couldn't be strong in front of the children, so it was just as well that they were away.

The doorbell rang. She got up to open the door. There stood Håkan, awkwardly clutching a bunch of flowers in one hand, and a bottle of wine in the other. He looked as if he might fall apart if anyone so much as blew on him.

'I'm sorry for losing my temper last time.'

'That's OK,' she replied, giving him a hug. 'We're all feeling a bit off balance.'

Beata and John appeared a second later. They'd made lamb kebabs and potato salad. John took Håkan outside to put the lamb on the barbecue. Beata started bustling about the kitchen without really doing anything. She knocked a bowl of snacks on the floor, where it landed with a bang.

'I'm so sorry,' she cried. 'How clumsy of me.'

Andrea was already taking the vacuum cleaner out of the cupboard. She cleaned up the mess while Beata perched on a stool at the kitchen island, holding a glass of wine and watching helplessly.

When Andrea was finished, she took Beata by the hand.

'Come on.'

They went out to the deck, where Håkan was already seated, looking like a forlorn puppy. Andrea poured more wine for everyone, and John turned the kebabs on the rack. No one spoke for a while. They didn't have to ask how everyone was feeling since they knew each other so well. The outburst from the last time they'd met was forgotten.

Then the kebabs were ready.

'Here,' said John, holding out the serving dish. They each took a kebab and helped themselves to the potato salad and Beata's freshly baked bread.

No one commented on the food as they ate. Finally Beata broke the silence.

'What did the police say about that horrible phone call?' she asked Andrea.

'They came over here, and then stayed all night in a patrol car outside. But they can't very well give me round-the-clock protection just because of some pervert breathing down the phone.'

'But your husband was just murdered,' said Beata. 'Wouldn't that make the police take this more seriously?'

'I think they *are* taking it seriously. They asked me whether I could stay with friends for a while.'

'Of course you can! You can come and stay with us,' Beata quickly replied.

Andrea dismissed the idea with a wave of her hand.

'Thanks, but that's not necessary. We have a really sophisticated security system. I just have to be better about turning it on when I'm at home.'

'Who do you think made that call?' asked John. 'Do you think it's somebody you know?'

'That seems unlikely. Who would do such a thing? I think it might have to do with Sam's death and all the media attention. As soon as your name appears in the newspapers, you run the risk of attracting all sorts of loonies.'

Andrea lit a cigarette. Normally she didn't smoke, but right now she felt the need for some kind of drug. And she thought it was better to smoke than to resort to consoling herself with food, which would just make her fat.

'Who the hell could it be?' John glanced around at the others. No one had any suggestions. 'It's damned unpleasant, at any rate. Wouldn't you rather come and stay with us for a while? We have plenty of room for both you and the children.'

'Thanks, but no thanks. I really need to be alone right now.'

'Håkan, what are the police doing about finding Stina?' asked Beata.

'They're not saying much. I phone them several times a day to find out how it's going, but they're being really secretive about what they're doing. Of course they're looking for some connection between Sam's death and Stina's disappearance.'

'Who have they interviewed?' asked Beata. 'Aside from us, I mean.'

'I don't know. They won't tell me anything. But I've seen them knocking on doors around here, and I'm sure they've talked to all the neighbours.'

'Do you know whether—?' Beata ventured cautiously.
'No, I don't think so,' Andrea interjected before Beata
could finish her sentence.

Her trip to Stockholm had to be postponed. With Knutas off sick, and the discovery of the dead man in Latvia, Jacobsson couldn't possibly take time away from work. The meeting with her daughter would have to wait.

On Sunday an investigator from the Visby police had flown to Latvia along with Valter Olsson's sister, Märta, to identify the body. Any doubts had now been erased about whether he was the one who had drifted ashore in a rowing boat. Offshore winds had driven the boat towards the Latvian coast and the town of Ventspils, which was located right across the sea from the east coast of Fårö. Since the winds had later subsided, the boat had probably bobbed about for quite a while before it finally drifted close to land.

Kihlgård was sitting in Jacobsson's office, ready to discuss the latest developments. He stuck his hand into a bag of crisps. The crunching sound that he made as he frenetically chewed was really getting on his colleague's nerves.

'Now we have two murders and one missing woman,' said Jacobsson. 'We have to be grateful that the media hasn't yet found out about Valter Olsson. But I'm sure it's just a matter of time.'

Kihlgård chewed pensively before he replied.

'With every day that passes, I'm more and more inclined to think that Stina Ek has also fallen victim to the murderer.'

'So we're talking about a serial killer?' Jacobsson sighed. 'If that's true, what do these three people have in common? OK, I know that Sam and Stina belonged to the same circle of friends. But what about Valter Olsson? What the hell does he have to do with the case?'

'You sure swear a lot,' complained Kihlgård, giving her a disapproving look. He took out another handful of crisps made from genuine Swedish potatoes.

'Let's go back to the beginning. It feels as if it all started on Fårö. That's where Olsson lived, and he was friends with Ingmar Bergman. That's where Stina was last seen, and she was apparently on her way to Bergman's house for some reason. It seems Bergman is the common denominator.'

'What did Sam Dahlberg have to do with Bergman?'

'He was a film director, so they shared a profession, which might not be an insignificant factor in the case. Sam was also an ardent fan of Bergman's work. He'd seen all his films and read most of the books written about him. You've read the transcripts of the interviews with Sam's wife, haven't you? They even used to watch Bergman movies on Sunday mornings while they were having breakfast.'

'Sure, but what does that really signify? There are plenty of people who like Bergman. Why should it have any connection with the murders?'

'I have no idea.' Jacobsson shrugged. 'But maybe that's the angle we should be taking. Something to do with the actors . . . Maybe Sam had a score to settle with some crazy celebrity.'

'That seems like a long shot. Maybe we should focus more on the actual setting of Fårö – from a purely physical point of view. That's where Sam, Stina and Valter were. And they all had some connection to Bergman. I'm starting to wonder whether Stina ever left Fårö.'

'What if . . . ?' Jacobsson fixed her eyes on her colleague. 'What if that's where we should be looking? On Bergman's property. What if Valter Olsson happened to find Stina out there and tried to get her to leave? What if a third person is involved?'

Kihlgård stared at her in astonishment.

'A third person who killed both Stina and Valter. He drifted ashore in Latvia. So where in the world is Stina?' he said.

Jacobsson didn't reply.

She had stood up and was already heading for the door.

It took a couple of hours to get Chief Prosecutor Smittenberg to issue a search warrant for Ingmar Bergman's property.

Three police cars parked outside the gate. Two officers with dogs were also present.

Kihlgård and Jacobsson went first, accompanied by Valter Olsson's sister. The gravel crunched under their feet. Erik Sohlman had asked to have the area cordoned off, just to be safe. Even if they didn't find a body, it was best to take preventive measures. If the theory turned out to be correct, that Stina Ek and Olsson had been murdered in the vicinity, every piece of evidence would be crucial.

Suddenly they caught sight of the house between the trees. It blended in beautifully with the natural setting – a long, one-storey structure surrounded by a high stone wall that hid the property from view. So this was the world-famous director's home, which had been kept private from outsiders all these years. Jacobsson couldn't help feeling a little excited.

'Bloody hell, it's a long building,' she exclaimed.

'There you go again, swearing,' said Kihlgård drily.

To reach the side facing the sea, they had to go through the gate next to the house. Jacobsson couldn't help peeking in through the windows. First a long hallway. To the right a modest kitchen with pine cupboards and a table next to the window. A few simple chairs.

'You'd think he would have indulged himself with something a bit more luxurious,' said Jacobsson in surprise.

'He was probably content to enjoy the luxury of being alone and left in peace. It's a big house, after all. And look at the view,' said Kihlgård with a sigh. 'It's not something that just anyone could afford.'

They went over to the veranda, which faced the sea. There they stood in silence for a moment, looking out at the horizon and the entire rocky shoreline.

Jacobsson peered into the library. The walls were covered with books, and in the middle stood bookcases holding rows of files and folders. It almost looked like a public library, with a ladder and everything. At the far end stood a beautifully designed office chair in black leather next to a desk.

'So that's where he sat, gazing out at the sea and writing. How bloody marvellous!'

'Watch your language, Karin,' admonished Kihlgård. 'Now, if you're done peeping in the windows, maybe we should get to work.' He turned to the dog-handlers who were standing nearby. The dogs were panting and yapping and tugging at their leads, eager to start the search. When the two Labs were let loose, they immediately began sniffing at every centimetre of the property.

Suddenly both dogs set off for the sea and the fence that separated Bergman's land from Valter Olsson's. They jumped at the enclosure, barking like crazy. Officers came running from all directions. The dogs soon found a big hole in the fence, and they easily slipped through.

'There's something on the neighbouring property,' said one of the dog-handlers. 'Without a doubt. Over there on the other side.'

'OK,' said Jacobsson resolutely.

The police followed. At the water's edge they found the upside-down rowing boat that Jacobsson had noticed on their earlier visit to Olsson's cabin. The dogs dashed straight for the boat and continued to bark.

The two dog-handlers lifted up the boat and moved it away.

The dogs sat down nearby as the two officers began to dig. It didn't take long before their shovels struck something, and slowly a decaying body came to light. Bloated and greenish-grey in colour, the skin had come loose in several places, and maggots were crawling all over the corpse. The eyes were sunken and cloudy. The hair a shiny black. Jacobsson turned away and threw up in the water.

Kihlgård gloomily studied the dead woman, who was wearing only a skirt and bra. In spite of the sorry state of the body, there was no question about the victim's identity.

'So at last we've found Stina Ek,' he murmured.

That afternoon, the entire area surrounding Ingmar Bergman's domain was cordoned off, and it didn't take long before journalists began turning up on Fårö. Rumours spread quickly, and reporters from all over Sweden flew to Gotland. Later that evening the foreign press also began to appear, mostly from Germany, where interest in Bergman was especially strong, since he had lived in Munich for almost ten years.

Word got out that a murdered woman had been found on property belonging to Bergman. When the foreign reporters realized that the victim had actually been discovered on a neighbour's land, their interest waned.

But the Swedish media was difficult enough to handle, and police spokesman Lars Norrby asked for help after only a few hours.

'This is fucking sick,' snapped Jacobsson to Wittberg as she hurried along the corridor of the Criminal Division, on her way to the late-night meeting of the investigative team. 'We can't even do our job because of all the media hysteria. Those journalists are nothing but a bunch of lunatics. We're going to have to call in the armoured troops on Fårö to keep the reporters away.'

They'd already heard that the police officers on the scene were having a hard time keeping out curiosity-seekers. Wittberg merely shook his head as they entered the conference room. At that moment Knutas phoned Jacobsson, but she didn't take the call. She'd ring him later, after the meeting was over.

'All right. We now have a lot of things to discuss,' she began, looking at her colleagues gathered around the table. 'We found the body of Stina Ek near Valter Olsson's home on Fårö. Only twenty metres or so away from Ingmar Bergman's property. The body was buried in the sand underneath an overturned rowing boat, so there's no doubt about the fact that she was murdered. What we don't yet know is when she was killed, but the ME will be able to determine that from the post-mortem. I've requested top priority for this case, and the ME has already flown over from the mainland. He's on the scene right now, along with Erik Sohlman and the other crime techs. Stina Ek was last seen when she cycled past Arne Gustavsson's farm on the afternoon of Saturday, the twenty-eighth of June. Sometime around three or four o'clock, after leaving her husband behind at the Slow Train Inn. An hour later she phoned him to say that she'd met a childhood friend. Then later that evening, as you know, he received a text message saying that she'd been called in to work.'

'So she must have been killed after sending the text

message – if she was the one who sent it, that is,' said Wittberg. 'But why did she lie?'

'Why did she want to stay away?' Jacobsson asked.

'And why did no one besides this Arne Gustavsson notice her?' interjected Kihlgård. 'She was quite striking in appearance. Not somebody who could disappear in a crowd.'

'Not a single witness seems to have seen her other than Gustavsson,' Jacobsson confirmed. 'And all indications are that she headed straight for Hammars, turned off the main road, and then took only side roads. Sheep are the only living things to be found out there.'

Wittberg ran his fingers through his blond mane.

'How did she happen to end up at Valter Olsson's place?'

'Either the perpetrator found her there, or if they ran into each other near Bergman's house, Stina may have tried to flee through the neighbour's property. Maybe she was being chased. Or else she was killed on Bergman's property and then her body was dragged next door, even though that's a long way. The question is: Who was in the vicinity at the same time Stina was there?'

'Well, it happened during the Bergman festival,' said Wittberg. 'So plenty of people could have been out there.'

Jacobsson was interrupted by the ringing of her mobile. When she saw that it was Sohlman, she took the call.

The others seated around the table watched her in silence as she listened to the crime tech. When he was done with his report, she turned to her colleagues.

'That was Sohlman. They've found blood on Bergman's veranda and on the wall of the house facing the shore. And one more thing. In a nook of the veranda they found a top and a thong, neatly folded. They seem to be Stina's size.'

'So they weren't just tossed there?' asked Kihlgård. 'They were folded up, nice and neat?'

Jacobsson nodded.

'What about the bicycle? Have they found it?'

'No, they haven't.'

Kihlgård looked thoughtful. He took a banana from the fruit platter on the table, peeled it slowly, and then said: 'Maybe Stina Ek contacted someone. She must have been ecstatic about finding Bergman's house. What would you do in that sort of situation?' Kihlgård waved the banana in the air as he went on. 'You'd want to share the experience with somebody. So she phoned someone. The question is: Who? And why did she take off her clothes? Apparently she did it voluntarily. It was planned.'

'Her husband?' suggested Wittberg. 'Maybe she was bold enough to want to have a tryst out there.'

'Or . . . could it have been someone else?' suggested Jacobsson. 'Someone she was having an affair with? Sam Dahlberg, for instance? He was such a Bergman fanatic. Maybe that was something they shared.'

'What if he was the one? Who went out there, I mean. Where was Andrea Dahlberg at that time?'

Jacobsson leafed through her notes.

'She was at the Bergman Centre in the late afternoon. That's where she ran into an old friend from school. They had coffee together, so she wouldn't have noticed if her husband slipped away. He could probably have been away for at least a couple of hours without drawing attention.'

'Have we talked to this childhood friend?' asked Kihlgård.

'It's been very difficult to get hold of her,' Jacobsson admitted, noticing to her chagrin that her face had turned crimson.

'Do we know this person's name?' Kihlgård patiently went on.

'Andrea Dahlberg couldn't remember her name, and she found it embarrassing to ask. Of course we've gone through the class lists from Andrea's school years in order to pinpoint this person. Unfortunately, she doesn't have any school photos from that time. That would have made it easy.'

'Because I think it's really strange,' Kihlgård stubbornly continued. 'On that afternoon Stina Ek meets an old friend from her school days – or from middle school, to be more specific – and the two of them go to a restaurant together. Then at almost exactly the same time Andrea Dahlberg runs into a childhood friend and they have coffee together at the Bergman Centre. Doesn't it seem a bit odd?'

'Who provided us with this information?' asked Prosecutor Smittenberg.

'Both Håkan Ek and Andrea Dahlberg.'

'Håkan and Andrea – the spouses of the two murder victims,' muttered Kihlgård. 'Quite a coincidence.'

'Yes, you might say that,' replied Jacobsson. 'Let's stay with Andrea Dahlberg for a moment. She contacted the police over the weekend after she received that phone call from an unknown man who was apparently right outside her door. We need to check up on that. I want us to knock on more doors in the neighbourhood and talk to people who live in Terra Nova, to find out if anyone saw anything suspicious. Evidently Andrea has felt someone watching her for quite a while. Up until Friday night, she had dismissed it as just her imagination. But not any more. We've asked her to stay with a relative or a good friend for the time being, but she refused. At least the children are staying elsewhere.'

'Did she recognize the voice?'

'No. The person who called seemed to be disguising his voice.'

'I went out there to talk to her, and she was really upset. But she had no idea who the person could be,' said Kihlgård. 'And none of the neighbours had noticed anything unusual.'

'Then there's Valter Olsson. We need to work out how

he fits into the picture,' Jacobsson went on. 'We also need to knock on doors in both Hammars and Dämba – in fact, all of Fårö. From Broa up to Sudersand. We've received surprisingly few leads so far. We can only hope that the discovery of Stina's body will jump-start things. We've checked out everyone's alibi, but we'll have to do it again. And if it's true that Sam and Stina were having an affair, then there are two people of key interest to the investigation at the moment. Andrea Dahlberg and Håkan Ek.'

The phone call that Johan Berg had been longing to receive finally came on the day after Stina Ek was found murdered in Hammars. He never would have thought that he'd be so happy to hear the voice of Max Grenfors, editor-in-chief in Stockholm.

'Hi, how's it going? Listen, we're swamped right now because of the murders on Gotland, and we don't have anybody else to send. Here at TV headquarters it's swarming with summer replacements, and we can't do without the few good reporters we have. Not a chance. So could you possibly fill in? Just for a couple of days, until the worst blows over. We've already sent over another cameraperson for Maddie, so you can take Pia with you.'

Johan paused before answering. He was enjoying keeping his boss, who was usually so overbearing, on tenterhooks.

'Hmm. I'm not sure. I've got a lot to do, with the kids and all.'

'OK, you can consider the whole job as overtime. Every fucking hour of it. That means double pay.'

'That'll work. When do I start?'

'Right now. The police have scheduled a press conference in an hour.'

Fortunately it was no problem for Emma to take care of the kids. Her parents were out of town, as usual, so she had already planned to drive out to their house on Fårö for a few days. Her best friend, Viveka, was going with her so she wouldn't be there alone. The weather was sunny and warm, which meant they'd have a good time. The house was in a beautiful location, right on the beach. That eased his guilty conscience. So far he'd managed to make it through a month at home with the children without working. But he wondered again how he was going to make it through the lengthy paternity leave from his job as planned.

At the same time he couldn't help revelling in the adrenalin rush. He loved his job, especially when things were happening. Like now. Up until today the editorial office had kept him out of the summer's big murder case. He'd offered to contribute in one way or another, but he'd been refused. He wasn't needed even when he got the tip from Arne Gustavsson. But now they were tooting a different horn. He was in demand, so it was no wonder that he was feeling pleased.

The important thing was to get up to speed before the press conference. He rang Pia as soon as he got into his car.

'God, it's so great that you can do this,' she panted.

He assumed that she was on her way over to the car.

'Maddie has booked a super-important interview on Fårö, so she had to go out there right away.'

'What could be a higher priority than attending the press conference?'

'The thing is, the Latvian police are arriving on Fårö today, in just a couple of hours, and she was incredibly lucky to get the investigative team leader to promise her an interview. It was set up just a little while ago.'

'What the hell are you babbling about? The Latvian police? What do they have to do with any of this?'

'Oh, I forgot. You wouldn't know about that. Here's what happened. A fisherman who's friends with one of my uncles told him that an old fisherman from Fårö was washed ashore in Latvia, in his rowing boat. Dead. And apparently he was murdered. The Latvian police are handling the case, but they're cooperating with the police force over here.'

'Good Lord, what a mess. So I assume there must be some sort of connection between the two murders. What are the police doing out there today?'

'After we got the tip, Maddie rang Latvia, and she talked to some guy on the police force who surprisingly gave her a lot of information. The police are going over to the old man's house on Fårö today. And it was on his property that Stina Ek's body was buried. And you know what? The old man was a neighbour of Ingmar Bergman.'

Johan's pulse quickened. The story kept getting better and better. And once again they'd had the benefit of

knowing Pia Lilja's extended family, who lived all over
the island. Her six siblings and all her other relatives
were a reporter's dream as a source of information.

'When was he found?'

'I have no idea. Maddie knows more, but she's on
her way to the airport right now to pick up the cameraperson from Stockholm. But anybody can see that it's
absolutely certain he was murdered and that his death
is connected to the other murders. This is turning out to
be big, Johan. A fucking big story.'

The room was packed for the press conference. The buzz of voices subsided when Jacobsson, Kihlgård and County Police Chief Malin Lundblad took their seats on the podium. The tension in the air was palpable. All the major media organizations in Sweden were represented: TV, radio and the newspapers. The microphones had been set up and cameras positioned as the reporters sat ready with their notepads.

Jacobsson opened a bottle of Ramlösa mineral water and poured herself a glass. She took several big sips. Even though there were so many people crowded into the room, it was dead silent as she finally began to speak.

'At four fifteen yesterday afternoon, Stina Ek's body was found. She had been missing since Saturday, the twenty-eighth of June. There is no doubt that she was the victim of foul play. The body was discovered in Hammars on Fårö on private land, next door to Ingmar Bergman's property. Since rumours have been circulating that her body was found on Bergman's land, I just want to clarify immediately that this was not the case. The cause of death has not yet been determined, but the victim's injuries indicate that she suffered a traumatic blow to the head. The body has been taken to the Forensics Division in Solna for examination. A large area surrounding the site has been cordoned off, and police crime technicians are working to secure evidence. The victim was a thirty-seven-year-old mother of two. She was married and lived with her family in Terra Nova in Visby. Stina was employed as a flight attendant on Scandinavian Airlines. She has no previous police record and, as far as we know, had no connection to the place where her body was found. She was last seen on the day when she disappeared, meaning Saturday, the twenty-eighth, at around four p.m. At that time she was riding a bicycle past a nearby farm. The police are currently in the process of knocking on doors in the area and, as I mentioned, the technicians are now on site.'

Jacobsson paused and looked out at the crowd of reporters. Everyone's eyes were fixed on her, and for a moment she lost her train of thought. Then she collected herself and went on.

'At this time the police have no suspects, and we're working on a broad front. You're now welcome to ask questions. I need to request that you raise your hand, otherwise it's going to be impossible to keep order.'

Hands began eagerly waving in the air. Jacobsson wanted to answer as many questions as she could. She had the help of two officers who each had a microphone to take questions from reporters in the back of the room.

'Exactly where was she found?'

'I can't discuss that at the moment.'

'How was the body found?'

'Police dogs located the remains.'

'How did you happen to know where to search?'

'Due to the on-going investigation, I'm afraid that I can't answer that question.'

'She was found very close to Ingmar Bergman's property. Is there any reason to think that someone from Bergman's family was involved?'

'There are no indications that any of Bergman's relatives or friends have anything to do with the murder.'

'Is there any connection between Stina Ek and the owner of the property where she was found? Or between her and Ingmar Bergman?'

'Not that we know of.'

'What if you go further back in time? For instance, could she be an unknown daughter of his?'

'I think we can rule out that possibility. Stina Ek was adopted from Vietnam.'

'Why do you think she was killed at that particular site?'

'If we knew that, we'd be making good progress in the case.'

'Did the murdered woman have a particular interest in Bergman?'

'Not as far as we know.'

'Apparently Stina Ek was a member of an Internet club called Friends of Bergman. Do you know anything about that?'

Jacobsson fixed her eyes on Johan Berg from Regional News. Was he back on the job? It was so typical that he'd come up with something like that. She was completely unprepared for the question. She hadn't heard anything about it before. For several seconds she was at a total loss for words, but then she recovered her composure.

'In the early stages of an investigation, it's a matter of collecting a lot of facts from all possible directions. We look at everything and carefully weigh the significance of all the information. That's the phase we're in at present. Stina Ek's body was found yesterday afternoon, less than twenty-four hours ago. We're going to be following all possible leads.'

'But you haven't answered my question,' Johan persisted.

'Precisely,' Jacobsson curtly replied and then turned to another reporter.

'What can you tell us about how the murder was committed?'

'Only that the perpetrator used a blunt instrument to deliver a blow to the victim's head.'

'Did the body have other injuries?'

'Not that we know about at the moment. We'll need to wait for the post-mortem report.'

'Are you positive that she was killed where her body

was found? Or could she have been taken there from some other place?'

'We're quite certain about that. The murder was committed at the scene. Traces of blood and other evidence clearly indicate this.'

'What does the property owner have to say?'

Jacobsson's face changed colour. She was prepared for the question, but the investigative team had decided not to reveal anything about the fact that Valter Olsson had been found murdered in Latvia. They needed to take one thing at a time.

'Due to the on-going investigation, I won't discuss that at the moment.'

An increased tension was clearly evident in the room. The reporters took Jacobsson's response to mean that Olsson was a suspect.

'Who owns the property where she was found?'

'He's an elderly man, seventy-five years old, who lives there alone and spends most of his time fishing. I have nothing else to say.'

'Were he and Bergman good friends?'

'I'm not going to discuss their relationship.'

'Is the property owner a suspect?'

'I can't comment any further on the subject. Let's move on to something else.'

'Do you have information from any witnesses?'

'At the moment we're collecting statements, but we've just begun that part of the work.'

'What are the police doing now?'

'We're undertaking a proper investigation – which means carrying out a technical examination of the crime scene, interviewing potential witnesses, knocking on doors in the area, and finding out the details of Stina Ek's life, including what she was doing in the period before she disappeared. In addition, we are of course looking at the significance of the crime scene itself.'

'How is this connected with the murder of Sam Dahlberg?'

'Naturally we see a link between the two homicides, since both victims belonged to the same social circle.'

'Do you think they were killed by the same person?'

'We're not ruling that out, but we can't assume that it was the same perpetrator. As I said, we're working on a broad front, and keeping all doors open.'

Jacobsson was beginning to tire of all the questions. The police didn't have much to say. She cast an enquiring glance at the county police chief, who took the hint and gave an almost imperceptible nod. It was time to end the press conference.

'All right then. That's all we have to say at the moment. Depending on how things develop, we're planning another press conference for tomorrow since there's such great interest in the case. We will not be available to do individual interviews, since we need to devote all of our energy to the investigation. I hope you'll respect this decision. If you have any further questions, please direct them to the police spokesman, Lars Norrby.' She motioned towards her colleague, who hadn't uttered a single word during the entire conference. Then Jacobsson got up and quickly left the room.

In the corridor outside she found her way blocked by Johan Berg and Pia Lilja, who had her eye pressed to the TV camera, as usual.

'Karin, I need to ask you about something,' he said with a serious expression.

Foolishly enough, she stopped.

Johan spoke directly into the microphone.

'Sources tell me that a murdered Swedish man was found drifting ashore in a rowing boat off the Latvian coast. The man was supposedly Ingmar Bergman's closest neighbour, and from what I understand, he also owns the property where Stina Ek's body was found. His name is Valter Olsson. What can you tell us about this?'

He held out the microphone to Jacobsson.

She was dumbfounded.

With a wave of her hand she pushed the microphone aside and quickly strode off down the corridor.

Jacobsson was annoyed that the press conference had ended in such an ignominious fashion. She hated being caught completely off guard like that. It was a mystery how Johan Berg had found out that Valter Olsson's body had been discovered in Latvia. Norrby, she thought. Had he blabbed again? The police spokesman had in the past displayed a tendency to talk too much. But surely he couldn't be that stupid. And she hadn't known anything about that group called the Friends of Bergman. She had immediately asked Wittberg to check up on the association, which turned out to have a website on the Internet. Stina was listed as a new member.

She leaned back in her chair and clasped her hands. She shut her eyes, allowing images from the investigation to come and go in her mind. Sam Dahlberg's mangled body out on Stora Karlsö, pecked apart by seabirds. The well-kept neighbourhood of Terra Nova with the friends who stuck together, come hell or high water. What were they hiding? Valter Olsson, who'd gone out fishing and then floated ashore in Latvia. The Bergman festival with all the social functions and film showings. Stina Ek who disappeared on her bicycle and whose body was found on land next door to Ingmar Bergman's property. They had finally discovered her bike in the woods outside the fence. What happened to her on her way over there? Who did she meet?

Then there was the group of friends whose pleasant trip was supposed to mark the beginning of the summer holidays but instead ended in tragedy. She thought about the people in that social circle. During all of the interviews in which Jacobsson had participated, she'd had an uneasy feeling that they were hiding something. She seemed to detect a vague feeling of guilt.

New interviews had been conducted with every single one of them over the course of the day, but none had produced anything new. Håkan Ek was subjected to a cursory questioning at the hospital, where he'd been taken after he learned of his wife's murder. He could barely muster a word. The poor man was totally devastated.

But there was something about that collection of friends that wasn't quite right.

She summoned up images of the individuals who had gone on the trip together. Most were in their early forties. Håkan Ek was the only one who was significantly older. Sam Dahlberg's wife, Andrea, seemed terribly reserved, but that might be her way of coping. Outwardly, she was almost perfect: beautiful long hair; make-up skilfully applied and so natural-looking that it was hardly noticeable; a physically fit body with high, firm breasts that could indicate plastic surgery. She gave the appearance of being a loving wife and devoted mother, but that might not be true at all. Maybe she was putting on an act.

So what about Håkan Ek? Jacobsson might as well start with those closest to the victims, since it was often in the immediate family that the killer was to be found.

At the very first interview she had felt a real empathy for him. He was considerably older than his wife – fifty-three compared to Stina's thirty-seven. So there was a difference of sixteen years between them. How had that affected their marriage? Jacobsson leafed through Håkan Ek's file.

The photograph showed a man in his prime, looking fit, energetic and suntanned as he smiled at the camera. Laughter lines around his eyes and white teeth. And it looked as if he dyed his hair, so he was apparently a bit vain. In the photo he radiated a self-confidence that she hadn't noticed when she met him in person. This picture could have been lifted directly out of an advert for the Dressmann clothing chain, she thought. Håkan had been married twice before, and he had children with two different women, in addition to the two that he and Stina had together. The oldest, a daughter named Klara, was twenty-five years old and lived in the Östermalm district in Stockholm. The thought of her own daughter flitted through Karin's mind, causing a pang in her heart. The two young women were the same age. Håkan's first wife, Ingrid, had remarried and lived in the wealthy Stockholm suburb of Djursholm. He had divorced her in 1985, when their daughter was only two years old. Three years later he had already married his second wife, and they'd had a son named Robin in 1989. Another divorce in 1990, before Håkan married Stina that same year. Jacobsson raised her eyebrows. He was certainly a fast worker. The son must have been only a few months old when his parents parted ways. How awful, thought Jacobsson as she studied the face of the suntanned, smiling man in the photograph.

My childhood home was located way out in the Uppland countryside in an area of historic importance, filled with rune stones and burial sites from both the Iron Age and the Viking era. The house stood high on a hill. It was painted brown, a splendid structure with several entrances and a view of the fields and meadows, with Lake Mälaren off in the distance. Outside the imposing main entrance with the circular drive and flagpole was a lush abundance of rhododendron bushes. At the back a stone stairway led down to the garden, which was filled with shrubs, apple trees, and arbours. We children used to cycle over to the church bell tower to play a game that pitted the Swedes against the Danes. We would fight with tree branches, pretending they were swords. Our bikes were horses in the tournaments we held, and pine cones were our ammunition. Out where we lived, there were no official playgrounds with swings and roundabouts like in the small town about thirty kilometres away where we went to school. The woods, the mountains and the open fields were our playgrounds. And we didn't complain. Each morning my sister and I would board the school bus near the bend in the main road and go off to school. By the time we came back home, our mother would often have a snack ready for us – usually milk and some of her homemade cinnamon rolls, which we ate in the kitchen. Then we'd go out to find the local kids. There weren't many people living out there. Four families lived in the nearby houses, and three of them had children. The narrow gravel road that passed through our little village was used mostly by visitors heading for the nearby country church or the agricultural school. It might seem strange to find a school in such a remote area, way out in the country, but it had been established by a wealthy woman in Stockholm who donated the money to start a boarding school for poor children. For the past thirty years it had functioned as a secondary school where the students studied agriculture and animal husbandry. Pappa, who was a farmer and ran the neighbouring farm, often held classes for the students. They would follow him around, helping to milk the cows, taking care of the pigs and sheep. Part of the barn had been turned into a stable, using money from the school, with space for eight horses. Sometimes my sister and I were allowed to ride them. That was our favourite thing to do.

Mamma worked the night shift as a nurse at the hospital in Enköping and was often away from home during the week. She would work three or four days in a row and then have several days off. I thought that was a fine schedule. Periodically we'd have Pappa all to ourselves, and then when Mamma was at home, she'd take over and Pappa would spend most of his time in the barn or out in the fields.

Every Sunday we went to church. It was a small white building with a single rectangular tower rising up over the landscape: golden fields of oat slowly undulating in the wind, flowering meadows, pastures where the horses and cows grazed in the summertime, and far below we could see the glittering water of Lake Mälaren. At exactly eleven o'clock, the bells would ring for the church service. The clear sound reverberated over the few houses in that little community, the stable and the barn, the school and the student dormitories. Occasionally a car would arrive, bringing people from the outlying areas to the church service. There might be ten or fifteen people in attendance in addition to my own family.

I don't know whether my parents' zeal with regard to churchgoing had to do with a strong belief in God or whether it was more a show of courtesy to their best friends, the pastor and his wife. They had three children who were much younger than us, so we didn't play with them very often, but my sister and I did sometimes babysit for them so we could earn some extra pocket money. The pastor's wife was both kind and generous, and she always paid us more than the usual fee. She and my mother belonged to the same sewing circle, and they spent a lot of time together. They used to go for long walks, and they were always running over to each other's house to have coffee.

We went to church every single Sunday, and to be honest I have to confess that no matter how much I complained to my sister, I actually enjoyed those Sunday mornings in God's house. It was a small church, simply furnished. The wooden pews were old and worn with thick timbers along the sides. The church had a brass chandelier, a painted window, a picture of Jesus, a beautifully ornate pulpit, and a humble altar. I liked watching how the sun's rays came through the high windows in the deep niches, casting light on the bare, white-plastered walls. I can still recall the faces of the parishioners sitting in the pews and the intoning voice of the pastor. Everything was always exactly the same. The same prayers, hymns, and turns of phrase. I knew them inside and out. When I was little, I still had a childlike faith; I believed in God and everything that was said in church. The pastor's words were sacred. Although it did seem a bit strange to see him there in church, this man who came so often to our house, with his loud laughter and effusive manner. But I also felt a certain pride that he was actually one of our friends, that he could sit in our kitchen and tell funny stories to Mamma while she peeled potatoes and doubled over with laughter at his jokes.

No one could make her laugh the way he did.

Pappa and the pastor spent just as much time together as the two women did. Pappa was a reserved man who didn't make friends easily. And he rarely said much; the words had to be practically dragged out of him. He had a hard time even talking to his own children. For some reason, he seemed to feel inhibited.

A memory that is still fresh in my mind is of one morning when I awoke unusually early. I was about twelve at the time. I went to the toilet, but then I heard a sound from the kitchen downstairs and wondered what it could be. The floorboards, gleaming in the morning sunlight, creaked under my bare feet. The house was very quiet. Everyone else was still asleep in bed. Cautiously I tiptoed down the wide stairs. Someone was in the kitchen, but at first I didn't know who it was. I remember standing in the doorway. At first I didn't see anything; then I recognized my father's striped bathrobe. He was sitting with his back to me, utterly still, and looking out of the window at the garden, the lilacs, the blossoming apple trees, the bright-green leaves of the birches. And off in the distance, the gleaming water.

Pappa suddenly seemed like a stranger as he sat there. Motionless. Unaware that he was not alone. Usually he was in constant motion. Taking big strides in his wellington boots, he would cross the yard on his way to tend to the livestock. He would drive the tractor around and around out in the fields, spend time working on a piece of machinery behind the barn, or go out to mow the grass. He was always dashing about, always busy with something. He never sat still, the way he was doing on that morning. Maybe that was why he seemed like a stranger to me.

I sank down on to the staircase and sat there without

announcing my presence. I don't know why I did that. The air seemed oppressive in the room. The mood seemed inexplicably unpleasant and unfamiliar. As if the walls were closing in with anguish.

I heard Pappa sigh. He leaned his head on one hand, ran the other through his hair. I wondered what he was thinking about at that moment. I wondered if he was worried about something. If there was anything I could do to help him. Beloved Pappa. My stomach churned with anxiety. Maybe he needed comforting. I was just about to get up when he turned around. Our eyes met. I will never forget the expression on his face. I opened my mouth to say something, but he beat me to it. The strange silence was shattered, and his face broke into a smile. His voice sounded the way it always did.

Everything was as it should be. I breathed a sigh of relief.

Karin was sitting alone in her office, paging through the preliminary post-mortem report. It had been difficult to ascertain the precise time of death, but the ME thought Stina Ek had been dead for about two weeks. The cause of death was a violent blow to the head, delivered by a blunt instrument, most likely a rock. Karin felt sick when she read that part. The victim had suffered extensive skull injuries, but it had been impossible to determine much else because the body had already started to decay as a result of the heat and the exposed location near the water. However, the ME did find bruises and scratches on her forearms, neck and chest. The victim also had shreds of skin under her fingernails, all of which indicated that she had put up a fight. DNA samples had been taken, and Jacobsson had asked the techs at the Swedish Crime Lab to put a rush on their report, but it would still take at least a few days to get back the results.

Jacobsson took out the ME's findings on Sam Dahlberg and Valter Olsson. She spent the next hour comparing all the facts that the police had collected so far regarding the three homicides. Was it possible to determine that the same person had committed all three murders? By all indications, Stina had been killed before Sam, so they could rule her out as a possible suspect. Both she and Valter had died as the result of a blow to the head, but Valter's body exhibited no signs of a struggle. What did these three people have in common that would make somebody want to kill them?

Of course there were many things connecting Sam and Stina. They were neighbours, members of the same social circle, and good friends. But what about Valter?

The only common link that she could think of was Ingmar Bergman. Sam was almost fanatically interested in the acclaimed director, while Stina had become a member of the group called the Friends of Bergman. Olsson had lived next door to Bergman for many years, ever since the director's house had been built in the 1960s. The old man seemed to have had a good relationship with Bergman. Was it because of that relationship that he had died?

Throughout my childhood I secretly harboured a strong admiration for my sister, even though I would never openly admit to it. Emilia hated receiving compliments. She felt burdened by such remarks, and she usually thought that people were exaggerating when they praised her for something that she'd done or accomplished. She also loathed hearing any comments about her appearance. If anyone said that she was attractive or beautiful, she would merely snigger.

But she was both of those things. She had long, shiny dark hair, very straight. A pale, heart-shaped face with freckles, and a dimple in her chin. Brown eyes with thick lashes. Nice teeth, although they were seldom seen because she almost never smiled or laughed.

The only time I remember her ever being truly happy was when she petted animals, especially the puppy that she received on her sixteenth birthday. She loved that dog with all her heart. More than she loved any people. Definitely more than Pappa, but me and Mamma too. I'm very sure about that. She said that deep inside people were evil. I didn't like it when she talked that way. Emilia often talked about death. She claimed not to be afraid of dying; she said she viewed death as a friend that could set her free whenever she chose. Her words scared me. I didn't understand. She noticed and would always try to reassure me. It made me happy when she showed that she cared about me, but that rarely happened. Yet in her heart I'm sure that she was fond of me. At least it makes me feel good to think so. Now. After the fact.

She was four years older than me. The age difference was probably the reason why we were never really close. I looked up to her, the way a little sister usually does. Emilia could do everything better than I could. Skating, riding, cycling. She could bake sponge cakes and blow-dry her hair. She did better at school too; she was more diligent. Emilia loved school. She almost always got all the answers right in exams. She used to sit in the kitchen and do her homework while Mamma cooked dinner. She often asked me to test her, and she could answer all the questions. Sometimes it felt as if she just wanted to show off in front of me, to let me know how much she knew. Sometimes I wonder why she felt the need to do that. Maybe she was trying to prove something to herself. Emilia never stayed home from school, no matter how sick she might be. Even when she had a fever and Mamma said she should stay in bed, she would refuse. I really didn't understand what attracted her to school. She was four years ahead of me, but when we were still going to the same school, I would sometimes see her at break, and she was usually alone.

Occasionally I would go to the cafeteria when she was there, and she would be sitting on her own at a table. I pretended not to see her so as not to embarrass her or myself. I was always surrounded by friends; you might even say that I was terribly popular, but nobody ever sought out my sister. I don't recall that ever happening the entire time she was in school. So I felt sorry for her, but also powerless to do anything. I wanted to help her, invite her to come with me and my friends. But it was hard for me to do anything, since I was so much younger. I didn't want to upset her. And now, when I think back on it, I sometimes wonder whether her loneliness was of her own making. She deliberately withdrew. She seemed to have no interest in being with other people. And after Mamma gave her that puppy as a birthday present, it seemed as if she didn't need anyone else. The dog followed her everywhere she went and slept in her bed every night.

That was probably the only period when I saw my sister really happy.

On the following Sunday morning Karin awoke with a jolt. She'd been dreaming that she'd met Hanna, but when she told her daughter who she was, Hanna had run off. Karin tried to follow, but never managed to catch up with her.

She lay in bed, staring at the ceiling and unable to go back to sleep. She was thinking about all those lost years.

She wondered what sort of upbringing her daughter's adoptive parents had given her. At least it seemed likely that they'd had plenty of money, considering their upper-class surname, so Hanna probably hadn't wanted for anything in that sense. Karin hoped that she'd received as much love as she had material things. She wondered whether Hanna knew that she was adopted and, if so, why she hadn't made an effort to look for her biological parents. Was it because she was afraid of what she might find? That they might be drug addicts or criminals? That she was the produce of incest or some form of sexual assault? And the latter assumption was actually the truth of the matter.

Karin was terrified by the idea of telling her what

happened, and she'd been considering other options in order to spare her daughter the truth. Would it be possible to lessen the trauma of the event in some way?

She still broke out in a cold sweat whenever she thought back on that moment. How long did the rape actually last? Ten minutes? Maybe fifteen? Fifteen minutes out of a whole lifetime.

The riding teacher's assault had caused suffering that had lasted all her life. First the nine months of her pregnancy. The nausea in the mornings. The shame, the humiliation. This was the riding teacher who had taught her the half-pass and collected gaits with military precision at the riding school. He had tackled her to the floor of his living room with all the happy family photographs hanging on the walls above them. Then he had forced his way into her next to the TV and coffee table where his family gathered in the evening. There he had robbed her of her virginity. And a significant portion of her life. Sometimes the hatred would surge inside her so strongly that the world turned black. It was lucky that the riding teacher had died before she turned twenty. Otherwise she might have murdered him.

In some ways it felt as if she were living her life in a straitjacket, and she could never be rid of it. A corset tied tight with strings from the past. At long last she had decided that there was only one means of escape. She had to contact her daughter and find out who she was.

Finally she gave up any attempt to go back to sleep.

She got out of bed, made a pot of strong coffee, and took a shower. After breakfast she decided to go out. It was a beautiful day, and she was restless with impatience. She thought about the circle of friends from Terra Nova. What was it about those people? Bergman seemed to be somehow connected everywhere she looked, but it was among the group itself that she'd find the answer. Two of them were dead, and none of the others seemed able to contribute any concrete information that might carry the investigation forward.

Jacobsson had been to Terra Nova only once after Dahlberg was murdered. She glanced at her watch. Eleven fifteen. The perfect time to take a bike ride out there.

Quickly she tied her shoelaces and left the flat.

When she reached the other side of the wall, she realized that she'd left her mobile back home on charge, but she resisted an impulse to turn around. People used to get along just fine without mobile phones, and she wouldn't be gone long.

She passed Lindh's big nursery and turned on to Norra Glasmästargatan. She pedalled slowly along the road, looking at the houses and gardens, each one more beautifully tended than the last. She stopped in the middle of the development, in the small car park. There she got off her bike, locked it, and looked around. The Dahlberg family home looked empty and dreary. Jacobsson walked around the cul-de-sac and then continued along the deserted street. Anyone who hadn't left on holiday was probably spending the hot day at the seaside.

The police had done several interviews with the four people in the Terra Nova group who had survived the holiday trip, but without any significant results. For once the police had taken the unusual step of questioning the older children, too, asking them both about their parents' activities and what they thought of the apparent harmony among neighbours in the area. Unfortunately, this hadn't produced anything of interest. The colleagues, grandparents and siblings of those involved had also been interviewed. The more time that passed, the wider the investigative circle had been expanded from the core group. Maybe it's time to broaden our approach beyond Terra Nova, thought Jacobsson. Maybe we should talk to people outside the inner circle. Maybe there's somebody who wanted to become a member but was pushed aside. Somebody who was so upset by this that he or she wanted revenge.

It wasn't unreasonable to think that those who remained might be threatened, but so far no one other than Andrea seemed to need police protection.

Jacobsson reached the end of Norra Glasmästargatan. The three couples involved in the case lived ridiculously close to each other in their houses on the small cul-de-sac. Andrea and Sam owned a large wooden house in the early-twentieth-century style; then came Beata and John's house, which was the biggest and most ostentatious, built of white sand-lime brick; and finally the home belonging to Håkan and Stina, painted a pale lavender with blue trim around the doors and windows. The outbuilding was the same lavender colour. Jacobsson looked at the house, feeling great sympathy for Håkan. He had completely fallen apart after Stina's body had been found, and he was still in the psychiatric ward of the hospital. He was willing to talk only to his children and his first wife, Ingrid. No one else seemed able to get through to him. The police interview would have to wait until his condition improved.

Next she thought about Beata and John. He was American, and she was a red-haired, long-legged Barbie doll who seemed absurdly naive. Jacobsson had met them before, since they belonged to Emma Winarve's social circle. Five years ago she had questioned them in connection with the murder of Emma's best friend, Helena Hillerström, who had fallen victim to a killer. They had also been friends with Helena. What a strange coincidence, mused Jacobsson, but her thoughts were interrupted by someone tapping her on the shoulder. She gave a start and turned around to see a man in his forties with a Dalmatian puppy on a lead. The man looked friendly and agreeable.

'Can I help you with anything?'

His hair was cut short and smoothed down with gel. He had a gentle yet manly face with high cheekbones, a distinctive jawline with the trace of stubble, and widely spaced eyes that were slightly slanted, which gave his face character. He had a sensitive mouth, which looked both resolute and tender in a way that made him seem unusually attractive to Jacobsson. His voice was dry and a bit gruff. She was surprised by her own reaction, feeling almost weak at the knees as she stood there. The puppy leaped around her, wagging its little tail. She squatted down and let the dog jump up and lick her face.

'Oh, what a sweet little guy,' she exclaimed. 'How old is he?'

'Nine weeks. I just got him.'

'He's fantastic. He really is. What's his name?'

'Baloo. Like the bear in *The Jungle Book*.'

Jacobsson stood up and looked at the man.

'Do you live around here?'

'Yes. Over there, in the last house. The yellow one.'

She saw a lovely wooden house with white trim set slightly back from the street. The property was surrounded by a tall lilac hedge.

Jacobsson showed him her police ID and introduced herself.

'Karin Jacobsson. Police detective.'

'Janne Widén. Photographer. I know who you are. I recognized you.'

Jacobsson noticed to her chagrin that her cheeks were hot. A grown-up woman, standing here and blushing.

'Is that right? Well, I'm here with regard to the murders, you know. I was thinking of talking to some of the neighbours. Do you have a moment?'

'Absolutely. I just need to give Baloo some water. He's dying of thirst in this heat. Would you like to come over and have a cup of coffee?'

Jacobsson hesitated for a few seconds. But why not? She might find out something important. And that's why she was here, after all. To meet people in the area who weren't connected to the group of friends.

'OK.'

They went through an iron gate between the lilacs. A grey sports car was parked in the drive. The man led the way around the side of the house. At the back was a wooden deck and a lawn facing the woods. There the lilac hedge continued, shielding the garden from view.

'How lovely,' said Jacobsson, and she meant it.

'Thanks. Have a seat. Would you like coffee or something cold to drink, or both?'

'I'd like something cold. Water would be fine.'

Jacobsson sat down in one of the armchairs on the terrace. A large umbrella provided shade from the sun. The puppy was trying hard to jump on to her lap. Janne Widén quickly returned with a tray holding a carafe of iced water and two glasses. He set down a bowl for the dog, who eagerly began lapping up the water.

'How long have you lived here?' asked Jacobsson as she raised the frosty glass to her lips.

'Over ten years.' He gave her a crooked smile. 'Just like everybody else, I moved here when the development was newly built. Back then I had a wife and kids, and we thought this place was perfect. Unfortunately, the marriage didn't last. We got divorced five years ago. The children moved with my wife to the mainland.'

'But you chose to stay here?'

'I have my business here, and I love this house, in fact the whole neighbourhood, even though it might not seem like anything special to an outsider. But it has a particular atmosphere that makes it hard to move away.'

'Atmosphere?'

'Yes, a sort of community spirit, or whatever you want to call it. Everyone helps everyone else, and we all care about each other. You're never alone unless you want to be. I thought that was especially nice after I got divorced. I was used to having a house full of kids and their friends, and suddenly it was empty. The children wanted to live with my wife when she moved in with her sister, who runs a kennel. The kids love dogs; they always have. Baloo is from there too. I try to see them as often as possible, of course. I'm a freelance photographer, so I can set my own schedule.'

Jacobsson was surprised by the man's candour. She hadn't asked about his personal life. She took a couple more sips of her iced water.

'This sense of community spirit that you mentioned seems to work well around here.'

The man sitting across from her laughed.

'Well, some people show more community spirit than others.'

'What do you mean?'

'I'm referring to that group over there in the cul-de-sac – because I assume that they're the ones you're interested in. And they've always been rather extreme.'

'In what way?'

'A lot of us think that they've gone a bit overboard. They do everything together and always check with each other before making a decision. Almost as if they have to apologize if they want to have dinner with someone outside the gang, or if one family books a trip without consulting the others first. They just really seem to go too far.'

Widén had an inscrutable expression on his face that Jacobsson couldn't read.

'What are you thinking of? Is there something else that I should know?'

'They're pleasant enough, but it's a really closed circle. They don't allow anyone else in.' He paused for effect. 'I think they have a lot of secrets.'

Jacobsson was instantly on the alert.

'What do you mean? What kind of secrets?'

'About a year ago there was a rumour circulating. Well, it was actually more than just a rumour. Everyone was talking about it.'

'About what?'

'People said that the group was interested in . . . hmm . . . special arrangements. Whenever they had parties together, they would exchange partners with each other. Swinger parties.'

Jacobsson nearly choked on the water she was drinking. She could hardly believe her ears.

'Are you sure?'

'As sure as I can be without having been to those parties myself. And I just remembered how the rumour got started. It was on a Sunday, and one of them who'd been at the party, Beata Dunmar, was talking to another young woman here in the neighbourhood who's not part of the group. Her name is Sandra. Beata told her that they'd exchanged partners. Someone had seen a film on TV in which all the neighbours put their house keys in a basket and then took out one at random and went home with whoever the key belonged to. She said that's what they'd done on Saturday night.'

'Do you know who participated in these parties?'

'Sam and Andrea Dahlberg, Stina and Håkan Ek, Beata and John Dunmar. Plus a couple who don't live here any more.'

'What's their name?'

'Sten and Monica. They lived here for less than a year, but I think they somehow managed to worm their way into that group. For some reason they were allowed in.'

'What do you know about them?'

'Not much. They lived over on Bryggargatan, and they didn't have any children, as far as I know. They moved away after only a year.'

'What's their last name?'

Widén paused to think.

'Hmm . . . I'm sorry, but I can't remember. But I'm sure the others would know.'

'How long did these sorts of parties go on?'

'I think there were actually only a few of them. I don't think it worked out. I heard that the parties got out of hand and somebody was jealous . . . All I know is that something happened, and then they stopped.'

Jacobsson stared in astonishment at the man sitting on the other side of the table. She tried to make sense of what she'd just heard. This was an entirely new lead that cast a different light on the investigation. Could this be the explanation for the murders? The next step was to get hold of the couple that had moved away and then interview the rest of the group again. None of them had ever said a word about swinger parties. Jacobsson stood up and was about to thank Widén when he held out his hand.

'It was nice to meet you. I'd love to see you again, if you're interested.'

Surprised, Jacobsson reached out to take the business card he wanted to give her.

'Call me, if you like.'

He smiled at her, and in his eyes she saw genuine appreciation. She couldn't help smiling back. It had been a long time since a man had shown any interest in her. She could hardly remember what it felt like.

Moving a bit unsteadily, she left Janne Widén's back garden.

As Jacobsson was walking to work on Monday morning, she got a phone call from Wittberg. She could tell from his voice that he had something important to tell her.

'I was out at Svaidestugan last night. You know, that orienteering place in Follingbo. In the sauna I met a guy who told me something very interesting.'

'Really?'

'Just listen to this. He works as a chef in town and does a lot of running in his free time: ordinary running and orienteering. One evening in May he went out after work to go running. It was late, after ten o'clock, so he chose the route that has electric lights since it was dark. Well, as dark as it gets in May – dusk at any rate. After jogging almost the whole route, he was on his way back when he discovered a couple having sex in the woods, right above the marshy area up there near Svaide.'

'And?' Jacobsson was wondering what this had to do with the investigation.

'At first he just heard some strange sounds in the dark. He thought it sounded like somebody was sick

336

or needed help. A woman was crying and whimpering. But when he got closer, he saw a couple a short distance away from the path. There was a full moon, so he could see them quite clearly. A naked woman tied to a tree, and a man having sex with her. At first glance, he thought she was being raped, so he was about to rush forward to rescue her. But then he realized that even though she was . . . making a lot of noise, and bound, she was actually enjoying it. Apparently she was wearing a blindfold too. So then he just kept on running. The couple never saw him.'

'What's so interesting about all of this, other than that he had a different sort of running experience that day?' asked Jacobsson, yawning.

'He saw their car. It was a purple Corvette.'

'And?'

'Don't you remember? Andrea Dahlberg's sports car. We talked about how cool it was. It's a purple, or plum-coloured Corvette.'

'Oh, that's right.'

'And this guy even remembers that the registration on the number plate started with "O".'

Jacobsson uttered a sigh of relief. It would be child's play to find a purple Corvette with a number plate starting with 'O' on the small island of Gotland. Finally something was happening in the investigation.

'Did he give you a description of the couple?'

'It all happened so fast, but he recalls that the man looked very fit, without being a hunk. That's all he could say about him. The woman was thin and apparently had dark hair. And he recalls that she had small breasts.'

Jacobsson frowned. So that ruled out Andrea Dahlberg. It was impossible not to notice that she wore a size-C cup. Had someone borrowed her car?

'What about their age?' asked Jacobsson.

'He guessed thirty-five or forty.'

'OK. The meeting starts in fifteen minutes. I've also got some news to report.'

A feeling of anticipation hovered over the meeting of the investigative team. A good deal of new developments had surfaced. Both Kihlgård and Sohlman were present. Lars Norrby wasn't there, but that was no great loss. Wittberg was in the process of checking out the few Corvettes to be found on Gotland. They had convened in the usual conference room. Jacobsson raised her eyebrows at the sight of two chocolate cakes on the table, decorated with French flags.

'Is it somebody's birthday?' she asked her colleagues as they took seats around the table.

'Today is Bastille Day in France,' Kihlgård told her solemnly. 'And I think that's worth celebrating. Help yourselves.' He motioned for everyone to take a piece of cake.

Jacobsson smiled to herself. Celebrating this particular holiday with Kihlgård had practically become a tradition at police headquarters in Visby. She strongly doubted whether a comparable celebration of the

Swedish independence day ever took place at a police station in France.

After everyone had taken a piece of cake, Jacobsson began by telling them about the couple that had been seen near Svaidestugan, and the car that was parked nearby.

At that moment Wittberg stuck his head in the door.

'We've found the car. Guess who it belongs to?'

'I'm not going to guess,' replied Jacobsson with ill-concealed impatience.

'It's just as we thought. Andrea Dahlberg.'

'OK,' said Jacobsson, picking up her phone. 'Let's bring her in.'

Then she reported on the wild parties that the group of friends had evidently indulged in only a year ago.

Everyone stared in surprise at their boss. Even Kihlgård stopped eating.

'Swinger parties? Good Lord,' exclaimed Wittberg. 'Do people really do that sort of thing? And right there in those fancy houses in Terra Nova? Imagine that – it's actually sort of cool.'

'Maybe so,' said Jacobsson. 'But so far this information is just based on rumours. Our first priority is to conduct new interviews and find out if there's any truth to it. I don't know how many times we've asked these damned Pollyannas – and I'm actually starting to get really fed up with them – whether there's anything else we should know about their relationships. Even though two members of their group have fallen victim to a murderer, they've all been as quiet as mice. I'm going to be bloody pissed off if these rumours are true.'

'Swearing again.' Kihlgård gave Jacobsson an admonishing look.

She pretended not to hear him. What was his problem? He was turning into a regular language cop.

'The question is: What does this mean for the murder investigation?' Jacobsson went on.

'Maybe some of them kept playing the sex games,' suggested Wittberg. 'Maybe they simply couldn't resist.'

Jacobsson noticed that he seemed delighted by the idea. Wittberg had undoubtedly conjured up a whole bunch of interesting images in his mind.

'Sure, that's one possibility. Maybe it was Sam and Stina out there near Svaidestugan. He could have borrowed his wife's car.'

'But who would want to kill them because of that?' Kihlgård objected. 'It would have to be one of their spouses, either Håkan or Andrea.'

'What about the other two?' asked Wittberg. 'The couple that moved away and were part of the group for only a short period? Apparently that was during the period of time in question. And there was something odd about that. Why were they admitted to the group so easily when other people are rarely let in? And why did they disappear after attending those sex parties? Seems fishy, don't you think?'

'Definitely. Could you try to track them down? I don't know what their last name is, or where they live now, but someone in the group must be able to tell us.'

'One possibility is that Stina and Sam continued the sex games with that couple, and then something happened to make them quit. Or one of them, at least. They lived in the neighbourhood for only a short time, so they couldn't have got to know each other very well. Maybe they were a couple of lunatics.'

'But the others should have known if something like that happened,' Kihlgård interjected. 'At least Håkan and Andrea should have known. But they both claimed over and over that they had very happy marriages – which almost makes me suspicious.'

'Exactly,' murmured Jacobsson. 'I've felt from the beginning that there was something wrong with that whole "one big happy family" idea. I sensed something desperate about all of them. They seemed to be hiding something. And now we know. Sex parties. Bloody hell.'

'You're swearing again,' said Kihlgård.

Jacobsson gave him a furious look. At that moment her mobile rang. Since she saw that the call was from the ME, she answered.

'Hi, am I interrupting anything?'

'We're in a meeting, but that's OK.'

'Well, I wanted to call you because we just finished the post-mortem on Stina Ek, and I assume that you'd like to know about this at once.'

'Yes?'

'Stina Ek was pregnant. About three months along.'

Knutas was starting to get impatient. The doctor had insisted that he take sick leave for another week, even though he was feeling perfectly fine. When it came to the murder investigation, Jacobsson had been keeping him updated, but over the weekend he hadn't heard a thing. She had sounded strange on the phone when he talked to her at the end of the previous week, but she hadn't wanted to discuss it when he asked what was wrong. 'We'll talk about it later,' she'd simply said. 'After you get back.' Right now there was nowhere he'd rather be than back on the job. In the meantime he'd been doing his own investigative work. It helped to quell the impatience and he was hoping that it might prove useful.

At the heart of the whole case was the group of friends from Terra Nova, and that ought to be the starting point for the police investigation. It had all started when they went on holiday. Now two of them were not only dead, they had been murdered. And apparently the deaths had occurred only a couple of days apart. In Knutas's opinion, there were two possible avenues to take. Either they started by digging into the past of these people, going way back in time; or they followed their footsteps very closely, trying to find out every nano-event that had taken place during that brief trip to Fårö and Stora Karlsö. Knutas had realized that the easiest thing for him to do was to start by finding out everything he could about the past of these friends.

He'd been working on the case all weekend. By now he had separate piles of printouts detailing the story of each individual. On top of each stack was a photo of the person. It was a very tidy collection. He'd concluded that no one could be described as average in this circle of friends, in terms of either appearance or background. He'd started by looking at their family relationships, their jobs and education, as well as memberships of any associations. He already knew that none of them had any debts or financial problems, and none of them had ever been convicted of a crime.

Yet he had managed to uncover a few secrets. His eyes fell on the oldest member of the group: Håkan Ek. He seemed to be the one to worry about: he had the messiest past. This conclusion was reinforced by the fact that he'd been married three times and had children with three different women. He'd moved a lot during his life and had never lived very long in any one place. The exception was when he settled in Terra Nova with Stina. Then it seemed as if he'd finally found his home. He'd lived there fifteen years and had held the same job even longer; his colleagues had nothing but praise for him. Maybe he and Stina were two lost souls who had finally found each other.

His gaze moved to Stina. He felt a pang in his heart when he looked at the picture of the young woman smiling so warmly at the camera. She was truly charming, thought Knutas. She reminded him of Karin because of her petite size. And she had that soft, feminine side that Karin was so good at concealing. Knutas had the feeling that Stina had been something of a loner who went her own way, choosing to remain more or less on the sidelines. In that sense she was also like Karin.

And then there was Sam Dahlberg. The director had made his breakthrough five years ago with a film that attracted a great deal of attention. But after that, nothing. Only now had he started shooting another feature film. Dahlberg had studied at drama school and then done an internship with Swedish TV. After that he'd spent several years working as an assistant for one of the great directors, Bo Widerberg. Sam didn't seem to have had any major difficulties in life. He came from a culturally involved family in Visby. His mother was a librarian, and his father ran the Roxy Cinema in town. Maybe that was where Sam had got his interest in film. When he was a little boy, he started going to work with his father, helping out at the cinema. He had grown up with movies. Both of Sam's parents were still alive, and he had two sisters. He seemed to have had strong ties to his family. What a tragedy for them to see their son fall victim to a murderer, thought Knutas.

Then he moved on to Beata and John.

John had left the United States with Beata, who was a native Gotlander from a stable middle-class family in Klintehamn. After a brief modelling career in New York and Los Angeles, she had met John Dunmar, a bartender from San Diego, who fell head over heels in love with the beautiful Swede. Beata soon became pregnant, and they decided to settle down in Sweden. John received both a residence and a work permit relatively quickly, and he learned Swedish so well that after only a year he was able to open his own bar in Visby. His business was thriving, and he was well liked by his colleagues and customers. Beata continued to work in the fashion world, as the buyer for a large clothing company. They'd had three children in quick succession and were the happy, proud owners of one of the biggest houses in Terra Nova. Knutas had found nothing noteworthy about them whatsoever.

Finally he came to Andrea. Without a doubt, she was the most complex and interesting of the lot. She was also the one who seemed to have the most secrets. Knutas studied the picture of the dark-haired woman with the sharply etched features. Her expression was inscrutable, impossible to interpret.

Knutas needed to get in touch with Jacobsson.

But before he picked up the phone, he leaned back and read through all the material one more time.

The police had gone to Andrea Dahlberg's home, but she was away, visiting her children who were staying with their grandparents in the Stockholm archipelago. They had gone on a sailing expedition, and no one knew exactly where they were at the moment. The police got hold of a cousin who said that they'd planned to be away at least a week, and it would be hard to track them down.

Jacobsson tried numerous times to get through on the mobiles belonging to various family members, but without success.

Then she discovered that she had missed several calls from Knutas. She tried to ring him, but the line was busy. Oh well, it could wait. Right now she was fully occupied with the investigation, looking into this whole business about the swinger parties and what the significance might be. In addition, there was the discovery that Stina Ek had been pregnant, in her third month. DNA samples had been sent to the lab to determine who the father was, but Jacobsson was not at all convinced it was Håkan.

The first person they managed to get hold of was

Beata, and half an hour later the woman was sitting in an interrogation room at police headquarters. Her red hair was swept up in a loose knot on top of her head, with decorative ringlets framing her face. She was casually dressed in a denim skirt and an especially low-cut T-shirt. She looked self-conscious as she sat at the table across from Jacobsson.

'Why am I here again? You've already questioned me numerous times. I was in the middle of baking. We're having a big family party tomorrow.'

'I'm sorry we had to interrupt your housewifely duties,' said Jacobsson without a trace of sympathy.

Beata Dunmar pursed her lips.

'You've been asked to come here because some new information has come to light in the case, and we want to talk to you about it. We've learned that you and your group of friends have held swinger parties. Is that right?'

Beata opened her eyes wide. She stared at Jacobsson for a long time, apparently feverishly trying to work out how to respond to what she'd just heard.

Jacobsson remained silent, her eyes fixed on Beata, waiting for her to say something.

'What do you mean?' she finally managed.

'Exactly what I said. We've heard that you and your friends have held swinger parties. You, John, Stina, Håkan, Sam and Andrea, along with another couple who moved away from the area. Sten and Monica.'

Beata seemed to realize that the game was up. It

would do her no good to deny the claim. She stared in shame at the table as she answered.

'That's true,' she said in a low voice. 'But only a few times.'

'How many times exactly?'

'Three.'

'What happened during these parties?'

Beata fidgeted a bit before replying.

'The first time it started out as an ordinary party at Sam and Andrea's house. Their children weren't home, so we had the place to ourselves. We drank an awful lot of wine at dinner and everyone got very drunk. We went on drinking afterwards as we sat in front of their big fireplace in the living room. They have big, comfy sofas and armchairs, and we ended up sprawled all over them. Somebody started talking about a film they'd seen. I think it was *Ice Storm*. It took place in an American suburb, rather like our own, with educated and established people who knew each other well, much as we do. They held parties where they put their house keys in a bowl in the hall when they arrived. Later, after dinner, all the women would take out a set of keys and go home and have sex with the man whose keys they'd chosen. They had worked out some sort of system so that nobody would ever get her own husband.'

'I see. So what happened then?'

'First we joked about it. What if we did the same thing? Then someone started teasing John because he's American. Saying things like: Is that how you do things where you're from? And John jumped in and said that he'd always had the hots for Stina and wouldn't mind exchanging keys with her. At first we were all a little shocked, but at the same time there was an excitement in the air, because it was obvious that he really meant what he'd said.'

'And how did you react to that?'

'I pretended this was news to me, even though I'd noticed it long before. He tried to hide it, but it was perfectly clear that he thought Stina was super sexy. Whenever we had a party, he would always dance with her. Preferably all night long.'

'What did you think about that?'

'It didn't really bother me. John and I have an open marriage. We've agreed that we can have sex with other people as long as we don't expose each other to any diseases or feel compelled to report on our escapades. Neither of us believes in the illusion that people can stay together for a whole lifetime without being attracted to anyone else. And why shouldn't a person be allowed to act on his or her desires? We've got only one life, at least as far as we know. Why should you have to deny yourself a lot of pleasurable experiences? For whose sake? For what reason? Because of an unrealistic, romantic and naive notion that there's only one love in your life? Neither of us believes in that sort of shit.'

'So you thought it was OK for John to have sex with Stina?'

'Yes. I would like to have been there, sitting in a

corner of the room. I've often fantasized about making love to a woman.'

Jacobsson took a sip of water. She knew that Wittberg, sitting at the back of the room in his role as witness to the interview, was thoroughly enjoying this unexpected turn in the questioning. He also probably found it terribly amusing that Jacobsson was the one conducting the interview. He'd always accused her of being a prude.

'Let's go back to that first evening. What happened?'

'Well, after John said that about Stina, the mood changed. There was an unusual tension in the air. You could see by the way everyone was moving about that they weren't averse to the idea of experimenting, so to speak. Then Stina did something incredibly surprising.'

'What did she do?'

'She asked John what he thought was so sexy about her.'

Without being aware of what she was doing, Jacobsson leaned closer.

'He told her that it was mainly her breasts. They were so different from mine. Small and pointed. Then Stina went a step further. She got up, went over to John, and unbuttoned her blouse. Everyone was so surprised that they didn't say a word. Håkan sat there, stunned. John stroked her breasts and that's when it really got started. New pairs formed, and little by little one couple after the other disappeared. I ended up with Sam in their bedroom upstairs.'

'Oh,' said Jacobsson, taking another sip of water.

'We had great sex, Sam and I. I've always found him bloody attractive. When we were done, we joked about the whole thing. It was a wonderful feeling, very natural, at least between the two of us. Then I went home, but John wasn't there. I fell asleep, and in the morning he was lying in bed next to me. We didn't talk about it. As I said, we have an unwritten rule not to discuss our sexual adventures, so we didn't in this case either, even though we both knew what had happened. I think we wanted to protect each other. No one wants to hear that his or her partner has had amazing sex with somebody else. Even we draw the line there.'

'So what happened when you met the others again?'

'It was still exciting. Everyone seemed a bit on edge, as if we were all just waiting for the next party.'

'And what happened then? The next time you had a party?'

'Everybody drank more than usual, as if to avoid taking responsibility. And since the boundaries had already been breached, things moved faster than before. We were at Sten and Monica's house.'

'Why did you stop having these parties?'

'The third time we were again at Sten and Monica's house, and it was very clear that Sten only wanted to be with Andrea. He was after her right from the start, as if he took it for granted that they would have sex later on. At the first two parties, everybody had gone through the motions in the beginning. We had aperitifs and dinner and carried on conversations, putting on a good show until everyone was sufficiently drunk to lose their inhibitions. But that night Sten showed an interest in Andrea right from the start, kissing her and stroking her thigh and making sexual references throughout dinner. I could tell that Monica was getting really annoyed because he wasn't following the rules of the game.'

'What about Andrea? How did she react?'

'She seemed flattered, laughing and flirting with him as if it were the most natural thing in the world.'

'So they both went too far? Is that it?'

'Yes, you could say that, even though I didn't think Sam cared very much.'

'What happened then?'

'Well, after dinner everyone helped to clear the table, so there was a lot of commotion. A few people went outside to have a smoke; some stood around talking and drinking wine. And suddenly we noticed that Andrea and Sten had gone.'

'And?'

'The laundry room was right next to the kitchen, and I remember standing in the hallway between the kitchen and the living room, and suddenly I heard somebody screaming. It was Monica. She had opened the laundry-room door and found Andrea and Sten going at it.'

'So they'd jumped the gun, so to speak?'

'Yes, and Monica was furious. Obviously this was too much for her, and she really flipped out. She started punching both of them, hitting and biting and acting like a crazy woman. By that time she'd had a lot to drink. I remember noticing her guzzling down the wine all evening. She was probably cross about how Sten had been behaving ever since Andrea arrived, so when she caught them, she went out of her mind. I've never seen anybody get so hysterical.'

'What did the rest of you do?'

'At first everyone was totally shocked, and it took a few minutes before we fully grasped what was going on. Monica was a tall, stout woman, so it wasn't easy to overpower her. I know that Håkan and John and Sam had to work hard to get her out of there. They were forced to wrestle her to the ground. The rest of us stayed out of their way. I don't really know how it all ended.'

'Did you ever talk about this afterwards?'

'No. It was as if everyone was embarrassed and found it too unpleasant. We took the easiest way out by keeping silent. John and I did talk about it with each other, of course, right after it happened. He told me that Monica finally calmed down. Or rather, her anger gave way to despair, and she sobbed for several hours. She thought she'd made a fool of herself, and after that she and Sten stayed away. Just a few weeks later, they moved. That didn't upset the rest of us. They'd only lived here a short time, they had no children, and we really hadn't got to know each other very well.'

'Yet you had group sex with them! How was that possible?'

'I've wondered about that too. I mean, we're such a close-knit group that we really don't need to let anyone else into our inner circle. There are a lot of people living in the area. Everybody spends time together, having dinners, and crayfish parties, and Midsummer celebrations. But our small group is especially close; we have our own circle inside of the larger social circle, so to speak. And now that I think about it, in hindsight I wonder why we let those two in so easily.'

'So what's your theory?'

'I don't really have one. I know that Sten somehow became friends with Håkan, and he was the one who decided to include Sten and Monica. They came to a few dinners and were terribly nice, and I suppose that's how it happened. Maybe we felt a little sorry for the two of them. They were such outsiders, with no children, working here on a trial basis, and only renting their house. Maybe we saw them as temporary visitors who wouldn't threaten or change our friendships. And so we were more generous towards them.' Beata looked pensive as she stared at the opposite wall. Jacobsson chose to change tack.

'A witness saw a couple having sex outdoors near Svaidestugan in Follingbo late one night at the end of May. And the car they'd arrived in belonged to Andrea Dahlberg. Do you have any idea who those people might have been?'

Beata looked surprised.

'No. That sounds strange. I mean, if it wasn't Sam and Andrea trying to spice up their sex life.'

Jacobsson decided not to say anything about Stina's pregnancy. For the time being the police didn't want to make that information public.

'Let's go back to those parties of yours. How did the whole group continue after that? Did you talk about what happened?'

Beata shifted her gaze back to Jacobsson, although she still looked preoccupied. A smile flitted across her lips.

'That's what's so funny about it all. Even though we consider ourselves to be such good friends, we never discussed the matter. We pretended to each other that nothing had happened. As if we all thought that if we stuck our heads in the sand, the memory of the whole mess would simply disappear.'

'And did it?'

Beata sighed.

'No. I honestly don't think so. We tried hard to pretend that everything was back to normal, that it wasn't important. But certain things had definitely changed. That much was clear.'

'In what way?'

'Our friendships felt strained, as if we had to keep up the pretence at all costs. But I think everyone could feel how holes had begun to appear in the fabric of our relationships. Stina, especially, seemed to change afterwards. She withdrew more, and she stopped going for walks with us. Suddenly she started jogging instead. She seemed more involved with the kids and with her job.'

'What about Sam? Did you notice any difference in him?'

Beata shook her head.

'No, not really.'

'What about you?'

'It didn't bother me. I can separate sex from other kinds of relationships.'

'But what about the fact that your husband was attracted to Stina? Didn't that bother you?'

'Not at all.'

'You'll have to excuse me, but I have a hard time believing that,' Jacobsson persisted. 'It didn't upset you in the least?'

'No. It was just a sexual attraction. Nothing more. And I can handle that.'

Beata reached for the glass of water on the table. Jacobsson noticed that her hand was shaking. She dropped the subject for the moment.

'What about Andrea? Do you know if she ever saw this man named Sten again?'

'No, I really don't think she did. He and Monica moved away and, as far as I know, nobody has heard from them since. Andrea was also terribly in love with Sam. She adored him beyond all reason, as if he were a

Greek god. As if they never had any problems in their marriage.'

'And yet she behaved that way at the party, with Sten?'

'I think it was mostly to get Sam's attention, to make him realize that other men desired her.'

'Why would she feel the need to do something like that?'

'Even though Andrea is sexy and attractive and she's used to having men look at her, I think she compared herself too much to Stina. And, in her own eyes, she always fell short. Stina enchanted people. There was something magnetic about her eyes, and she radiated a charm that made men fall all over themselves. I think Andrea was jealous, and that's why she gave in to Sten like that. It was a way of showing off, of saying: "See, I can do it too." Both to Stina and to her husband.'

Jacobsson shook her head. The whole thing sounded awfully naive. Was this really the way grown-up people behaved?

'Do you think she'd noticed that Sam was attracted to somebody else?'

'Maybe. Although I think his job took up most of his time.'

'So what do you think about the murders? Do you have any idea who might have killed them?'

'I've been thinking a lot about Sten and Monica. And, in hindsight, I think it was the two of them who initiated the whole thing. Or rather, he did. He was the one who urged us on.'

'What's their last name? Do you remember?'

'They weren't married. Her last name was Nordin, and his was . . . Oh, that's right, it was Boberg. His name was Sten Boberg.'

By Tuesday Andrea Dahlberg still hadn't been in touch with the police, and the interview with Håkan Ek had produced largely the same information that they'd gleaned from Beata Dunmar. The police had of course mentioned Stina's pregnancy to Håkan. He seemed genuinely surprised and claimed that he hadn't known anything about it. Jacobsson was inclined to believe him; he seemed sincere.

When it came to the parties, it sounded as if Beata and Håkan had discussed the matter. It was an experiment that had got out of hand, and everyone wanted to forget about it, even though that had proved hard to do. Naturally Håkan had noticed certain changes in Stina, and he'd already told the police about that. But as Håkan said, she was getting close to forty and had been thinking more than usual about her past. He'd said that life often caught up with a person at that age, and Jacobsson felt strongly affected by his words. That was exactly what had happened to her.

At the same time, the police had finally received a concrete and tangible lead to follow. Wittberg had been in contact with Monica Nordin on the phone, and she told him that she and Sten had split up long ago. They had never been married, just lived together for about a year. First for a few months in central Stockholm, and then Monica's job had taken her to Gotland. Sten, who had his own business, had followed, even though they'd only been together a short time. They found a house to rent in Terra Nova, and their plans for the future had included both children and a dog. But their relationship had begun to deteriorate, and the situation got worse after the parties started. Sten talked about nothing else. Several times she'd caught him spying on Andrea, and after the last party, their relationship was over. Monica had not only moved away from Gotland, she'd also split up with Sten. She wanted nothing more to do with him.

It had been more difficult for the police to locate Sten Boberg. His business no longer seemed to be functioning, nobody answered the phone, and the email address wasn't working. He'd apparently moved around to various addresses, but Wittberg finally tracked him down to a block of flats due to be demolished in Upplands Bro municipality, about thirty kilometres north of Stockholm. Wittberg had asked the Stockholm police for help in bringing Boberg in for questioning.

Now they were just waiting for their colleagues in the capital to report back.

After countless attempted phone calls, Jacobsson finally reached Andrea's mother, Marianne, late Tuesday afternoon.

'We're looking for your daughter. As I understand it, she's been on a sailing trip with you. Is she there now?'

'No, I'm afraid not,' said the woman on the phone.

Her voice was so faint that Jacobsson had to strain to hear what she said.

'Maybe I misunderstood, but her cousin told us that she and the children were staying with you.'

'The children are here with me and my husband, but Andrea decided to stay at home.'

'Do you know why?'

'She changed her mind.'

'When was this?'

'Just before we were supposed to leave,' said her mother with a sigh. 'Everything was all set, and we were standing on the dock . . .'

'Yes?'

'Well, she just decided not to come with us.'

'Do you know why?'

'She got a phone call.'

'A phone call?'

'Yes.'

'Then what happened?'

'She took the call and afterwards she told us that she needed to go and see somebody.'

'Do you know why?'

'No.'

'Do you know who she was talking to?'

'No.'

Jacobsson felt a growing annoyance. She practically had to drag every word out of this woman.

'But you'd made plans to go sailing for a whole week with her and the children. What explanation did she give for not going with you?'

'None. She just said that she'd meet us later.'

'When?'

'The next day. At least that's what she said.'

'And did she?'

'No.'

'Have you talked to her since then?'

'No, actually, I haven't. I've tried to phone her, but it's hard to get through from out here in the archipelago.'

'Do you have any idea where she might be?'

'No, I don't. I have no idea.'

One day when my sister came home from school she stopped talking. I asked her a question – I can't remember what it was about – but she refused to answer. She wouldn't say a word. I was completely bewildered. I could tell from her expression that she had made up her mind. She wasn't going to talk any more. Mamma was at the hospital, and Pappa was out in the fields. Ploughing, or whatever it was that he was doing. I got upset, asked her what was wrong, what had happened. She just gave me a solemn look, shook her head, and then went to her room. Later Mamma came home and began cooking dinner. I told her that Emilia was refusing to talk. She thought I was joking. 'Oh, what kind of foolishness is that?' She dried her hands on her apron and went upstairs. She called to Emilia on the way up, but received no answer. I followed at her heels, worried about what would happen. Both Emilia and I had great respect for our parents. Would Emilia dare to defy Mamma?

'Hello, dear. Why didn't you answer when I called you?' said Mamma reproachfully as she pushed open the door to Emilia's room.

Emilia was sitting on the bed with her diary on her lap. Pale and sombre, she looked at Mamma without saying a word.

'What's wrong with you? What's this all about?'

At first Mamma just sound irritated, but when Emilia persisted in keeping silent, Mamma grew desperate. She scolded and cursed, but nothing helped. Emilia refused to speak. Mamma grabbed her by the shoulders and shook her. My sister just sat there, seemingly unaffected. As if it didn't bother her in the slightest that Mamma was screaming and carrying on. Horrified, I watched the scene unfold before me. Mamma was angrily trying to make my sister open her mouth, forcing her lips apart with her fingers. Emilia offered no resistance; she seemed almost apathetic, just staring into space, her eyes glassy. Nothing seemed to reach her. Mamma then started to cry, pleading with her daughter. She fell to her knees next to the bed, took Emilia's hand in her own, and begged her to say something. But Mamma's efforts were in vain. Not one word crossed Emilia's lips.

That was when I understood how serious the situation was.

And that I would never again hear my sister speak.

Knutas had tried to contact Jacobsson all afternoon without success. He was in the kitchen making himself an omelette for dinner when she rang.

'Finally you called me back,' he said, taking the frying pan off the burner. He slid the omelette on to a plate while he clamped the phone between his ear and shoulder.

'I'm sorry. It's been crazy all day. There have been a few developments in the case at last.'

'Really?' said Knutas with interest. 'What are they, if I might ask?'

'It turns out that this nice little group of friends used to sleep around. With each other.'

Jacobsson then told him what they'd found out, and about the couple, Sten and Monica.

'Well, I'll be damned,' exclaimed Knutas. 'And nobody breathed a word about this?'

'Actually, that's not so hard to understand,' said Jacobsson. 'It's not exactly something that you'd want to make public.'

'This Sten sounds like a real scumbag. Have you got hold of him yet?'

'We're working on it. Was there anything special that you wanted to tell me?'

'Yes, as a matter of fact, there is. Don't be cross with me, but I was feeling so bored here at home that I decided to do a little research. Do you know about Andrea Dahlberg's tragic background?'

'No. What do you mean?'

'Do you know that her father was convicted of sexually assaulting her older sister when Andrea was only thirteen?'

Knutas paused for effect. He could hear Jacobsson gasp.

'No. How do you know that?'

'I've been checking up on everyone in the group, looking into their past and going further back in time than we've done previously. I've basically gone through everything since they were born. The person who turned out to have the most secrets was Andrea Dahlberg.'

'Tell me what you found out.'

'When she was twelve her sister committed suicide. Andrea was the one who found her at home in bed, unconscious after swallowing a lot of pills. They couldn't save her. A short time after her sister's death, it came out that her father had been raping her sister for years. He was sentenced to five years in prison. Andrea's mother filed for divorce, and they moved to Stockholm. As far as I know, she's never had any contact with her father since then.'

'What a tragic story. But what does this have to do with the murders?'

'Maybe nothing. I just thought you should know about it. We've questioned everyone involved so thoroughly, but Andrea has never mentioned any of this.'

'Maybe it would be too difficult for her to talk about it.'

'Of course. But I think we need to interview her again.'

'Definitely. There's just one hitch. Andrea Dahlberg has disappeared.'

Jacobsson walked home on Tuesday evening. It had been an eventful day, and it was nice to get outside, breathe in some fresh air and clear her head. She took a detour, heading towards town and through the Botanical Gardens, and then continued along the shoreline promenade. She had just stepped on to the path when a little spotted dog came dashing towards her. Right behind him was somebody she recognized at once. Those shoulders, that hair, that posture. It was impossible to ignore the tremor that passed through her body like hot lightning. It was him, Janne Widén, the photographer who lived in Terra Nova. He saw her and gave a cheerful wave as he came running after his dog.

'Hi again! I'm sorry, but he's hopeless. He refuses to listen to me the minute he sees something interesting.'

'It's all right,' said Jacobsson with a smile. She patted the dog, whose joy at seeing her again seemed to know no bounds.

'Do you live nearby?' he asked with interest.

She noticed that his eyes were greyish-green.

'No, not really. I live on Mellangatan, but I thought it'd be nice to take a walk after work.'

'I came out here with Baloo, to let him swim and run around for a while. He's been keeping me company all day while I worked, and that wasn't much fun for him. Is it OK if I walk with you for a bit?'

'Sure.'

They started walking in the direction of the hospital. The sea was glittering and still in the evening sun. A few ducks were soundlessly gliding around on the mirror-like surface. The puppy leaped around at the water's edge, jumping and splashing about.

'How's the investigation going? Have you got any suspects?'

Jacobsson smiled.

'If we did, I wouldn't be able to discuss it.'

'Of course. Sorry. I'm just interested. Since I'm a neighbour and everything. What a senseless thing to happen; it's hard to believe it's all true. That it really did happen, right in our midst.'

'How do you think the other neighbours are reacting?'

'They're shocked and puzzled, of course. Something like this creates a lot of uneasiness. Some people won't let their children go outdoors to play on their own in the evenings. People are being more careful about locking their doors. And no one sleeps with the windows open any more. Everyone has become more cautious. There isn't the same relaxed atmosphere we used to have.' He shook his head, and then tossed a ball for the dog. 'I really hope it gets resolved soon, so that things will go back to normal.'

They walked in silence for a while.

'How did you happen to join the police force, by the way? I mean, don't take this wrong, but you seem too soft somehow for that type of work.'

Jacobsson smiled, feeling suddenly embarrassed.

'I don't know. I suppose I wanted to do something useful. Something real, if you know what I mean.'

He laughed, kicking aside a stone on the ground.

'Not like me. I just take pictures of people. And food. Lately I've been mostly photographing food. You know, because everyone's talking about "culinary Gotland". It's so trendy at the moment. All those chefs and cookbooks and newly opened restaurants and cafés. Speaking of food, are you hungry?'

They had reached Tott's newly opened restaurant down on Norderstrand. Both a luxury hotel and a block of condominiums were being built nearby. The restaurant had outdoor seating right on the water, and they could smell the fragrant aroma of grilled meat.

'As a matter of fact, I am.'

'Baloo is getting tired, so he won't want to walk much further. Shall we sit down for a while?'

They chose a table that had a splendid view of the water. Then they ordered grilled steaks and salad, along with a bottle of wine. Karin thought it all seemed totally unreal. Here she sat with a man in a restaurant for the first time in ages, and she'd forgotten how to act. But Janne turned out to be a charming companion. They chatted about all sorts of topics. Baloo fell asleep under the table after having a piece of meat and some water.

'What's it like being a police officer, anyway? How do you cope with all the misery you have to see?'

'I don't know,' replied Karin. 'You get used to it, to a certain extent. And when you're working, you focus on the professional side of the job, so that's a way of protecting yourself. I suppose I shut out my emotions a lot in order to concentrate on the work.'

'What about when you get home?'

'That's when the feelings can surface,' she admitted. 'That's when you return to being yourself, in a way. Although I try not to let in too many emotions. You have to learn to separate the work from your personal life. Otherwise it would be intolerable in the long run.'

'I think it's so admirable that you're able to do that. I don't know if I could handle it. I'm too sensitive.'

'You are? In what way?'

'I always cry at sad movies, for instance. It can be a problem. If I go to the cinema with my friends, they think I'm really embarrassing. I think so too, but I can't help it. It just comes over me.'

Karin laughed. She took a sip of her wine, aware how happy she felt in Janne's company. She gazed out at the sea and thought that, in spite of everything, life was good.

*

They left the restaurant around midnight. Janne carried the sleeping puppy in his arms as he walked Karin to her door.

'How will you get home?' she asked.

'No problem. I'll get a cab.'

'OK,' she replied. 'Thanks for a nice evening.'

She gave him a quick hug.

In the stairwell on the way up to her flat, she realized that she hadn't felt this happy in a long, long time.

The next morning Karin Jacobsson was the first to arrive at the offices of the Criminal Division. That wasn't unusual. Now that Knutas was on sick leave, she was often alone in the office, at least for the first few hours of the day. Normally Knutas was always there with her, since they were both early risers. She missed him more than she'd expected, on both a professional and personal level.

She got a cup of coffee from the vending machine in the corridor before she went to her office. On the threshold she stopped abruptly, hardly able to believe her eyes. On the desk was a vase with a huge bouquet of red roses. Slowly she moved closer and found an envelope among the flowers. The card inside said simply: *Will you have dinner with me again soon? Hugs from Janne in Terra Nova.*

Karin sank on to her chair. She couldn't help smiling. Was he courting her? She could hardly remember what it felt like to be the object of someone's attention – that hadn't happened for such a long time. And she couldn't recall ever receiving a bouquet of red roses.

She sat there staring at the flowers. They were big,

long-stemmed, and blood-red. Very beautiful. But red roses, she thought to herself. Is he crazy? Did anyone send flowers like this after meeting only twice? Didn't red roses signify love? Was this a warning that he might be a psychopath? No, she swore to herself the next second. Why do you always have to think like that? Knocking down anyone who shows a little appreciation? Karin was well aware of her inability to accept gifts and compliments. She always felt embarrassed and thought people were putting on an act; she never thought they were sincere. She couldn't explain why she'd ended up this way. But at least now she knew that's what she tended to do.

She picked up the card and read it again.

There was a knock on the door. Wittberg appeared in the doorway. He was about to say something but stopped when he caught sight of the flowers.

'What's going on? Is it a big birthday? No, that can't be right. You're already over forty.' He grinned. Wittberg was always teasing Jacobsson about her age. 'I know – you've got a lover! About time. Congratulations!'

'Shut up,' said Jacobsson, moving the vase off to the side. 'How come you're here so early? What do you want?'

'Seriously. Have you met someone?'

'No. But even if I had, you'd be the last person I'd tell. Come on, tell me what you want.'

'I'm here early because I never went home. Kihlgård and I and a few others from the NCP have been up all night trying to locate Andrea Dahlberg while you were home in bed. We've checked out all the possible places we could think of, but she's nowhere to be found. Not at home, not in her shop. None of her friends know where she is, or any of the neighbours in Terra Nova, or anyone else in her gigantic social circle. A couple of officers drove over to her house and went inside. No one was there, but they didn't find any sign of where she might have gone. The whole thing seems really weird. It's been three days since anybody saw her.'

Jacobsson felt an uneasiness clutch at her stomach. Not another victim.

'What about Sten Boberg? Is there any news about him?'

'Yeah, listen to this. We had an address for him outside Stockholm, and our colleagues went over to his flat during the night, but it was empty. We just found out that it was the wrong address. He no longer lives in Stockholm. He lives here on Gotland.'

Jacobsson jumped out of her chair.

'What the hell are you saying?'

'And his place is very close to Andrea's house. He lives in Gråbo – on Jungmansgatan. He moved there six months ago.'

Jacobsson grabbed her jacket and service weapon and was already out of the door.

The parsonage was about a kilometre from our house. I cycled over there. I was going to return a pie plate that had been left behind after dinner a few days before. Now the pastor's wife needed it back. She had been out picking blueberries and wanted to surprise her husband with his favourite pie. When I reached their house I stopped at the grand iron gate and walked my bike up the gravel path to the forecourt. It was a short distance from the church, beautifully situated on a hill with a view of the fields and meadows. The parsonage consisted of a main building with a wing on either side. One was used for visitors and the other served as the pastor's office. Mamma and Pappa had been here many times after Emilia's death. I still could barely comprehend that my sister had actually killed herself. That she no longer wanted to live. It was hard to accept. And we never talked about it at home. But it seemed so empty at the dinner table and in front of the TV in the evening. Emilia had left behind a terrible void. I don't remember what my thoughts were right after it happened. I felt like I was on automatic, eating the food put in front of me, going to school, doing my homework. The school counsellor had tried to talk to me, but I wasn't interested. It felt as if she wanted me to say a lot of things that I had no intention of saying. As if I were sitting there for her sake, so that she could feel that she'd done her job. Mamma just lay in bed with the blinds drawn. Pappa had been forced to move out of the room. She refused to let anyone in. I longed for her to hug me, comfort me, but she couldn't. She was too immersed in her own sorrow. People came over to visit. They sat at the kitchen table and drank coffee, fidgeting because they didn't know what to say. People talked about a 'cry for help'. A cry for help that nobody had heard. That made it even worse. As if it was our fault that Emilia had taken her own life. Take care of your mother, they told me. Pappa sought refuge in his farm work. Nobody cared about me. I closed off my grief; my defence mechanisms set in and made me able to get through the days.

As I cycled up to the parsonage on that day, I saw that our car was parked at the side of the building. Pappa was here. I could hear low voices coming from the pastor's office. Someone was crying, and I assumed it was Pappa. It was a hot day, the air was stifling, and the window stood open. Instinctively I pricked up my ears and hesitantly crossed the gravel forecourt so as not to draw attention. I stopped next to the wall of the house, so no one could see me from the window, and listened intently. Now I could clearly hear Pappa sobbing inside the room.

'It was my fault,' he said. 'All my fault. I've killed my own daughter.' At first I was filled with tenderness. Poor Pappa. He shouldn't shoulder all the blame for Emilia's death. She'd been suffering from depression, and it was worse and more serious than anyone could have imagined. It was no one's fault. I heard the pastor murmur something, and then Pappa spoke again.

'It's my fault. But I couldn't help myself.'

I was stunned and felt an icy shiver race through my body at the implication of Pappa's words.

'Now, now. Now, now,' said the pastor.

Pappa went on, whimpering pitifully: 'You know what I mean. I told you about it from the very beginning. I should have realized when she stopped talking. In my heart I knew it was an intolerable situation, but I couldn't help myself. I felt like sick demons were egging me on. I'm just a man after all, and Margareta never wanted to do it.'

'We talked about that,' said the pastor sternly. 'What you did is a sin and perverse and I told you so many times that you needed to stop. You can't blame your assaults on male urges.'

The words echoed inside my head. It was impossible to take them in, impossible to understand. Had Pappa . . . ? I was breathing hard, my head started to spin, and I dropped the pie plate on the ground. Suddenly everything was crystal clear.

The nausea came without warning. I threw up in the rose bushes. From far away I could still hear Pappa's churning, whining voice. It had been going on for several years. And our good friend, the pastor, had known what was happening the whole time but had never said anything. Not a single person had said a word about what was happening to Emilia.

I managed to get back on my bicycle and then left the parsonage behind.

I was never going back there again.

The blocks of flats, plastered a dirty grey, stood in a row in the run-down residential district on the outskirts of Visby. In the car park was a mangy-looking caravan as well as several rusty old bangers that looked as if they were at least twenty years old.

Jacobsson turned off the engine and pulled on the handbrake.

'OK, how shall we do this?'

Wittberg took a piece of paper out of his jacket pocket.

'He lives at Jungmansgatan 142.'

'It'd probably be best if we surprise him.'

They quickly walked over to the first building. A dilapidated sign on the peeling façade told them that it was number 120. They continued along the deserted street.

Jacobsson gave an involuntary start when a person appeared from around the corner. A young guy wearing a cap pulled down over his forehead came walking towards them with a pit bull on a chain. Jacobsson and Wittberg were not wearing uniforms, but he gave them a scornful look and spat on the pavement as he passed. I'm sure we smell like cops, thought Jacobsson. When they came to number 142 they found the letters 'KSS' sprayed in black paint all over the front entrance. It was the acronym for 'Keep Sweden Swedish'.

'Nice neighbourhood,' muttered Wittberg. They paused at the door. The glass in the top part was broken.

Jacobsson looked up at the façade of the building, then she stepped inside. What a contrast it was to the sunlight outside. Dim lighting, the walls a speckled brown, and a faint smell of rubbish. Wittberg took the lead and headed up the narrow stairs. Not a sound was audible. One storey, two. Each floor had four plain doors leading to the flats.

When they reached the third floor, they found what they were looking for. A handwritten piece of paper had been stuck in the nameplate: 'Sten Boberg'. And above the letter slot there was another sign. 'No junk mail, please'. Jacobsson and Wittberg took up position on either side of the door and then they rang the bell. The sound reverberated inside the flat. They waited thirty seconds. No reaction. Jacobsson rang the bell again. They waited. Still nothing. They exchanged glances. A few more attempts with no results. Wittberg pushed open the letter slot as far as it would go and shouted: 'Police! Open up!'

Suddenly they heard the clattering of a lock from the floor above, and a weak, trembling voice said: 'What's going on?'

Jacobsson ran up the stairs in three bounds. The door in the corner was slightly ajar. A bleary-eyed old woman was visible in the gap. A thick security chain prevented the door from opening further. Jacobsson guessed that the woman was in her eighties. She was short, with white hair, wearing soiled trousers and a nubbly old cardigan. She seemed almost blind.

'I'm sorry to bother you,' said Jacobsson. 'We're from the police, and we're looking for Sten Boberg, who lives on the floor below. It's nothing to worry about. We just want to talk to him.'

'What? What's going on?' the old woman repeated. She smelled strongly of urine. Jacobsson noticed a bunch of rubbish bags in the hall inside the flat.

'We're from the police,' she said, raising her voice and showing her police ID. 'We're here to talk to your downstairs neighbour, Sten Boberg. Do you know if he still lives here?'

The old woman turned pale and looked terrified.

'No, I don't want any. I don't want any, I tell you. Do you hear me?'

And she shut the door. More security chains clattered.

Silence descended over the building once again. Jacobsson sighed. The old woman seemed utterly confused. She hesitated for a moment, but then rang the bell. She glanced at the nameplate, which was made of white plastic, with officially printed letters. It had been attached to the door by the municipal housing association. Nothing happened. Then Jacobsson heard the sound of a TV. Someone was talking in a loud voice that was quickly drowned out by accordion music.

Wittberg appeared in the stairwell.

'What's happening?' he asked.

'Just an old woman. But I'm going to try again.'

Jacobsson rang the bell. After a moment she heard the rattling of chains, and the door opened slightly. The old woman peered out as if she'd never seen Jacobsson before.

'Yes?'

'Hi,' said Jacobsson, giving the woman her friendliest smile. 'My name is Karin, and I'm from the police.'

She didn't get any further before the old woman lost her temper.

'Are you from the home-help services? I told you I didn't want any help. Can't you understand that? I can clean my own home. I've done that my whole life, and I'm not going to change.'

'Excuse me,' said Jacobsson, her voice a bit sterner. 'But I'm not from the home-help services. I'm a police officer.' Again she showed the woman her ID. 'POLICE. We're looking for your neighbour.' She pointed downstairs, to clarify whom she meant. 'Your neighbour, whose name is Sten Boberg. Do you know where he is?'

For a moment the old woman looked confused. Her gaze shifted and her lower lip quivered. Jacobsson was afraid that she was going to burst into tears.

'It's all right,' she said soothingly. 'It's nothing to worry about. We just want to have a little talk with the man.'

She pointed again and then held up her ID.

'I have his keys. If he's not at home, you can go in and wait for him.'

Jacobsson gave the woman a doubtful look.

'You have his keys? Well, how fortunate. Could we borrow them?'

'Just a minute.'

Jacobsson watched in surprise as the old woman disappeared into the dimly lit flat. She heard drawers opening and closing as the woman muttered to herself the whole time. It almost sounded as if she were scolding someone. After several minutes she was back behind the security chain, holding out a gnarled, trembling hand to give Jacobsson a key ring.

'I have the keys from when Asta lived there. Before she died. I used to water her flowers when she went out of town to visit her son on the mainland. Gunnar. He was a nice boy. He always brought flowers for his old mother. Such a nice boy. But now Asta is dead, and everyone else is too. I'm the only one left, except for that man, who comes and goes. I don't trust him, so I didn't tell him that I had the keys. Here you are, young lady. Take them.'

'Thank you so much.' Jacobsson grabbed the key ring. 'I'll bring them back when we're done.'

'That's not necessary. I have no use for them any more. Asta is dead, and soon I'll be gone too.'

'Unbelievable,' Jacobsson whispered to Wittberg, who was sitting on the stairs, having resigned himself to wait. 'One minute the old woman was totally confused, and the next she was sharp as a tack.' She waved the keys before her colleague's eyes. 'And she had his keys. It's too good to be true.'

'You're out of your mind. We can't just barge in. We have nothing on him. He's not under suspicion for any sort of crime.'

'Right now I couldn't care less. But OK, I'll phone Smittenberg.' Without waiting for a response, she tapped in the phone number for the prosecutor. No answer.

'What a shame,' she told Wittberg with a grin. He didn't reply.

And before her colleague could object, Jacobsson unlocked the door.

Knutas woke up early. The ache in his wrist was almost gone. He was alone in the bed because Lina was out of town again. Lately she'd done nothing but take time off from work, using up any holiday time and days off in lieu that she was owed. The kids weren't at home either. He was almost starting to think that he was getting used to the solitude.

He thought about his wife and how she had changed. Maybe it has something to do with the menopause, thought Knutas, but then he was ashamed of such an idea. Why did people always blame hormones as soon as a woman wanted changes and started to make demands or to seek more time for herself? He wasn't going to fall into that trap. Maybe he should just leave her in peace.

Andrea Dahlberg's face appeared in his mind. His first impression of her was that she was extremely controlled. Even though her husband had been murdered in the most cruel way, she had been composed during the first interview he'd had with her at police headquarters. She hadn't shed a single tear.

Andrea seemed determined to maintain a façade.

Every time he'd seen her she had been amenable; she had been well groomed and properly dressed. She wore her long hair loose, but it was beautifully styled. She kept her home in perfect order, and the shop that she owned on Adelsgatan had been meticulously arranged and designed down to the smallest detail. Andrea seemed to be someone who left nothing to chance.

Now she had sent her children to stay with their grandparents, but she herself had decided not to join them for the sailing expedition. She'd changed her mind at the last second. Knutas wondered why. Apparently someone had contacted her. Was it a friend of hers? How could she leave her children like that when they'd just lost their father? And strangely enough, she'd made herself unavailable, even though her husband and best friend had just been murdered, and the police might need to contact her.

Within a short time she'd lost the two people who meant the most in her life, other than her children. How had that affected her? He thought again about what had happened in her childhood. That must have been tremendously traumatic. First her sister's suicide, and then finding out the reason behind it: their father's sexual assaults. A terrible betrayal back then. A terrible betrayal now.

Suddenly Knutas sat up in bed.

Andrea Dahlberg had switched off her phone and left the children where they would be safe. She had lost everything. A thought refused to leave him. Was that possible? If so, how and where? There was really only one place that seemed likely.

Now Knutas knew exactly what he had to do. Impatiently he got out of bed and checked the timetable on the Internet.

The front hall was cramped and dark. Wittberg crept in first, his gun drawn. Jacobsson followed close behind. It was possible that Boberg was in the flat and had just refused to open the door. They continued along a narrow hall with doors on both sides. The floor creaked faintly under their feet, and a clock ticked on the wall. The kitchen was empty, as was the bedroom. Jacobsson opened the door to the bathroom and a clothes cupboard. No one there.

They quickly concluded that the flat was empty. In the living room they found a white leather sofa, a glass table with lion's feet, and a large porcelain Dalmatian set in one corner.

'Good God, how ugly,' exclaimed Jacobsson.

The kitchen was long and narrow with a modern white plastic table next to the window. A fruit bowl holding fresh bananas indicated that the tenant had recently been at home. The flat was clean and tidy.

'He seems to be an orderly person, at any rate,' said Wittberg as he continued over to another room at the end of the hall.

The door was locked.

'I don't suppose we're likely to find the key,' murmured Jacobsson. 'And he could come home at any moment.'

Wittberg kicked open the door.

And whistled.

'I'll be damned.'

The room was painted bright red, and the entire ceiling was covered with mirrors. Strings of tiny red lights were hung around the windows. The walls were papered with hundreds of pictures, all apparently of one woman, showing her in various settings. Wearing a quilted jacket on a skating rink, in a white summer dress with a flower wreath on her head at a Midsummer celebration, wearing shorts and a top as she clipped the hedge. Naked with only a hat on her head, wearing a black negligee in the bedroom, in various provocative positions as she apparently posed for the photographer. A bizarre cavalcade with Andrea Dahlberg in the leading role. The photos had been professionally done. The photographer seemed to know his stuff.

'Good Lord,' gasped Jacobsson. 'Looks like we're dealing with a stalker.'

'And potentially a triple murderer. Judging by all of this, it looks like Andrea might be his next victim.' Jacobsson suddenly went ice cold. 'And she's been missing for three days, or more. Shit, shit, shit.'

She looked around. A thought had begun to take shape in the back of her mind. It had something to do with the porcelain dog in the living room. A Dalmatian.

Jacobsson's gaze fell again on the photographs, taken by a professional. Slowly she realized what it might mean. She pictured Janne Widén's smile and greyish-green eyes. His business card on which it said 'Photographer'. He was the one who had told her about the sex parties. Red roses in her office. The man she'd had dinner with last night. They'd been practically flirting with each other. She'd felt something that resembled a budding attraction as they said good night outside the door to her building. What an idiot she was. A sense of betrayal burned in her stomach. For the first time in ages she had felt appreciated as a woman. She'd thought he was really interested in her. And he was single. Her cheeks burned with indignation. Was Janne Widén really Sten Boberg?

She sank down on the sofa in the living room and pulled off her jacket. Thoughts were tumbling through her head. Could the situation be that bad? She felt totally confused.

'What's wrong?' asked Wittberg, who had seen Jacobsson's face go from pale to bright red.

'It's nothing. I just thought of something. Have you seen any indication that he owns a dog?'

'No.'

Jacobsson forced herself to push the feeling of humiliation aside so she could focus on the job they were there to do. They searched the flat, looking for further leads. Boberg had collected extensive documentation about Andrea: newspaper clippings, photos, notes about the business she ran, but nothing that revealed where she might be right now. Jacobsson was just about to notify her colleagues when they heard a key turn in the lock.

'Shit,' hissed Wittberg.

He shoved Jacobsson into the clothes cupboard and stepped in after her just as the front door opened.

Knutas got into his old Mercedes and drove south towards Klintehamn. The traffic was light this early in the morning, even though the tourist season was at its peak. Gotland is actually more beautiful after the summer holidays are over, thought Knutas. Especially from mid-August to the end of September. The weather was often lovely, and the sea surrounding the island was quite warm. That was when the beaches were deserted and most inviting, and it was possible to walk through the streets of Visby without constantly bumping into other people.

Waiting on the dock were about ten people besides himself. He didn't know a single one of them; they were probably all from the mainland. Usually Knutas cursed the fact that he couldn't remain anonymous. He'd been the police chief for so long that he knew everybody who lived on Gotland. Sometimes he put on a baseball cap and sunglasses just to avoid being recognized, as if he were a pop star.

When the ferry docked in Norderhamn, Knutas was the first to disembark.

He walked quickly along the stony path, grateful that he'd been wise enough to wear comfortable shoes. He soon reached the bay where the group from Terra Nova had stayed.

Everything seemed more real now that he was actually here. He could picture them swimming and relaxing together. He imagined the tension that must have existed at the thought of what they'd done at those parties only a year earlier.

He continued past the cabins near the bay and headed up the steep stairs to the lighthouse. He met no one and assumed that most of the people were taking the obligatory tour of the island. He'd been given special dispensation so he didn't have to participate.

It was nice and calm at the top. Knutas paused for a moment to look at the original lighthouse, which was eighteen metres tall and built of stones from the island where it stood. The house looked like a small castle that he'd once seen on a trip to France. The lighthouse on Stora Karlsö was not constructed in the usual form of a free-standing round tower. Here the tower was built into the house that had served as a residence for the lighthouse-keeper and his family. If it weren't for the big lamps in the windows at the very top, it would have been hard to tell that this was actually a lighthouse.

He made his way over to the first bird mountain and stood at the fence, gazing at the cliffs and the narrow ledges. All the birds had now left.

He turned around and went on to the next bird

mountain, which was some distance away. This was where Sam Dahlberg had been murdered. The sun was warm on his back, so he took off his jacket. It was almost eleven o'clock, and it was starting to get hot. Suddenly it occurred to him that it was almost exactly the same time of day when somebody pushed Dahlberg off the cliff. What a coincidence. He rounded the curve and the bird mountain was right in front of him. Eagerly he picked up the pace, keeping his eyes on the ridge. So that was where it happened. That was where Dahlberg had met his killer.

Suddenly Knutas gave a start. Someone had appeared up there on the cliff edge, pausing to look out at the sea.

He recognized her at once.

With a muted bang the front door closed again. Someone locked the deadbolt and lifted the security chain into place. Sten Boberg was obviously meticulous about keeping out unwelcome visitors. If he only knew, thought Jacobsson. A brief cough, shoes being removed. A jacket hung up on a hook. Footsteps only centimetres away from where both police officers were hiding, standing close together in the small cupboard. Jacobsson was holding on to the back of Wittberg's jacket so as not to lose her balance. A hanger was jabbing her in the back. Someone went into the toilet without closing the door, judging by the sound. Then the person flushed and came out again. Jacobsson poked her colleague, took out her gun, and motioned for him to step out. Wittberg raised his hand to stop her.

'Let's wait a moment,' he whispered. 'He might have Andrea.'

Water was running from the tap in the kitchen. Saucepans clattered. Was he making tea? Creaking footsteps heading for the living room, and then the TV went on. Apparently he stood there for a moment, using the remote to surf the channels as one sound was replaced by another: thudding pop music, the babble of a newsreader, loud moaning from what sounded like a porn film. To Jacobsson's relief, he quickly changed the channel to a sports report, and then music again. It sounded like movie music from some American drama. Footsteps went past again, going back to the kitchen. The clicking sound as a burner was turned off. Every little sound was audible through the thin cupboard door. Boberg seemed to be alone.

At that moment Jacobsson froze. As she stood there with her nose against Wittberg's back, she remembered that she'd taken off her jacket when they were searching the flat. It was lying on the sofa in the living room. Damn, she thought. Her mobile was in her jacket pocket.

She murmured a silent prayer that he wouldn't notice it. Her mouth was dry, and her heart was pounding so hard that she was afraid he'd hear it. The man went back to the living room. They immediately smelled smoke. Their first thought was that he'd lit a cigarette, but it didn't take long before they realized it wasn't the usual tobacco sold in the shops. Sten Boberg was sitting there smoking hash. So now he's going to get high? thought Jacobsson with growing frustration. She poked Wittberg. It was too crowded for him to turn around. She ventured a whisper.

'What the hell should we do?'

Before her colleague could answer, the volume on the

TV soared. Voices thundered through the flat, revealing that the music they'd heard before was definitely from some American film. Jacobsson froze. Why had he turned up the volume so loud?

For several minutes they stood there in confusion, unable to guess what was happening beyond the cupboard door. Wittberg tried to take out his mobile but rammed his elbow into a hanger. Jacobsson grabbed the hanger just as silence fell over the flat again. Suddenly they heard the door to the cupboard being locked from the outside. Then came the sound of furniture being dragged across the floor.

Boberg was in the process of blockading the door.

He'd found their hiding place, so there was no longer any need to remain silent.

'Police!' shouted Wittberg. 'Open up!'

'I'm sure he knows who we are,' hissed Jacobsson, who was still wedged in behind her colleague. 'My police badge is in my jacket, which I left on the sofa.'

No answer. Just more scraping and thudding.

Wittberg threw himself against the door, which abruptly gave way, and both officers tumbled out of the closet, only to see a man's back disappearing through the door. They ran down the stairs after him and out on to the street.

Just as they came outside, they saw the man they were chasing vanish around the corner.

'Let's split up,' said Jacobsson. 'You go after him, and I'll cut him off on the other side.'

They headed off in different directions. Jacobsson dashed around the dilapidated building and came out on a narrow side street.

She slowed down and then cautiously proceeded forward. Looking in all directions, she didn't dare shout to Wittberg, for fear of warning Boberg.

She crept along the side of the building. Suddenly she heard a crunching sound behind her. Abruptly she spun around. For a second she saw his face. It was not Janne Widén. She felt a momentary relief before she was shoved to the ground. She heard Wittberg yelling.

'Halt!'

Then silence. Jacobsson cautiously raised her head. Wittberg was standing in the deserted street, pointing his gun at the man whom she assumed was Sten Boberg. For a moment it seemed as if everything stopped. No one spoke; no one moved. Then the man slowly raised his hands in the air.

It was over.

Karin Jacobsson began the interrogation as soon as they arrived at police headquarters with Sten Boberg. Wittberg insisted on being present in the role of witness.

Boberg's face was white, and he seemed very nervous as he was led into the interview room in the basement. Jacobsson switched on the tape recorder and then studied the man sitting in front of her. He had classic features and wavy, ash-blond hair. His eyes were an unusual deep blue. Dark eyebrows and long, thick lashes. A real dreamboat, actually. But his eyes kept shifting, and he was constantly licking his lips. Jacobsson estimated his age to be about forty. He was tall and muscular, dressed in jeans and a navy-blue tennis sweater.

'Tell me about your relationship with Andrea Dahlberg.'

Boberg cleared his throat and again licked his lips.

'We met a year ago when I moved to Terra Nova with my girlfriend of the time. We met Andrea, her husband, and some other neighbours, and we spent a lot of time with them. But we didn't live there for long. Monica and I split up, and we moved away.'

'How would you describe your relationship with Andrea?'

'Good. Actually, it was fantastic.' Boberg rubbed the bridge of his nose.

'We know about the swinger parties you had. Was there anything in particular that happened between you and Andrea in connection with those parties? Did you meet at other times too?'

'No. I wanted to, but . . .'

'But what?'

'She insisted that it was all just a game. That it was OK at the parties, because everybody else was doing it too. But she didn't want to see me at other times.'

'So you didn't have sex outside of the parties.'

'No.'

'Not even once?'

Sten Boberg shook his head.

'Then how were you able to take pictures of her?'

'I brought my camera to one of the parties. She was in some of the pictures. Then I secretly took other pictures of her.'

'What's your relationship with Andrea today?'

'I love her, and I want to spend the rest of my life with her.'

'And you feel so strongly about her that you'd be willing to kill her husband?'

The man on the other side of the table met her eyes. He suddenly seemed perfectly calm.

'No. I didn't murder anybody. I've just been trying to get in touch with Andrea.'

'Couldn't you have found a better way to do that than spying on her in the middle of the night and taking a lot of photographs in secret? You could have phoned her, for example.'

'I did that, but she didn't want to talk to me.'

'Why not, if the two of you have such a good relationship?'

'There were problems. I'm sure you know all about it. Monica was jealous, and everybody in the group got upset and wanted us to leave. I tried to forget Andrea, but then I found the cardboard box with those photos of her, and all of the feelings came flooding back. I tried to contact her again, but I knew that she was afraid of what her husband would think. I thought that if I went out there, we might run into each other, but I didn't want to scare her, so I started by just watching her.'

'And you also took pictures, right?'

'Yes.'

'A lot of pictures. The fact is, you took a perverse number of photographs. We also have statements from witnesses who saw you sneaking around in her garden, and you were even bold enough to enter her house.'

Jacobsson was taking a gamble. The police knew only that a man had been seen sneaking around, but they didn't know whether it was Boberg.

He hid his face in his hands for a moment.

'Yes, but it was only because I wanted to see her. Be close to her.'

'Where is Andrea now?' Jacobsson finally asked him.

'I don't know.'

'You don't know?'

'No, I don't.'

'When did you last meet her?'

'The day before yesterday.'

'Where was this?'

'Here in Visby.'

'How did you happen to meet her?'

'I'd been trying to contact her for a long time, but she refused to talk to me. Finally I managed to get hold of her, so I lied and said that I knew who had killed Sam and Stina. I thought that would make her want to see me. She was really shocked and wanted to know who it was. But I said we had to meet, and I would only tell her in person. So she agreed to meet me the following day.'

'Then what happened?'

'We had coffee together and talked. No more than half an hour. Then she left.'

'What did you talk about?'

'I tried to talk some sense into her, but it didn't go very well.'

'Talk some sense into her? What do you mean by that?'

Suddenly the man on the other side of the table got angry. He rose halfway out of his chair.

'Nobody, not even Andrea, can deny how good the two of us were together. There was a special chemistry between us, something you find maybe once in a hundred years; the odds are maybe one in a million that you get to experience something like that. She gave herself to me. Do you understand? Totally and completely! I could do whatever I wanted with her, and I mean anything. But somebody like you can't possibly imagine what that's like. I tried to get her to remember what we'd had together – when things were good, and before the others intervened and ruined it all. They sabotaged everything for us; they put ideas into Andrea's head and made her lose confidence. So I was trying to get her to realize that it's the two of us now. Sam's dead. He doesn't exist any more, so there's nothing standing in our way.'

He sank back on to the chair. Jacobsson had listened without changing expression.

'Was that why you killed him? To get him out of the way?'

Boberg sighed heavily.

'I didn't do it.'

'Where is Andrea now?'

'I don't know.'

'So your meeting didn't turn out the way you'd hoped?'

'You might say that.'

'How did you react when she wanted to leave?'

Boberg threw out his hands.

'What was I supposed to do? She was suddenly in a big rush. I said that I'd be in touch again soon, and she just nodded. Then she was gone.'

'And you haven't seen her since?'

'No.'

'And you have no idea where she might be?'

'Not a clue.'

'OK.'

Jacobsson ended the interview.

'Can I go now?'

'No, you're staying here.'

Prosecutor Birger Smittenberg decided during the course of the afternoon to arrest Sten Boberg, on suspicion of murdering Sam Dahlberg, Stina Ek and Valter Olsson. But one question kept reverberating through Jacobsson's mind.

Where was Andrea Dahlberg?

I will never forget that terrible day. When I told Mamma what I'd heard at the parsonage, she fell into despair. But at least she believed me and immediately rang the pastor. We went over there together; Mamma demanded that I go along. He looked nervous when we came in, as if he knew. We sat in his office, and Mamma confronted him with what I'd said, without any attempt to disguise what she meant. He started shaking, trembling all over and sweating profusely. Almost as if he were the guilty party.

'I'm so terribly sorry,' he apologized. 'Lennart told me about it in confidence, and as a pastor I'm obliged to remain silent, no matter how awful that may sound. I have a pact with God, and it's something that I cannot break.'

I cast a sidelong glance at Mamma. She looked furious.

'A pact with God? Are you out of your mind?' she snapped. 'You knew about this for all these years, but you never said anything? You just pretended nothing was going on? You and your wife have been to our house for dinner, sat there with our whole family, including Emilia. And you're talking to me about a pact with God?' she repeated, hardly able to stay seated. Her expression was thunderous, and she was spraying saliva on the pastor's polished desk. I had never seen Mamma so angry before. Her knuckles were white as she held on to the edge of the desk. 'How could you possibly not say anything? You knew what Emilia was being subjected to, but you never intervened. You're just as guilty as he is. May you burn in hell!'

'Please, Margareta. Calm down,' the pastor pleaded, his voice quavering. 'There was nothing I could do. My hands were tied; my lips were sealed by our Lord God. Somewhere on this earth there has to be someone who listens to a fellow human being without revealing to anyone else what that person has said. Somewhere in this earthly life there has to be a means for release, a single person who can be trusted, someone you can confide in and at the same time feel completely sure that the confessions will go no further. No matter what the confessions may concern. Do you understand?' He gave my mother and me an imploring look. 'And it applies to both murderers and rapists; to anyone at all. There has to be a place of refuge for people on earth. I could not betray my pact with God.'

'But you betrayed Emilia.' Mamma spat out the words. 'You betrayed Emilia and now she's no longer here. Now she's dead, and she's never coming back. Do you understand what you've done? You're a murderer.

You killed her, just like he did. What does God the Almighty say about that? You killed a child!'

The pastor's face was as white as chalk.

'Please, Margareta. Please.'

All of a sudden Mamma was completely calm. She stood up, and all she said was: 'Come on, Andrea. We're leaving.'

Somehow the knowledge of what Pappa had done to Emilia didn't destroy Mamma. On the contrary. She was suddenly yanked out of her apathy and took action. She filed a police report, which was followed by official charges and a trial. Pappa was sentenced to five years in prison for having raped Emilia over a three-year period, starting when she was fourteen. Mamma and I moved away and got a flat in town, and we never went back. I haven't spoken to Pappa since. It's as if he no longer exists. But he destroyed my life when I was only a child.

I thought that I'd already had my share of hell on earth. But I hadn't. My world was going to be destroyed once again. In the same disgusting, brutal fashion, my happiness was smashed to pieces. The whole orderly and harmonious life that I'd managed to create, in spite of everything, was gone in a matter of seconds. Over. Shattered. It happened on that second day out there on Fårö, while Sam was in the shower. Suddenly his mobile rang, and he had a text message. I couldn't help reading it.

To my surprise, the message was from my best

friend. *Found Bergman's house. Completely deserted. Wild strawberries is the password. I want you. Now. Want to play somewhere that's better than anywhere else?*

She also sent a picture of herself. Wearing only a bra and a skimpy skirt, she was lolling on a deckchair. She had her legs spread wide, and I couldn't help noticing that she wasn't wearing any knickers.

Even though it should have been crystal clear what this all meant, it took me a few minutes before I grasped the whole picture. And understood what was going on.

That's when I lost control.

Knutas climbed the ladder up the slope. Far below lay the rocky shore and the sea. Andrea stood only thirty metres above him, her back to him, not moving. She looked so small, almost as if she'd shrunk since he last saw her. She was wearing jeans and a white sweater. Her hair hung down her back in a thick plait. He approached cautiously, uncertain what her state of mind might be, afraid that she was about to jump. When he was close enough, he spoke her name.

'Andrea.'

With a start she turned around and stared at him in astonishment.

'Take it easy,' he admonished her. 'It's me, Inspector Anders Knutas. Don't you recognize me?'

Andrea Dahlberg flinched as if she'd been struck. She looked as if she might topple over. Since she was standing at the very edge of the steep cliff, Knutas reacted instinctively. He threw himself forward and grabbed hold of her. Then he pulled her towards him and cupped her face in his hands. She offered no resistance.

Her body went limp, and tears ran down her cheeks.

'There, there,' Knutas consoled her. 'It's all right.'

He sat down on the cliff, holding Andrea in his arms, gently rocking her as she sobbed loudly. He stroked her hair.

'There, there,' he repeated. 'Everything's going to be fine.'

The poor woman, he thought. She must be totally devastated with grief.

Knutas continued to speak gently to the despairing woman, and gradually her sobs subsided. He handed her a packet of tissues that he dug out of his jacket pocket. After she calmed down, she looked up at him.

'That's the first time I've cried. I haven't been able to cry the whole time. I haven't shed a single tear since Emilia died.'

'Go ahead and cry,' said Knutas. 'That's good for you. I know what happened to your sister.'

'But I didn't want it to happen,' she said tonelessly. Her lower lip quivered.

Her big grey eyes were expressionless.

'There, there,' he comforted her.

'I didn't want that to happen,' she went on in a low voice, almost a whisper. 'I didn't want her to die.'

'Of course you didn't,' said Knutas. 'It wasn't your fault. Not at all. It was her own decision.'

'I suppose you could say that it was her decision. She took sides against me. She betrayed me. Do you understand that? She fooled me. She was pregnant, and she said that she loved him. That it was his child, his and hers. That they were going away together to get married. He said the same thing to me, up here on the bird mountain. He said that he didn't love me any more, that he loved her. Do you understand? They'd been secretly cheating on me. Both of them. We stood here, on this very spot.' Andrea pulled away from Knutas and pointed with a trembling finger. 'We were standing right here. And I was planning to tell him about the present. I was going to show him the card that I'd made for him and everything. We were going to Florence. It was supposed to be a surprise. But he didn't react the way I thought he would. He said that he wanted to live with her. That Stina was the one he loved.'

Knutas hadn't moved. Her words were starting to sink in, and at last he saw the whole picture.

'They had to die. Don't you see that? Although that wasn't my intention at first. I hadn't planned to kill her. I was just so angry that I wanted to hit her. But she fought back. Screaming hysterically. Saying that she was in love with Sam. Do you understand? And she was my best friend. My very best friend. And there she stood, practically naked, telling me that she loved my husband, that they were together now. She was expecting him, she'd sent him a text message and wanted him to come out there to have sex with her. But the thing is, I happened to see her message while Sam was in the shower. I got in the car and drove over there. She'd even included directions.

'When I saw her, wearing only a bra and sitting on the veranda in a deckchair, I hit her. I hit her over and over again. She fought back and screamed like crazy. She tried to get away, but I chased her over to the property next door. That's where I picked up a big rock and slammed it against her head. Finally she stopped screaming. But suddenly her body went limp. She wasn't moving at all, and blood was running from her head. Lots of blood. My clothes were totally soaked with it. And her eyes were blank, as if the light had gone out of them. I had killed her.

'Then I heard someone shouting behind me. It was that fisherman. He'd seen everything from out on the water and had rowed ashore. He was standing up in his boat, yelling and waving his arms about. I hit him on the head with a shovel, and he collapsed into the boat. I saw an anchor lying on the bottom, one of those collapsible kinds. I picked it up and slammed it against his head as he lay there. Then I pushed the boat out into the water as far as I could. I don't know why I did that, but I wanted to separate those two from each other.

'But that's what I regret the most. Killing that poor man. He just happened to get in the way.'

She gave Knutas a pleading look now, as if seeking his understanding. He gave her a slight nod.

'Well, then I realized how late it was. I had to go back to the others and clean myself up because I was covered in blood.'

'What about Sam? Why did you kill him too?'

'We went for a morning walk. I'd brought along the card that was my gift for him. For the trip to Florence.

I'd hidden Stina's body so well that she would never be found. And then I wanted everything to go back to normal. We were standing here, in this very spot, and then I started talking about Stina. Of course I didn't tell him that I'd killed her, but I said that I knew about their relationship, or at least that they'd been sleeping together. I was so sure that he'd tell me it didn't mean anything . . .'

'Then what happened?'

'He said that he loved Stina and wanted to live with her. That our marriage was over. Then he took out a cigarette and was just about to light it. That's when something snapped inside of me. I just stepped forward while he was fumbling with the cigarette and shoved him as hard as I could. So hard that he fell off the cliff and plummeted straight down, all the way down. That's what happened.'

Andrea fell silent. Knutas's face was stony.

'What about the sleeping bag?'

'I panicked after killing Sam. I thought I needed to do something that would shift the blame to Stina. I had her hair ribbon, and I thought her body might never be found. So the police would think she was the one who did it.'

A trembling sigh escaped from her lips. She didn't say another word.

Finally Knutas spoke.

'Shall we go home now?'

Andrea simply nodded.

The news that a man had been arrested for the three murders was out within the hour. Lars Norrby had insisted that the police send out a press release at once. Finally they'd had a breakthrough in this high-profile case. It would calm down the governor, the county police chief, and the chairman of the municipal board, not to mention everyone who was involved with tourism on the island. The murders had not exactly been good PR for Gotland as an idyllic holiday paradise. The public needed to be reassured.

Pia and Johan hurried over to police headquarters as soon as they read the press release. As they were driving, Pia got a phone call. Her face changed colour as she listened to the person on the line.

'What are you saying? The coastguard? What could that mean? Hmm. OK. What time?'

She held out her wrist to look at her watch. Johan noticed that today her fingernails were purple. A nice combination with the lilac-coloured gemstone in her nostril.

'All right. I understand. Thanks. Talk to you later.' Pia turned towards Johan. 'You're not going to believe this. That was my friend who works as a guide on Stora Karlsö. She told me that the coastguard has just been over there to pick up two people.'

'And?'

'Guess who they are? None other than Knutas and Andrea Dahlberg.'

'What's that all about? What were they doing out there?'

'That's a good question. At any rate, it seems that they're on their way to the police station. They left Stora Karlsö half an hour ago, so they can't have arrived yet.'

Pia Lilja stomped on the accelerator, making the tyres shriek.

Outside police headquarters a crowd of reporters had already gathered, hoping for an interview. At the moment that seemed unlikely to happen. Johan tried ringing every officer in the Criminal Division. The police spokesman was not available, and he'd asked the officer on duty to say that for now the journalists would have to be content with the press release. Johan was filled with impatience.

'Come on, Pia. Let's go over to the other door, the side entrance that leads to the crime-tech offices,' he said. 'Maybe they'll try to slip in that way.'

Discreetly they started moving away. Pia pretended to be filming the façade of the building so as not to draw attention. When they came around the corner, they caught sight of a police vehicle just turning into the small car park near the entrance. Then Knutas got out.

And he had Andrea Dahlberg with him.

It was with mixed emotions that Knutas arrived at police headquarters late in the afternoon with Andrea Dahlberg and two colleagues.

He studied Andrea as she quietly sat beside him in the back seat of the police car, her hands cuffed in front of her. She had insisted that he sit next to her. She seemed to find his presence soothing. And she was clearly relieved that the whole thing was over. In silence, she stared out of the window. He wondered what she was thinking. Suddenly she turned to face him, putting her hand on his.

'Thank you,' she said in a low voice. 'Thank you for coming.'

As the police vehicle was about to turn into the car park in front of headquarters, they saw a crowd of journalists gathered outside.

'Damn it,' swore Knutas. 'I should have known this would happen. Let's go around to the side.'

Before the reporters noticed the car, it turned in the other direction. When it came to a halt, everyone quickly got out and hurried towards the entrance. Knutas immediately caught sight of two people standing near the door. Johan Berg and Pia Lilja. Of course. Making no decision how to handle them, he approached the door.

'Can you tell us what's going on?' asked Johan, looking down at Andrea's cuffed hands. Pia was unabashedly filming, without even considering asking for permission. As usual.

'Nothing that I can discuss at the moment. I'm sorry, but I can't comment.'

'Why is Andrea Dahlberg under arrest if the perpetrator has been caught?'

Knutas stopped abruptly to stare at Johan.

'What the hell do you mean by that?'

'Prosecutor Birger Smittenberg arrested a man on suspicion of murder just a couple of hours ago.'

Then something happened that no one could have expected. Before Knutas or any of the other police officers could react, Andrea leaned forward and looked Johan right in the eye.

'I'm the one who killed them. It was me.'

Then she continued moving forward, keeping her gaze fixed on the façade of the building.

The plane left at two in the afternoon. Karin had a window seat, so she watched as the flat Gotland landscape disappeared far below. About a week had passed since the murder drama of the summer had finally been resolved – and what a commotion there had been. Two potential perpetrators had been arrested almost at the same time, with a disappointing result for Jacobsson. She and Wittberg had been on the wrong track. It turned out that Sten Boberg was a stalker, but he'd had nothing to do with the killings.

Andrea Dahlberg had confessed, and technical evidence had also been provided by the crime lab. They discovered that the skin underneath Stina Ek's fingernails had come from Andrea. So the game was over, and now they were just waiting for the arraignment.

Andrea would have to undergo a psychiatric examination. Karin couldn't help feeling sorry for the woman. Life was a labyrinth, and the human being was such a fragile creature. She found it hard to judge anyone. I'm really too soft-hearted to be a police officer, she thought, looking out of the window as the plane rose through the cloud cover.

Now she was on her way to see her daughter. When Karin thought about that, she felt her stomach churn. She was glad the plane was only half full so she had the row to herself. She needed to retreat for a while. She'd decided to meet with Hanna von Schwerin face to face, but without phoning her in advance. She'd just have to wait and see how things went. Knutas was the one who had helped her make up her mind. He had offered support and encouragement all along. She pictured his face in her mind and couldn't help feeling both admiration and a bit of envy because he was the one who had actually caught the murderer.

The plane landed at Bromma Airport outside Stockholm, and Jacobsson headed straight for the taxi queue. She hadn't bothered to bring along any luggage. On the way she switched on her mobile and discovered a text message. It said: *Saturday 8 o'clock at Packhuskällaren? Interested? Hugs from Janne*. Karin smiled and replied: *Sounds great*.

She got into a cab.

'I'm going to Wollmar Yxkullsgatan 51,' she said, noticing that her voice quavered. If Hanna wasn't at home, she'd just wait outside. It didn't matter how long it took.

The cab stopped in front of a grand red-brick building with a beautifully carved door. Karin paid the fare and got out. Her heart was beating twice as fast as normal.

Through the glass panes in the door she could make out a gold nameplate engraved with the names of all the residents who lived in the building.

Hanna von Schwerin lived on the fifth floor, which meant that her flat was at the very top. Karin wondered if it faced the street. She backed up a few metres and peered at the façade from the opposite pavement. A beautiful ornamental wrought-iron balcony covered nearly half the width of the building on the top floor. Was that her flat? Karin assumed that it must have cost several million Swedish kronor. Her courage sank. How would this all end?

She walked back across the street and over to a small café. She sat down at a table nearest the door and ordered a caffè latte and a glass of water. She lit a cigarette, preparing herself for a long wait. She'd brought along some newspapers, which she absent-mindedly leafed through as she sat there. An hour passed. Then another. Several times the door opened and various people came and went. An elderly couple, a young man, a father with a baby in a pram. No one who could possibly be Hanna von Schwerin.

Karin needed to use the toilet, but she was afraid of missing her daughter. For a long time nothing happened, and she began to lose hope. What if Hanna was out of town?

It was past five o'clock when the front door opened again. First she saw the dog. A big, shaggy mongrel that was tugging at its lead. The next second a young woman appeared. She looked to be about twenty-five. Karin stared, holding her breath. She was just as short as Karin, with tousled dark hair under a cap that said 'Fuck You' on it. A hoodie, jeans and trainers.

'Come on, Nelson,' she said to the dog, which had spotted Karin sitting at the nearby table and had come over to say hello. Karin leaned down to let him lick her hand. And then she couldn't help it – she started to cry.

'I'm sorry,' said Hanna, who hadn't noticed Karin's tears. 'He loves people.'

Karin raised her head, with tears still streaming down her face.

Hanna's smile vanished. At first she looked surprised. 'Oh, what's wrong . . . ?'

Then her voice faded. Her gaze quickly took in Karin's face. The young woman froze.

Karin looked at her daughter. There was absolutely no doubt.

Hanna even had a little gap between her front teeth.

Knutas was sitting at his desk, filling his pipe. The corridor outside his office was quiet. It was past midnight. He had stayed on at headquarters to go through all of the paperwork that had piled up while he was on sick leave. It felt good to put that whole depressing murder case behind him. It was time to move on.

Besides, there were plenty of other things that required his attention. In spite of his good intentions, the whole summer had now passed and he hadn't yet decided what to do about Karin. A feeling of guilt kept nagging at him, and he couldn't stand it any longer. If only that double murderer, Vera Petrov, could be found, he thought. Then everything could be looked at in a new light – it could be worked out. But so far that hadn't happened, and there was no indication that an arrest was imminent. The police still had no idea where in the world Petrov and her husband, Stefan Norrström, might be. The international authorities were looking for her, but most likely she was staying put in one place. And as long as she stayed away from Sweden and didn't draw attention to herself, she would probably remain free.

Knutas stood up with a heavy sigh and went over to the window. He opened it to let the warm night air sweep into the room. He lit his pipe and exhaled smoke into the darkness.

The murder investigation had taken a toll on him, as usual. The whole story about Andrea Dahlberg's past was so sad. The tragedy that had struck her family. Her father's betrayal. And the pastor's too. Then, as an adult, she had experienced the same sort of betrayal all over again. She had truly believed that she had everything she could possibly want, but it turned out to be an illusion.

And Ingmar Bergman had wound up in the middle of the whole case. Actually, he didn't have anything to do with the investigation, but there did seem to be parallels between his depictions of people and the individuals whom Knutas had encountered while investigating the homicides this summer.

Knutas was reminded of a picture that hung on the wall in the Dahlberg home. It was a big black-and-white movie poster for the Bergman film *Persona*. It showed the actresses Bibi Andersson and Liv Ullmann in a tender pose, with their faces close together. Next to the poster was a small card with a quote from the film: *Can you be one and the same person, at exactly the same time? I mean, be two people?* That quote sums up this whole sodding case, he thought.

Knutas took one last puff on his pipe, then he tapped

out the embers and put it away in his desk drawer. It was time to go home.

Just then his phone rang. He cast a glance at the clock on the wall. Twelve forty-five. Who would ring at this time of night?

There was a crackling sound on the phone and someone rattled off a string of words in a foreign language. It sounded like Spanish. Then he heard a voice that he recognized.

'Hi, Anders. It's Kurt.'

Kurt Fogestam, inspector with the Stockholm police. They'd known each other for a very long time.

'I'm here on holiday in Las Terrenas in the Dominican Republic.'

'Did you say the Dominican Republic?'

'Yes, and wait till you hear this. Do you know who I just saw get into a car outside the hotel?'

'Who?'

'Stefan Norrström.'

Knutas sank on to his chair. His head was spinning. Vera Petrov's husband. So the tip they'd received earlier from the tourist was correct after all. They'd dismissed the information because the man had been drunk and the photograph was too blurry to make a conclusive identification. But had he really heard right?

'Who did you say?'

'Stefan Norrström, Vera Petrov's husband. I'm certain it was him. But I didn't see the number plate and I couldn't follow him. I was coming back from the beach, on foot, with my wife, and I caught sight of him just as he got in the car. At first I wasn't sure, so I ran towards the street and got a good look at his face as he drove past. I'm a hundred per cent positive. It was him.'

Acknowledgements

This story is entirely fictional. Any similarities between the characters in the novel and actual individuals are coincidental. Occasionally I have taken artistic liberties to change things for the benefit of the book. This includes Swedish TV's coverage of Gotland, which in the book has been moved to Stockholm. I have the utmost respect for SVT's regional news programme Östnytt, which covers Gotland with a permanent team stationed in Visby.

The locations used in the book are usually described as they actually exist in reality, although there are a few exceptions.

Any errors that may have slipped into the story are mine alone.

First and foremost, I would like to thank my husband, journalist Cenneth Niklasson, for his support, love, and encouragement.

Mari Jungstedt

Special thanks to:

Magnus Frank, detective superintendent with the Visby police

Martin Csatlos, the Forensic Medicine Laboratory in Solna

Ulf Åsgård, psychiatrist

Lena Allerstam, journalist SVT

Paola Ciliberto, managing director Film på Gotland

Balkan Kalka, tour guide Fritidsresor

Mani Maserrat-Agah, film director and owner of Café Cinema

My thanks to everyone at Albert Bonniers Förlag who helped with this book, especially my publisher Jonas Axelsson and my editor Ulrika Åkerlund – your support is invaluable.

A big thanks to Gilda Romero and my agents Joakim Hansson at Nordin Agency and Emma Tibblin, Poa Strömberg and Jenny Stjärnströmer at Stilton Literary Agency.

And thanks to my designer, Sofia Scheutz, for the wonderful cover on the Swedish edition.

And of course I want to thank my beloved children, Rebecka and Sebastian, who are the greatest gifts in my life.

Mari Jungstedt
Stockholm, April 2009
www.marijungstedt.se
www.jungstedtsgotland.se

dead good

For everyone who finds a crime story irresistible.

Discover the very best **crime and thriller books** and get tailored recommendations to help you choose what to read next.

Read **exclusive interviews with top authors** or join our **live web chats** and speak to them directly.

And it's not just about books. We'll be bringing you **specially commissioned features** on everything criminal, from **TV and film** to **true crime stories**.

We also love a good competition.
Our **monthly contest** offers you the chance to win the latest thrilling fiction, plus there are DVD box sets and devices to be won.

Sign up for our free fortnightly newsletter at www.deadgoodbooks.co.uk/signup

Join the conversation on: